UNHINGED

BLOOD BOND SAGA: VOLUME TWO

PARTS 4 - 5 - 6

HELEN HARDT

This book is an original publication of Helen Hardt.

Cover Design by Waterhouse Press, LLC
Cover Photographs: Shutterstock

Paperback ISBN: 978-1-64263-014-5

PRINTED IN THE UNITED STATES OF AMERICA

UNHINGED

BLOOD BOND SAGA: VOLUME TWO

PARTS 4 - 5 - 6

HELEN HARDT

WATERHOUSE PRESS

TABLE OF CONTENTS

To those who believe without seeing...

BLOOD BOND SAGA

PART 4

PROLOGUE

Erin

I tugged at my bindings, wanting desperately to touch Dante, to curl my fingers through his thick dark hair.

But I couldn't.

And I found, suddenly, that I was thrilled.

I was at his mercy, couldn't touch him though I longed to. I whimpered.

"What is it, love?"

"I want to touch you, Dante. To feel you."

"I know you do. You will. In good time." He smiled. "Would you like me to get undressed?"

"Please. I want to feel your skin against mine."

He stood and slowly undressed. Achingly slowly. With each new inch of fair skin exposed, my pussy quivered.

Finally he was naked, his gorgeous cock jutting straight out, a drop of fluid glistening at the tip. I wanted so badly to lick it off, to take him to the back of my throat.

But no. Not before he was embedded in my hot pussy.

"Please, Dante. Please come into my body. Come into me. We've waited so long for this."

"Yes, my love."

He sat down on the bed and then hovered over me, teasing my labia with his hard cock.

"I feel how wet you are for me, Erin. So wet." He inhaled. "I smell you. I smell how much you want me. I wish you could smell how much I want you."

I inhaled his salty cinnamon scent. Maybe I couldn't smell his arousal as I smelled my own, but I knew. In my heart I knew he wanted me as much as I wanted him. In his eyes, I saw it. I saw what I knew he was seeing in my own.

That fire. That passion.

That true love.

He groaned as he thrust inside me.

Such sweet intrusion.

"My God, Erin. I feel your warmth. I feel every ridge inside you, your walls closing around me. You were made for me."

I hadn't been able to find the words, but he'd said them perfectly. "Yes. Exactly. I feel it, too."

He stayed inside me for a moment, and I relished the sweet fullness, as if I'd never been filled before.

And never would be again by anyone else.

Only by this man.

Then he gritted his teeth, pulled out, and thrust back in.

I arched into him, tugging at my bindings, wanting so much to touch his smooth skin.

"I love you, Dante. I love you."

He thrust back in. "I love you too, Erin. My only love."

Thrust.

Thrust.

Thrust.

His pubic hair and bone nudged my clit with each thrust, tickling it, making it flutter.

So close.

So close.

Until I erupted, the orgasm taking me with a force I hadn't yet known.

My whole body vibrated, every cell humming the jazzy tune that drifted to my ears.

"Dante, I'm coming. I'm coming so hard."

"Yes, love. Come. Come for me." He thrust once more, filling me. Each contraction of his cock in rhythm with my own pulsing.

"Ah, God!" he cried out, embedding himself into me.

We climaxed together, each of us moaning, our bodies sliding together from the perspiration.

Savor this moment. Savor it.

Again I tugged at my bindings. I lifted my head, trying to reach his lips. Sweat from his brow dripped onto my face, from his chest onto mine.

And then, as the pulsing finally began to subside, he opened his eyes.

They were blazing and full of fire.

"Come, my love, and I will bring you to true completion."

ONE

DANTE

My blood was still singing from the orgasm, the intensity of coming inside Erin's tightness with no barrier. Only her and only me.

I didn't try to stop the tingling in my gums, the itching as my fangs descended. I was all in now. Too far gone.

I said the words again, this time showing her my teeth.

"Come, my love, and I will bring you to true completion."

She was still high on her climax. Her pheromones were thick with oxytocin and dopamine, adding to her already intoxicating scent. Her eyes were heavy-lidded.

Still, she gasped when she saw my elongated cuspids. "Dante..."

"Don't be afraid, my love. I would never harm you."

She tugged at the rope binding her. "You... You're..."

"A vampire, love. A vampire who loves you. *Trust me.*"

Though her mouth dropped into an O, she arched toward me, turning her head slightly, giving me access to her throbbing jugular.

I sighed, my fangs itching, and sank my teeth into the flesh of her milky neck.

All the anticipation, all the dreams, couldn't have prepared me for the sheer intensity of finally being able to bite into her. I held myself for a few precious seconds, simply relishing the intense feeling of my teeth in her flesh.

Her sweet blood oozed out of the two small holes created by my fangs, and the creamy red substance trickled against my lips and gums.

She relaxed beneath me, still in a post-climactic high. As she unwound, her blood flowed freely, and I did what I'd been dying to do since I'd first laid eyes on her.

I sucked.

I sucked that velvety elixir out of her jugular vein. It gushed across my tongue, tasting of everything Erin. Her scent—earthy dark chocolate and truffles, lusty red wine, coppery and fruity—was all in the flavor, except it was magnified.

It cascaded down my throat like the richest Bavarian cream, settling in my stomach where it sated me as if I'd never been sated before.

As I continued to feed from her, I knew I'd never be able to give her up.

Somehow, I'd make her understand what this meant for both of us.

A blood bond.

Now more than ever, Erin Hamilton was mine.

Mine to love.

Mine to protect.

Mine to take nourishment from.

Mine to give back to.

And I would give Erin everything, everything within my power.

I sucked harder, taking more of her into my body...until I sensed her tensing beneath me.

Had to stop. Couldn't drain her.

But God, so hard to stop!

Over and over her blood flowed like a rolling river along my tongue and down my throat, nourishing me, sustaining me, freeing me from isolation. Isolation I never knew I felt until now. For now, I was no longer a singular being. I was one with Erin. The two of us had become our own entity.

A blood bond.

Now, I understood.

Now, I felt sorry for every vampire and human who would never experience this wholeness, this completion.

Once bonded, never broken.

I felt more than thought the words.

I'd heard them before, somewhere long in my past. Perhaps another lifetime even.

And again, I sucked more of her essence into my body. Into my soul.

Until she stiffened beneath me.

Stop. Must stop.

But so, so hard!

Dante!

My name was harsh in my mind. It came from me but was not from me.

It was my higher self, warning me to stop.

I stopped.

I forced my teeth from her succulent flesh and licked her wounds to begin the healing. Her eyes were closed, and her lips stretched into a small smile of serene peace.

"Erin," I whispered. "Thank you." I lightly kissed her

cheek, leaving a red lip print.

I got up and went to her bathroom to clean myself. As I stared at myself in the mirror, my mouth and chin covered in the blood of my only love, feral feelings of protection and devotion came over me.

This was me. My true self.

Vampire.

For the first time, I felt like I truly knew what being a vampire meant. It wasn't about drinking blood or having skin sensitive to the sun. It wasn't about preferring night to day or the ability to glamour prey. It was about this. This bond with Erin. About the need we had for each other that transcended so far beyond the emotional and the spiritual that it culminated in the physical.

We would never be complete without each other now.

Taking her blood had given me this knowledge—not in words but in feelings. In pure emotion. I thought of this while I washed my face and hands and then wet a cloth to clean Erin.

Erin. My Erin.

She had accepted me. She had accepted her bond with me.

I smiled as I walked back into the bedroom, the warm wet cloth in my hand.

I sat down on the bed and nudged her. "Erin."

No response.

I nudged her again, a little more strongly. "Erin? Love?"

Her pallor was light, but it was always light. I bent to kiss her lips—

"Erin!"

Her beautiful lips were tinged with blue.

TWO

Erin

Did you see him?

See who?

The vampire.

I whirled in a cloud of climactic bliss. Dante rose above me, thrusting into me, finally giving me what I'd been craving forever.

I left my body for a few seconds, and then minutes. Oh, I knew it was my imagination, but I lost myself in the fantasy. In the sheer magnitude of what was happening to me. To us.

He felt it too.

Come, my love, and I will bring you to true completion.

His words. They echoed around me, the deep timbre of his voice creating drumming vibrations inside me.

True completion.

The words resonated within me, sliding me into new heights of pleasure, as if I had been catapulted into a fourth and then a fifth dimension.

Something tugged on my neck, and the sensation traveled to my pussy, increasing the throbbing of my orgasm and shooting out into every cell of my body. Then into the air around me, and I could actually see the orgasm. Pinks and blues and yellows and reds. I'd never known that orgasms had color.

But they did. They so did.

More tugging at my neck, and the beautiful sounds of Dante's satisfaction.

He was happy. I could feel how happy and satisfied I was making him.

And that elated me.

His cock was still embedded inside me, and though I knew he had climaxed, still he was gaining more and more from our joining. More and more and more and more...

Heady. So heady.

More orgasm. More shaking. More trembling.

So good...

Until...

Nothing.

⚜

Erin!

Erin!

Erin!

No. Don't want to leave here. Feels too good. So good.

Peace. Pure peace.

Peace and joy.

Erin!

Erin!

Erin!

Then warmth on my lips. A rubbing sensation. Rough terry cloth.

I opened my eyes. Dante sat above me, furiously rubbing at my lips.

"Thank God! You were breathing, but you scared the hell out of me."

Scared him? I was in the most wonderful place I'd ever known. With him. How could I have possibly scared him?

I opened my mouth to say all of that, but all that came out was a crackly rasp.

"Baby? Love? Please tell me you're okay."

Of course I'm okay. Of course.

Had I said that aloud?

No, I hadn't. He was still freaking out.

"I'm so sorry, love. So, so sorry. Please forgive me."

"F-For what?"

"Thank God! You're speaking. The first time. I don't have any practice. We'll get to know how much is too much for you. Never again. I promise."

"How much of...what?"

"You don't remember?" He rubbed his forehead. "I'm so sorry. I thought you were letting me... God, I'm so sorry."

"I remember..." My mind was muddled, still filled with pleasure and rapture and euphoric haze. "I remember..."

"Yes, love? What do you remember?"

Then I jolted into a sitting position, except that I didn't. I couldn't. My wrists were still bound. Dizziness overtook me. "You!" I touched my neck. He'd bitten me. Bitten me, and...

"So you do remember." He stood.

"You're a... You're a..."

He let out a slow breath. "Yes. A vampire. I'm a vampire, Erin."

"No. No." I tried to slide over to the edge of the bed, but my body wouldn't—couldn't—cooperate. I pulled at my restraints. "This didn't happen. None of this—"

He cupped my cheeks. "Yes. It happened. I love you. And you love me. My being a vampire doesn't change any of that."

"Doesn't change any of that? Are you insane?" God. Abe Lincoln. The marks on my thigh. But— "You didn't bite my thigh!"

"No, love, I didn't."

"Then who..."

"I don't know. But I will find out. I promise you that."

I closed my eyes then, willing myself to wake from this nightmare. "Only a dream. A terrible, horrible dream." Yet a beautiful, passionate, fulfilling dream.

"Not a dream, love."

My eyes shot open. "Stop it! Let me go back to sleep! I need to... I need to..." I tugged at my bindings. "Let me go! Untie me!"

He sighed, his countenance sad. "I will do whatever you want. I will never hold you against your will." He untied the rope that bound me.

I rubbed at my wrists, though they weren't red. "How...?"

"Synthetic fibers don't cause friction burn. I'd never harm you, Erin. Never."

"But you just..." I sat up and moved to the edge of the bed, suddenly ultra-aware of my nakedness.

"I just took your blood. I may have taken a bit too much, and I'm sorry. It won't happen again."

The sadness in his dark eyes was too much to bear. I gulped, looking away from him. Running away screaming seemed juvenile. I honestly didn't feel I was in any danger. He'd unbound me when I asked, and now he was taking great pains, from the longing on his face, not to touch me. Plus, this was my home. Where would I run?

One thing was certain, though.

This had to end.

Now.

I turned back to him, facing his troubled eyes, his distressed posture. “You’re right. It won’t happen again. None of this will ever happen again.”

“Erin.” His voice was low and husky. “Please. Let me explain.”

“Explain what?” I touched my neck, new images swirling in my mind. Dante walking the streets at night, searching for prey. Dante, lying down in a coffin to sleep. Dante, bursting into flames in daylight. Dante, struck dead by a silver bullet. I cringed.

Then a new picture, this one disturbingly clear. It was me. With fangs. “Oh my God. Am I going to become...one of you?”

He reached forward to touch my forearm, but I snatched it away and grabbed the sheet from the bed, wrapping it around me.

“No. You won’t become one of us. Vampires are born, not made.”

“But aren’t you...?”

“It’s all myth, Erin. We are people, just like you are. People who just happen to require blood for sustenance. You’ve seen me eat meals. You’ve seen me bleed. I’m a living being, not undead.”

“You go out in the sun.”

“Yes. Though our skin is particularly sensitive to it. We need strong sunscreen.”

"You don't burst into flames?"

He chuckled softly. "You've seen me in the sun. Did I burst into flames?"

Anger rose deep in my gut and burned through me. "Don't laugh at me. You've just challenged everything I believe. Everything I've been taught. How can you expect me to accept this?"

"Because you have to, Erin. I love you and you love me."

Yes, I did love him. I could never deny that. But I'd have to get over it. I wanted to crawl back in bed and go to sleep and forget any of this had ever happened. I fell back onto my pillow and closed my eyes.

Maybe this would all go away.

THREE

DANTE

She didn't return my sentiment, though I could see it in her eyes. She wasn't frightened, exactly. She was fraught with disbelief—that struggling duel when the mind and eyes are in conflict.

She would come around.

She had to.

I touched her cheek, the warmth of her blood tingling against my fingers. "Erin. What do you want? I'll do anything for you."

She opened her eyes. "Anything?"

I nodded, fearing what was about to come out of her mouth.

"Leave. Go and don't come back."

I nodded again. I would do so. I would leave.

But I would be back.

She would beg me to come back to her. In my heart, in my very soul, I knew that as much as I knew anything that was proven fact.

We couldn't live without each other. Not now.

⚜

River was still on sick leave, so it seemed logical to go to his place. I didn't want to talk to Bill, though I'd need to eventually.

Despite my sadness at Erin's rejection, I felt a renewed energy and purpose. I was sated beyond my wildest beliefs.

And I knew she was as well. She'd get up, and she'd feel it, and when the feeling dissipated, she'd know to come to me to find that feeling again.

More than energized, more than satisfied.

Reborn.

Once bonded, never broken.

Where had I heard those words? Maybe River would know.

"Yeah, come on in," he said when I knocked on the door.

I entered, and he sat on the couch in his living room, his laptop set up before him.

"Hey, Riv."

"Hey," he said, still looking at the screen. "I've been doing some research—" He looked up. "Dante? What the hell?"

"Yeah? What do you mean?"

His eyes widened. "You look...different somehow."

"I do?"

"Yeah. More... This won't make any sense, since we're vampires and all, but you have color in your cheeks. And your eyes... I can't put my finger on it, but there's something different."

I walked into River's bathroom and gazed at my reflection in the mirror. My eyes looked no different to me, but my cheeks had a definite pinkness. Not a lot, but some. I touched them, and they felt warm. Vampires had a normal body temperature of about a degree and a half below humans. We often felt cold to the touch.

Another side effect of the blood bond maybe? There was so much I didn't know. I walked back out to River.

"See what I mean?" he said.

"Yeah. Weird." Though really not weird at all. Nothing about me felt weird at the moment. In fact, I felt absolutely normal, as if I were finally where I'd always needed to be.

"What's up?" he asked me.

Where to start? What had transpired between Erin and me felt intensely personal, and even though River was one of the closest people to me in the world, telling him about it felt almost like a betrayal.

It wasn't a betrayal, of course, and I needed to talk to someone. I cleared my throat. "I was with Erin. I...took her blood."

He arched his eyebrows. "And?"

"It was the most intense and erotic experience I've ever had." Not that I had much experience in that area, but nothing could ever compare to what Erin and I had shared. I was sure of it.

River didn't flinch. "And...how did Erin take it?"

How had she taken it? When she'd come to reality, she hadn't taken it well at all, understandably. But during the feeding, when we were both in climactic bliss...

"Good and bad," I said. "And that's the God's honest truth."

"Okay. What exactly do you mean?"

"She accepted me. She didn't try to stop me. She allowed it, which made it all the more amazing. But afterward..." I shook my head. "I told her what I was and what had happened between us. She asked me to leave."

"Understandable."

"She's in denial," I said. "I could see it all over her face. We're a myth to her. She thinks we burn in the sun and live forever."

"That's what everyone thinks, Dante. We made it that way ourselves. Not us, maybe, but our ancestors."

"Yeah, I know. Perpetuating the lies so we could live in peace with humanity. I get it."

"She'll come around."

"I know she will. I know she'll come back to me. I'm not sure how I know, but I do. I'm necessary to her now, as she is to me. But I have no idea how long it will take her to accept the idea of us. That we're meant to be. That our love is only one small piece of what we are to each other."

"You're waxing a little poetic, cuz."

I laughed. "I guess I am. I have no idea how I know these things. I've had no experience at real life at all. I mean, I was..." I drew in a breath. I didn't want to think about my past now. Didn't want it to darken what I'd just experienced. "I can't really explain any of it. After finally tasting her, a whole new world opened up to me. I know things, Riv. I feel things I never knew existed."

"Like what things?"

How could I explain that my orgasm was a physical, tangible thing, with colors and shapes and melodies all its own? How could I explain that the taste of Erin was more than just the flavor of her fragrant blood, but the energy of her, her aura, everything that made her innately Erin? Words didn't exist for what I'd experienced.

"Everything's just brighter. More vivid." And even that wasn't close to what I wanted to say.

"I suppose that's a good thing. Maybe you just had really good sex." He laughed.

Could he be right? I had no experience other than my fumbling attempt as a teenager. It was possible.

"Does really good sex make you see things? Hear things?"

"Like what?"

Again, I couldn't explain. The sex had been amazing, but until I punctured her flesh, I hadn't felt the true release. The true intensity.

No, it wasn't just good sex.

Once bonded, never broken.

"I don't know." He wouldn't understand anyway, not unless he was lucky enough to form a blood bond with someone, and he probably never would. It obviously didn't happen often anymore. But those words... "Have you ever heard the phrase 'once bonded, never broken'?"

River twisted his lips. "No, I don't think so. Why?"

"They formed in my head after I'd taken Erin's blood. I could swear I've heard them before. I just can't figure out where or when."

Once again, the words forced themselves into my head.

Once bonded, never broken.

"No!"

Her voice. *Her* words.

"Fuck, no!"

FOUR

Erin

I didn't sleep.

How could I?

Several times, I'd walked to my bathroom and examined my neck in the mirror. Two marks. Looked like bug bites. But now I knew better.

Then I examined my thigh.

Two punctures.

Dante *hadn't* bitten my thigh.

Someone else had.

Our first encounter came crashing back into my mind.

He swept me into his arms and placed me on my bed. "Mine," he growled. "These lips are mine." He ripped my bra open at the middle. "These breasts are mine. That treasure between your legs is mine." He licked his lips, his eyes dark with desire. "You are *mine."*

"But yesterday," I whimpered. "You didn't want—"

"Forget yesterday. I want you now. And I will have what's

mine." He inhaled. "I can smell you. I can smell how much you want me."

I could smell it too. My lust was thick in the room, and it hadn't been there with Logan. Dante had brought it out in me.

Dante, who I hardly knew.

Dante, who was rude as hell.

Dante, who had broken into my home.

Dante, who I'd found vandalizing the blood bank.

Dante...who I wanted more than my next breath of air.

Couldn't think. Couldn't form words. All I wanted was his mouth on me. Everywhere.

He tugged off my shoes, then my jeans and panties. He spread my legs and closed his eyes. "Your musk is the sweetest thing I've ever scented."

Scented? Odd use of the word. But then he lowered his head, slithered his tongue over his bottom lip...

Opened his eyes...

And then his mouth, his eyes ablaze with rage.

"What the hell is that*?"*

Scented. I'd thought its use as a verb was strange, but he could smell me. Even that first night, in the blood bank, he'd sniffed at my neck, muttering words that hadn't made any sense. He'd said I smelled like truffles, chocolate, blackberries, tin. Tin? Copper? What did those things smell like? I had a vague idea, but I wouldn't pick them out in the midst of truffles and chocolate, two strong and distinct smells.

Cabernet Sauvignon. Fuck. Fuck, you smell so good.

I remembered every word. Every feeling the words had invoked in me. I should have been frightened, scared out of my mind.

But I hadn't been.

I'd felt fear, yes, but something else had overpowered it.

Need. Ache. Want.

That relentless pull I'd felt since Dante Gabriel catapulted into my life.

And now?

I still didn't feel fear. He would not harm me. He loved me. I knew that as much as I knew anything that was real and tangible.

He'd taken my blood. I still couldn't wrap my mind around that thought.

But there was another thought that was even more difficult to comprehend.

Someone else had taken my blood first. Blood from the femoral artery in my thigh.

What the hell is that?

Who tasted you?

He hadn't meant a kiss. Or even my pussy.

Dante had been referring to my blood.

I spent most of the night searching my memory, seeking one tiny recollection of someone biting my thigh, sucking my blood. I searched and I searched and I searched, and...

Nothing.

Then I remembered something else. I'd seen the same marks on Abe Lincoln in the ER.

I'd seen the same marks on my brother.

If Dante was a vampire...did that mean Jay's partner was also a vampire?

Had River fed on Jay? And did Jay remember?

Abe Lincoln had said that vampires hypnotized their victims so they wouldn't remember having been fed on.

I didn't believe in hypnosis. I thought it was mostly crap.

Of course, a few hours ago, I hadn't believed in vampires either.

Dante Gabriel, you have a lot of explaining to do.

But how could he explain if I never saw him again?

FIVE

DANTE

What's wrong? Dante, what's wrong?

My body shook with tremors. "Get out of my head!"

"What? No one's in your head, man. What's going on? You're scaring me."

I opened my eyes to reality. My body wasn't shaking on its own. River was shaking me.

Those words. Those words—words that had seemed so meaningful when they'd first come into my mind—had come from *her*.

"Stop," I said. "I'm okay. I'm okay."

River let go of me. "What was that about, Dante? You went into some kind of trance or something."

"It's just..." God, how to say this? "It's...nothing."

"Oh, hell, no. That was *not* nothing. I'm going to call Bill." He turned.

I grabbed his arm, yanking him back toward me. "No. No Bill."

"Then I'm taking you to the ER."

"No ER. What exactly are you going to tell them? That a blood bond is making me crazy? That words are making me crazy? They'll cart me off to some mental hospital and lock me up."

He sighed. "Yeah, we can't do that. How about that vamp doctor that Em sees? Dr. Hebert? I've seen him a few times. He's great."

"Jack. Yeah, he's cool."

"I'll take you there."

"No, Riv. I don't need a doctor. I need..." I shook my head. What the hell did I need? Counseling? Maybe, but where would I get it?

Once bonded, never broken.

"I remember where I heard the words. The female vampire who held me captive. She said them. To me."

"Oh, man. Okay." River sat back down and pulled his computer onto his lap. "You've got to let me find this bitch. Please. I can get her put away, and she'll be punished for what she did to you. I'll make sure of it."

"I don't want you going after her," I said softly.

"Are you fucking kidding me? I'm a detective. It's what I do. I solve cases and I put criminals behind bars. Do you want what happened to you to happen to someone else?"

"Of course not."

"Then let me do my job."

"It's not that simple," I said. "She's powerful. How else would she have been able to keep me for so long? I should have been able to break through those leather bindings. My muscles never weakened. The bindings were...enchanted or something."

River scoffed. "This is reality, Dante."

I scoffed back at him. "What the hell is reality, anyway?

To Erin, vampires aren't reality, but we're here. A month ago, I would have said werewolves didn't exist, but you've assured me they do. And now Bill believes in ghosts, despite what we've been told our whole lives. How much further is it to believe that maybe the leather bindings that held me down for ten years were enchanted? What other explanation is there? The goons who fed and tortured me were human, Riv. *Human.* I should have been able to overpower them, but I couldn't. Something else was at work. Something I don't want you prying into, for your own good."

"A little voodoo doesn't scare me, Dante."

"Voodoo, if it actually exists, is good magic. Whatever kept me captive all that time was evil. I felt it, Riv. There was evil all around me. I fought against it. I stayed strong and kept from crying out. But I couldn't overpower it. Believe me, I tried."

"The vampire who took you is evil."

"She is. I'm not denying that. But there was a force there. It was more than just her. Maybe she created it. I don't know. But it was there. It was dark and powerful, and you don't want to fuck with it. Trust me."

"All right. All right. I'll let it go." River scratched at his head. "I hate to ask this, but...do you think she'll come back for you?"

I drew in a deep breath. "The thought occurred to me, but I've been so consumed by Erin that I haven't been overly worried, even though I probably should be. But no, I don't think she will, at least not for the time being. She *let* me go, Riv. I'm almost sure of it."

⚜

Later, after River had gone to bed, I went out. It was after eleven, and I knew Erin would have already left for work. I needed to check something.

I drove to Erin's and sat in my car for a few moments. Was what I was about to do a violation? She'd asked me to leave, and I'd promised I'd do as she asked.

Yet here I was, about to check something I had no right to check. I was invading her privacy.

Still, I had to know. She was mine now—mine to protect.

I left my car and walked to her door. I didn't bother knocking because she wasn't home anyway.

I let my hand hover over the door knob for a few seconds before I grasped it.

It didn't turn.

She had locked her door.

SIX

Erin

I jolted when I heard my door knob. I walked briskly out of the kitchen and regarded it. Someone was trying to turn it. Trying to break in. I frantically searched for my phone. Had I left it in the bedroom? I'd used it to call in sick to work. I hadn't gotten a wink of sleep, and I'd be no good to patients in my current mental state.

I turned to go up the stairs—

But a veil of calmness settled over me.

Dante.

Dante was trying to get in. And I'd locked the door this time. I walked back.

"Who's there?"

"Erin?" His voice, of course. "Sorry. I thought you were at work."

"So you thought you'd break into my house?"

"Of course not. Look. This conversation will be a whole lot easier if you open the door."

My hand automatically reached toward the deadbolt. “I told you to leave.”

“I know. I did. I’ll leave again if you tell me to.”

Instinctively I knew he was being truthful. But why did I feel this way? After what had transpired, I should be frightened out of my wits.

Still, I was certain Dante would not lie to me. Not anymore. I wasn’t sure he ever had.

I turned the deadbolt and opened the door.

He wore jeans that encased his firm thighs beautifully and a black T-shirt with no logo. His hair was a mass of waves around his handsome and stubbled face. His dark eyes were mesmerizing.

So mesmerizing.

I could never shut the door in his face, though that was what my mind was telling me to do, despite my emotions saying otherwise.

“May I come in?”

Did I have to invite him in? Or would he tell me that was a myth as well?

I decided to do an experiment. “No.”

“All right. I guess we can talk like this, but it’s nearing midnight. You shouldn’t have your door wide open.”

I edged back a little and then feigned a stumble. He entered swiftly and steadied me.

“Another myth,” I said.

“What?”

“That you can’t come in unless you’re invited.”

“Erin, I’ve come in uninvited before. Remember? When you left the door unlocked and fell asleep on your laptop? And yes, that’s a myth.”

Right. Now I felt pretty idiotic. I shut the door and turned the deadbolt.

"What are you doing home?" he asked.

"I called in sick. I'm a mess, Dante. I didn't get any sleep at all. All I could think about was how my whole life has been turned upside down."

"You don't have to be afraid of me, Erin."

"Damn it!" I pulled at my hair. "I'm *not* afraid of you. I probably should be, but I'm not. I don't know why I'm not."

"I know why."

"Do you? Maybe you should explain it to me, then. Because if I don't get a handle on this, I won't get any sleep tomorrow either, and I won't be able to work. If I can't work, I can't pay my bills. What have you done to me?"

"I didn't do anything to you, Erin. What was done to you has been done to me as well. I don't fully understand it, but together, we can try to figure it out. Do you want to know why you aren't afraid of me?"

"Please. Enlighten me."

"Because you love me. And I love you. But even that love isn't the strongest bond between us."

My head was whirling. I'd been up for over twenty-four hours. I wasn't sure I'd be able to process anything he told me. Especially knowing the subject matter.

"Believe it or not, I didn't come to see you tonight. I thought you'd be at work, and I came to make sure you locked your door."

"Why is that any of your business?"

"Because your safety is my business! Because I'd die if something happened to you! Is that good enough for you?"

His words flowed into my mind, and though I

comprehended them, I also felt them. They moved me almost in a literal way as I found myself inching toward him despite my desire to stay away, to forget all of this, to go back to my simple life where vampires didn't exist.

But in that simple life, there was no Dante. There was no "most amazing sex I'd ever had." There was no orgasm that blinded me with colors and made me float on air.

"You can't stay away from me, Erin."

I gathered all my strength and forced my feet to stay glued to the ground. No more inching toward him. No more.

"I can, and I will."

"We're bonded. We need each other."

"Bonded? What the hell are you talking about?" My feet itched to continue their forward movement. I clenched my hands into fists, hoping the tension would force my legs to stay immobile.

"I don't fully understand it myself, but that pull you've felt since we met? That's part of it."

"But I'm not...one of you."

"Vampire. I'm a vampire, Erin. You need to say the word. I need to hear you say the word. To accept what I am."

I squeezed my eyes shut. "Vampires don't exist, Dante."

I popped my eyes open when he gripped my shoulders, his dark gaze searing into me. Already I burned from his touch, his nearness.

"They exist. *I* exist. Say it. Say I'm a vampire, Erin. Say I'm a vampire, and you love me."

"I...can't."

"You are human. And I love you, Erin Hamilton, with everything that I am. I will never harm you, and I will never allow anyone or anything else to cause you harm. I will die protecting you if I have to." His grip on me strengthened. "Now say it, damn it. Say 'you're a vampire, Dante, and I love you.'"

My mouth dropped open, and the words formed on the folds of my vocal cords.

You're a vampire, Dante, and I love you.

But they stayed lodged at the back of my throat.

My mind dueled with my heart. *Vampires don't exist. Yet this man sucked my blood, and when he did, I experienced the most intimate sensation of my life. But vampires don't exist.*

Vampires don't exist.

I couldn't. Couldn't let the words flow. If I did, I'd be admitting that everything I knew to be true in the world was a fabrication. Life would be forever changed.

"You *will* say the words, Erin. Maybe not today, but you will in the future. Sooner than you think." He loosened his grip on my shoulders. "I will leave now, if you ask me to."

I opened my mouth once more, ready to tell him to get out, but again the words wouldn't emerge.

I didn't want him to leave. Being near him seemed...right. Right in a new and wonderful way. That pull hadn't lessened at all. In fact, I felt it stronger than ever, like an invisible rope around my waist that he was yanking toward him, and I was powerless to escape.

No. That was a lie.

I didn't *want* to escape.

How could I turn my back on an intimacy I'd never imagined? Emotions I'd never encountered? Never dreamed could exist in this world?

I couldn't.

And that scared the hell out of me.

"Just say the words, Erin," he said again. "Tell me to leave, and I will. You know I'm not lying. I'll do whatever you ask."

This time words came, but they weren't the words I was thinking. The words I was trying, but failing, to will myself to say. Four completely different words tumbled forth.

"Kiss me, Dante. Please."

SEVEN

DANTE

I didn't hesitate.

After all, I'd told her I'd do whatever she asked.

I pressed my lips to hers, attempting a gentle kiss, but she opened instantly, and my resistance failed. I kissed her hard, with passion, with urgency, with all the love I felt for her in my heart and my soul.

With the force and strength of the bond between us.

When I felt the familiar tingle in my gums, I didn't try to stop it. This was me, and she knew who and what I was now. She would eventually accept it. She had no choice. Not if we both wanted to continue to exist.

I pulled her close to me, every inch of her touching every inch of me. Her nipples hardened through her tank top, and I felt them like pebbles pushing into my chest.

I kissed her harder.

My fangs had descended all the way, and my cock had become rock inside my jeans. I nudged her against a wall, flattening her and then grinding my erection into her soft belly.

Her groan vibrated into my mouth, into my body, and I answered with one of my own.

When one of my cuspids scraped her tongue and drew a drop of blood, the flavor took over my entire mouth as it trickled into me.

Then she pushed me away and placed her hands over her lips—lips that were swollen and dark pink from the feral kiss we'd shared.

I said nothing, just gazed into her fiery green eyes.

"You... My tongue..."

I made no attempt to hide my fangs as I spoke. "My teeth descend when I'm turned on. It's just something that happens, love, like my dick hardening, or you getting wet." I closed my eyes and inhaled. "And you're wet, Erin. I can smell you. I can smell your lust."

"But...do you need...?"

"Your blood? No, not yet. I had enough this morning."

"How often do you need to..."

Poor thing. She still couldn't bring herself to say the words. "I require blood every twenty-four hours. I can go a week without it if I have to, but it's like a human going without food for a week. I'd be starving."

"If you don't have mine... I mean, how do you..."

"We drink animal blood. Mostly steers and sheep. We get it from a local butcher."

"But the animals. How can you..."

"We don't kill animals, Erin. We don't kill anything. We're not killers. The animals we drink from are already dead. They're raised for meat."

"This is all so... How can you expect me to..." She closed her eyes.

I touched her cheek, the warmth of her blood barreling through me. "You're going to need to talk in complete sentences, Erin. You're going to need to accept this eventually."

Her lips trembled, but she raised her hand and placed her warm palm over mine. I figured she'd move my hand from her cheek, but she didn't. She simply stood with her hand covering mine. Her warm blood curled through her palm, her nerves jittery. I felt it. I felt it all.

"I'll ask again, Erin. Do you want me to leave?"

She closed her eyes, a light sigh escaping her throat. "I should. I *should* want you to leave."

"But *do* you?"

She drew in a breath and opened her eyes. "No, Dante. I don't want you to leave." She let go of my hand and bent down to remove the sweatpants she was wearing. She tossed them aside and stood, naked from the waist down, her painted toes digging into the carpet. "I want you to fuck me. Right here. Right now. Right up against this wall. I shouldn't want it, but I do. I want it so bad I might die without it. What is wrong with me?"

I unbuttoned and unzipped my jeans, sliding them over my hips and freeing my cock. "Nothing is wrong with you, love. Look at me."

Her gaze drifted to my erection.

"Not there. Here. Look into my eyes. See the love I feel for you." I lifted her and set her down on my cock, welcoming the warm suction of her pussy, her blood-filled walls gloving me in warmth and exquisiteness. "Nothing is wrong with this. How could it be? Do you feel it, Erin? Do you feel how perfectly we fit together? How can anything be wrong with this?"

She didn't answer, and I pushed her against the wall and

then shoved my cock into her once more. My teeth were out, and I buried my nose in her neck, scraping my fangs against her soft skin.

"No, Dante. No."

"Not now, love. I don't need to. You'll know when I need it. You'll need it too."

Still, my sensitive teeth were drawn to the pulse in her carotid artery, and I pressed my lips over the rapid thump. So sweet, so warm, so Erin.

She wrapped her arms around my neck, moaning my name as she held on. Still I pumped into her—thrust in, out, in—until her pussy clamped down on me with her climax.

"Dante! I'm coming. My God." She exploded around me, her heart beating faster, the rich pulse in her neck like a drumbeat over my lips.

I couldn't hold out any longer. I shoved my cock deep within her, letting myself go, spilling into her body, into her soul.

I stayed there for a few timeless moments, letting her milk every last drop of semen from me, her back pushed against the wall. I breathed heavily into her neck as her rapid pulse slowly faded back to normal. I pressed my lips to her skin as my fangs began to retract.

Then I eased away from her, gently moving her off me and steadying her as her feet hit the floor.

She touched her neck, touched the healing puncture wounds from this morning. "You didn't."

"No. But I will need to. In the morning."

She closed her eyes. "I can't let you."

I didn't argue with her. She *would* let me. She'd have to, for both our sakes. Now was not the time to tell her that if she didn't feed me, she'd condemn us both to death.

EIGHT

Erin

I still stood against the wall, my back sore from the friction of being pushed against the roughness. I'd seen him. Seen Dante. He had fangs.

And God help me, I found him attractive that way.

Something about the animalistic look, the fire in his eyes when his teeth were descended... He was a predator, and I was his prey.

And that excited me to no end.

What was wrong with me?

God help me, I'd gotten wetter. My pussy had throbbed harder when I saw him in his vampire state.

I'd wanted him to bite my neck again, suck my blood, take me to the top of the world with that feverish orgasm I remembered so well. Yet I didn't want it just as much.

Didn't want to want it. I'd told him I wouldn't let him take my blood again. Even as I'd heard the words, I knew they meant nothing.

I would do whatever he wanted me to do. Whatever he told me to do. I would obey him. Perhaps not without question. Not yet. But I would still do as he commanded. Just the thought inflamed me once again.

And frightened me just as much.

"Erin," he said.

I bit my lower lip. "Yeah?"

"I want you to get some sleep."

I huffed. "Easier said than done."

"Would it help if I stay here? So you'll feel safe?"

Safe? How could I feel safe with a man who wanted my blood? Worse, I *wanted* him to take my blood. I was terrified of being alone with Dante.

Yet the calmness I felt overruled my rational mind. Somewhere, deep in the recesses of myself, outside the realm of my logic, I felt ultimately safe with him.

Keep an open mind. A very *open mind.*

Those words from the man who'd helped me with my car. Did he know Dante?

So much to think about, and so little sleep for my brain to work on.

"Erin? Are you going to answer me?"

"No, I don't want you to stay, Dante. I need time. Time to process all of this. I'm just not sure how much time I need, or if there will ever be enough."

He reached toward me, lightly trailing a finger over my cheek and jawline. "There is all the time in the world. This won't be as hard as you think it is."

Just his small touch ignited me again. My nipples hardened, and an image shot into my mind. Dante, looking feral and gorgeous with his fangs descended, sucking on my nipple, fingering my pussy, and then sinking his teeth into the fatty flesh of my breast.

I crossed my legs to ease the throbbing between them.

This couldn't happen. None of this could happen.

"You need to leave," I said. "Now."

He dropped his arm to his side and pulled up his jeans and boxer briefs, zipping and buttoning them. "I understand. But I'll be back in the morning."

"Please," I said. "Don't come back."

Even as the words spewed out of me, I knew I didn't mean them.

And I knew he'd be back.

NINE

DANTE

Once bonded, never broken.

"We need each other now, Dante. I require your blood for sustenance, and you require mine."

I thrashed against the leather bindings. "If you need me so much, why do you let those goons torture me?"

"I have my reasons." She hovered over me, her fangs protruding and red with my blood that she'd just sucked from the femoral artery on my thigh.

Already the wounds were coagulating. I could feel each layer of my skin regenerating, the tingles and the itching.

"We are bonded now, Dante. And once bonded, never broken." She sank her teeth into my neck.

⚜

It was one a.m., and I didn't want to go back to River's or Bill's. I hadn't seen my sister in a few days, and though I was loath to return to the French Quarter, I found myself driving to the

Cornstalk Hotel, where she was a night manager.

The street lights illuminated the wrought-iron fence with the cornstalk posts that gave the pale yellow hotel its name. The actual building had once been a private residence, originally built as a home for the first attorney general of Louisiana. Like most other buildings in the Quarter, it was reputedly haunted, though Emilia and I knew better.

I rang the bell. Em was sitting behind the front desk, which was at the other end of the hotel, but she looked up and saw me through the window in the door. Good thing for acute vampire vision. She buzzed me in.

"What are you doing here?" she asked when I walked to the front desk.

"Just out and about, and I wanted to see how you're feeling."

"Okay. Nauseated a lot, but that's normal for a vampire pregnancy. Humans are lucky. The sickness usually ends around the twelfth week. I'll probably feel this way the whole nine months."

"Maybe not," I said.

"I hope I do. Jack says the sicker I am, the better the pregnancy is progressing and the better chance of a successful outcome."

"Oh. Then good." It felt strange hoping my sister would feel sick, but I wanted her to make it safely out of this pregnancy. Vampire females were rare. If River was right, and Erin's brother was the father of the baby, it wouldn't be a vampire baby. It would be human.

"So..." I began.

"Yeah?"

"Are you ready to tell us who the father is?"

She shook her head, chuckling. “I should have known you didn’t stop by just to chat.”

“Em, you’re going to have to at least tell the father. He has a right to know.”

She sighed. “I know, and I will. Eventually. I just need to get a grip, you know? I haven’t told anyone this, but you’re my brother, so I’ll tell you. I’m scared out of my mind, Dante.”

I nodded. “Because of what happened to Mom?”

“Of course! But I can’t have an abortion. I thought about it, but I can’t do it. This is my child. A life growing inside me. I want it. I want this baby.”

“I understand. You’re going to be fine, Em.” I hoped to God I wasn’t lying to her.

“I need you to promise me something, big brother.”

“Of course. Anything.”

“If I don’t make it but the baby does, I want you to take him. Raise my child as your own. You’re my big brother, and for so long I thought I’d lost you. Now you’re back, and I need you. You’ll be a good father, Dante.”

A good father? I was wrestling so many of my own demons that I couldn’t even begin to think about fatherhood. Plus, I couldn’t process the fact that Emilia might not survive the pregnancy.

But right now my sister needed my assurance, not my doubts.

“Of course, Em. But that isn’t going to happen. You’re going to be fine, and the baby is going to be fine.”

“I hope so. I’m doing everything I can. I’m following Jack’s instructions to the letter. No caffeine. No alcohol. No sex.”

“Easy, Em. There are some things a big brother doesn’t want to think about.” Though the fact that she was pregnant made me think them anyway.

"I shouldn't be whining to you," she said. "You've been through so much. If you need anything, or just to talk, you know I'm here."

"I'm all right. I've talked to River and to Bill a little." I couldn't tell my baby sister what had been done to me, especially not while she was in such a fragile state. She needed to be stress free until the pregnancy was over.

Time to change the subject. "Slow night?"

She nodded. "Weeknights sometimes are. The weekends are usually hopping, people coming in at all hours, but I don't work Friday and Saturday nights."

Good. Em didn't need the stress of the partiers coming in at all hours and waking up the other guests. "Do you get a break? Do you want to go for a walk?"

"Not for a few hours, but you're welcome to hang here if you want. Do you want a snack?"

"Sure. I'll get it. Where?"

"There's a fridge in the back. I keep some cold cuts and bread in there. Make a sandwich. In fact, make two. I'm starving."

"You need something else? I can get you—"

"Not at work. Even on a slow night. I can't take the chance of anyone seeing me. I drank before work."

"Got it." I walked back and found the refrigerator. I quickly made two sandwiches and brought them back to the front desk, handing one to Em.

After taking a few bites, I sighed. If I expected Em to be honest with me about her pregnancy, I had to tell her what was going on with me. The blood bond. But I didn't want to stress her out. I could at least tell her that I'd fallen in love.

"So...I have some news."

She swallowed her bite of sandwich. "Yeah? What?"

"I'm seeing someone. A human woman."

Her eyebrows shot up. "Really? Who?"

"Remember the nurse who came to our house?"

"Oh, yeah. She was nice. She told me to go to the doctor. I should have listened to her." Em laughed.

"If you had, maybe you wouldn't have ended up in the ER."

"Yeah, yeah." Em took a bite of sandwich. "Quit going all big brother on me," she said, her mouth full.

"Anyway, her name's Erin."

"I remember. She's Jay's sister."

Perfect opportunity to press her. "How do you know Jay?"

She laughed, nearly spitting out her sandwich. "In the biblical sense, so to speak."

I cleared my throat. "Oh?"

"Just one time. I doubt he even remembers me." She patted her stomach. "But I'll always remember him."

"He's the one, huh?"

"Yeah. Have you met him?"

"A couple times."

"Then don't tell me you didn't know he's the father. His scent must be all over me."

"My nose isn't working very well these days."

"Oh? Are you okay?"

"Yeah. I've seen your doctor. I'm fine." Fine? Maybe not exactly. But I didn't want Em worrying about me losing my ability to scent any human but Erin.

"River has to know who the father is. Jay is his partner."

"Has he said anything to you?"

She shook her head, swallowing.

"He probably thinks it's none of his business."

"Then he's right. I'll tell him and Bill eventually. Right now I just don't like talking about it. I'm scared I'll jinx the pregnancy or something." She rolled her eyes. "I know that sounds completely stupid."

"Is that why you haven't told Jay?"

She nodded. "Yeah. Go ahead. Tell me I'm being a moron."

After all I'd been through and the ridiculous thoughts that whirled through my own head, I'd never call my sister a moron or anything else derogatory.

"You do what you need to do, Em. Whatever keeps your stress level low. We'll all support you."

My phone buzzed against my thigh. I was still getting used to the constant texting. Being "on call" to everyone who knew my number was a little ridiculous.

I grabbed my cell phone and smiled.

Erin.

I need you. I'm okay,
but please come over.

TEN

Erin

Dante texted me back almost instantaneously.

In the Quarter. I'll be there
as soon as I can.

I was glad he was still up. Dawn was nearly here, and he was coming back anyway.

I'd tried to sleep. Tried herbal tea. A relaxing lavender bath. A self-massage. Meditation. Even warm milk, which was disgusting.

Nothing had worked.

My brain wouldn't calm down. Questions. So many questions. Some that I wouldn't even be able to verbalize.

I'd been so hung up on my inner duel between what Dante was and how he made me feel that I'd neglected to pay much attention to another issue. A *big* issue.

Someone *else* had taken my blood.

Dante said he'd find out who it was, but now the thought

had consumed me. Even as I'd tried to meditate, all I could picture was this ferocious animal of a person with a blurred face hypnotizing me and feeding on my thigh. The marks were perilously close to my gifts.

That didn't bode well.

If I didn't remember, other things could have happened as well. What if I'd been...raped?

Just thinking the word tormented me.

My nerves jittered under my skin, and I'd been pacing around my living room, rubbing my arms, when I'd finally decided to text Dante. I texted rather than called so I wouldn't wake him if he was asleep.

But if he hadn't answered the text, I would have called.

I was that desperate. That fucked up.

I poured myself a glass of wine, but after one sip I threw it in the sink.

While it might relax me, I didn't want my faculties impaired even in the slightest.

I had to face reality.

I had to face the fact that I'd been violated. Not only were vampires real—still having a hard time with that one—but one had bitten me and taken my blood without my consent. God only knew what else he had done.

I sat down on my couch, my knees jiggling, biting off the cuticle on my thumb. "Ouch!" I tore so much skin off that it bled. Just what I didn't need. My blood right in front of Dante's nose. I hurried to the bathroom and bandaged it.

As I stared at my reflection in the mirror, an uninvited image hurled itself into my mind. Dante, turned away from me, blood smeared on the kitchen floor in his grandfather's house. Yes, I'd been there. I'd run into the kitchen when I'd heard the commotion.

A bread knife. He'd cut himself with a bread knife. But now, in my mind's eye, I saw something else.

Not the jagged cut from a serrated knife.

No.

Two wounds. I touched my neck. Much like...

But no. That wasn't what had happened. He'd cut himself with the bread knife. The scene was clear in my mind, and my memory confirmed it. Where had the other image come from?

I blinked my eyes, and the picture was gone. Just my reflection again. My eyes looked sunken and tired, rimmed with dark circles. I was a mess.

I jolted at the knock on the door. I walked out of the bathroom swiftly and eyed my deadbolt. I had locked it. "Dante?" I said through the door.

"It's me, love."

I opened the door and pulled him inside, his very presence already soothing me. That veil of calmness I'd felt before.

I crashed into his body. His arms went around me and he held me. Simply held me, as though he sensed it was exactly what I needed.

It was.

I breathed him in. His masculine fragrance. His strength.

This man would never harm me. This man...

But he wasn't a man. At least not a human one.

He was...

Still couldn't form the word in my thoughts. Not when it came to Dante.

Did you see him?

See who?

The vampire.

I squeezed my eyes shut, forcing out the unpleasantness.

Just Dante. Just his hardness, his protection.

"What's wrong, baby? What do you need?" He pressed his lips to my forehead.

It was a comforting embrace, not the embrace of someone who wanted to fuck me.

Not the embrace of someone who wanted to suck my blood.

"I'm scared," I said.

He kissed my forehead again. "I know you are. You'll accept it in time."

I pulled away. "I'm not even talking about that."

"Then what are you talking about?" He took both of my hands in his.

"I'm freaking out more than a little here. Those marks on my thigh. Someone bit me. What if they did other things? Abe Lincoln said vampires—"

"Hold on a minute. Who is Abe Lincoln? Don't tell me you're communing with the dead." He smiled.

"Damn it! This isn't a time for paranormal jokes! A patient at the hospital. Abe Lincoln is his name, or so he says. Anyway, he told me that vampires feed on him, and he lets them. That they don't hypnotize him. But most vampires hypnotize their victims and then feed, so they don't remember it."

"Hypnotize? Actually, we call it glamouring, but it is a form of hypnosis."

I dropped his hands. "So it's true? It's not a myth?"

"That part is true. Vampires have the ability to glamour humans, but most don't do it. We consider it morally wrong. We only do it in a dire emergency. If we have to feed and there's nothing else available."

"Oh my God. Have you ever..."

"Of course not! I would never violate you in that way."

"So you never took my blood before..."

"Not before yesterday, no. I mean, I got a little taste when I accidentally nicked your tongue once, and then that night we were dancing in the Quarter, and I nicked your neck. But you remember those times, right?"

"Yes."

"There's your proof that I never glamoured you."

I breathed in slowly and let it out, trying like hell to calm my nerves. "But someone else did, Dante. Someone glamoured me and fed on my thigh. If I don't remember that, what else don't I remember? What happened to me? What happened?"

ELEVEN

DANTE

She was frantic. Her eyes had widened into circles and her whole body trembled. Her pulse thumped in her neck, and her heartbeat drummed in my ears, lending a beat to the whooshing of blood through her veins and the higher-pitched hiss as it flowed out through her arteries.

My gums tingled, but I suppressed my urge to feed. She needed me right now. She needed Dante the man, not Dante the vampire.

I kissed the top of her head and then slid my hands to her shoulders, pushing her away slightly, for my own sanity as well as hers.

While her blood didn't quiet, at least I no longer felt the thump of her heart against my body.

"Erin, love, I told you I'd find out who did this to you, and I will. Trust me on that. Believe me when I say I hate the idea of someone else feeding on you as much—probably more—than you do. You're mine. I've known that in some capacity since I first laid eyes on you. I will find out who did that, and it will not happen again."

"It's not even that." Her lips trembled. "What if they did something else to me? What if I've been raped, Dante? What if..." She closed her eyes, shaking her head. "I can't go there. This is all too much. My whole world is collapsing."

"Open your eyes, Erin, and look at me."

Her eyes stayed shut. "Don't you *dare* try to glamour me into some kind of submission to take away my agitation. Don't you fucking dare, Dante."

"Hey." I cupped her cheeks, easing my thumbs to her temples and massaging them. "I will never glamour you. You have my word."

She slowly opened her eyes, her fear showing within them. I felt her pain, felt everything she sensed as her heart continued to thunder loud enough for my enhanced hearing. I was in tune with her body and her heart, and I didn't think anyone had touched her in any other inappropriate way. If someone had, I'd know it, and I'd murder the motherfucker. Still, I had to be sure.

"Erin, have you had any strange pain down there? Any feelings of something being 'off'?"

She shook her head, her lips still trembling.

"I don't think you've been raped."

"Can you smell anything? Smell who did this to me?"

"Unfortunately, no. Vampires have no scent to each other. We can smell all other animals, but not ourselves. And even if we could, I'd be no help. Since I met you, I only smell you."

"What do you mean?"

God, where to start? I couldn't tell her about the blood bond. Not yet. She was already freaked to the hilt.

"I mean I can only smell *you*. Your scent overpowers all others."

"Even when you're not with me?"

"Yes."

"How? Why?"

"I don't know." I hated not being completely truthful. I actually *didn't* know for sure, but I had a pretty firm idea of what was going on.

"Then how will you find out who fed on me? And how will you make sure it never happens again?"

"Your scent may still be on whoever fed from you. I just need to find that vampire. I will. You can count on that." It could have happened anywhere. She'd been leaving her door unlocked since we met. I'd assumed it was because of the blood bond, but could she have been glamoured into doing so? To let someone in to feed?

I seethed. Damn it!

I had to maintain control. She needed me.

It could have happened at the hospital or anywhere else she'd been. It had most likely happened in the French Quarter, where most of the vampires hung out. Most of us didn't feed on humans, but a select few didn't share our scruples. Erin had gone out with Lucy the night we danced at the bar. She'd probably been out many times before with her friend.

"When was the last time you went to the Quarter?"

"The night we danced."

"I mean before that."

"I don't know. I'm not a big partier, but Lucy drags me out once or twice a month. Probably a few weeks before that time."

Time enough for the marks to still be visible. If I took Erin to the Quarter, her scent would drive out whoever had fed on her, and I'd make it clear that she was off limits.

"When is your next night off?" I asked.

"Friday."

"Okay. We have a date to go to the Quarter."

"Are you sure that's wise?"

"It's the only way. I'll find who did this to you, and I'll make it clear that you're mine. No one will touch you again. No one but me."

She melted into my arms then, and the calmness that overtook her was almost visible. Did my words have that effect? Or was it *me*?

I didn't care. I just wanted her to feel better. I wanted to keep her safe from harm. It was what I'd always wanted—no, *ached* for—since she'd found me covered in blood at the hospital.

Erin and I were meant to be.

Once bonded, never broken.

Where I'd heard those words no longer mattered. They belonged to Erin and me now. Always.

I inhaled. Her blood called to me, and my cock stiffened as my fangs elongated. I was done trying to stop them. My body would respond to her no matter what. What was important was how I responded to my body.

She nudged against my erection.

"I won't do anything, Erin. It's just a physiological response." I inhaled. Her arousal had been triggered. "Just like the one you're having."

River had said I'd learn to control my blood lust and my other urges. I hadn't had a lot of luck, but one thing had proved so powerful that it gave me control.

My love for Erin. My duty and obligation to see to her needs first, before my own.

She gave me the control I needed.

She pulled away from me slightly. “Will it always be this way between us? Will we always want each other so much?”

I laughed softly. “I certainly hope so.”

“There’s so much I’m not ready for yet. So much I don’t understand.”

“I know, love.”

“But one thing I do know. I want you to take me to bed. Right now.”

TWELVE

Erin

I couldn't fight the physical thing between us. I loved him. I knew that with my whole heart. And as much as I couldn't say the V word about him yet, I still needed him. Needed him in a physical and emotional way.

And he needed me.

He needed my blood.

The idea scared me but also veiled me in a warmth I was only beginning to comprehend. I liked that he needed me. That I could give him something no one else could.

"Are you sure?" he asked.

"You said... Every twenty-four hours..."

"Yes. But I can take blood from another source if I have to, Erin. At least for now."

"You mean...you *don't* need me?"

"God, no! I need you like I need air. And yes, vampires breathe."

"Don't," I said.

"Don't what?"

"Don't take blood from another source. Not today, anyway."

The thought of him sharing the intimacy we'd shared with anyone else made me want to throw things. I cupped his cheeks and pulled him into a kiss.

Our lips slid together, our tongues tangling, and within a few minutes he scooped me into his arms and walked upstairs to my bedroom.

He had me naked in an instant, and then I watched, nearly drooling, as he removed his own clothes. First his leather boots and socks. Then his shirt, baring that gorgeous chest. Last, his jeans and boxers, his cock already hard.

I tried not to look at his handsome face.

His fangs were out. I'd felt them during the kiss.

I knew it. I could handle it. I even found it attractive.

I just didn't want to look yet.

So I fell to my knees and licked the drop of fluid from his cock head.

He groaned. "Oh, God, Erin."

I sprinkled tiny kisses over his glans and along the bottom of his shaft, but then I pulled back.

I wanted to look at him. Commit his gorgeous cock to memory.

He was huge, and the skin was a hue darker than the rest of him. Two purple veins marbled over the top of the shaft, intersecting and then disappearing at the base. His balls were covered in a smattering of black hair, and they were already scrunched up close to his body. But the head of his cock—that was a true work of art. It was like a polished white door knob, a shape I knew well as I felt it nudge past my lips and into my pussy.

Now I wanted to feel it slide past my other lips.

I took it into my mouth and slid about halfway down before I needed to pull back. Yes, he was that long and thick. It would take some time for me to work him all the way to the back of my throat. I slid my lips over the top of his shaft, all the way to the base, and then pressed kisses to his black curls. He smelled musky and masculine, and I inhaled, closing my eyes, my pussy throbbing.

Then I returned to his head, taking it all into my mouth once more.

He groaned above me, threading his fingers through my hair but taking care not to move my head.

Scary, but I wanted him to. I wanted him to take charge, fuck my mouth, nudge the back of my throat.

Just as the thought crossed my mind, he grabbed both sides of my head and pushed me onto his cock.

I moaned, and then he pulled me back, all the way to the head, and I sucked at the knob.

"Erin, God, that feels so fucking good."

I smiled—as much as I could with my mouth full of cock—and then he pushed me back onto him again.

I relished his groans, his warm hands in my hair and on my scalp.

But then he pushed me off again.

"Can't," he said. "Not yet. Need to be inside you."

He picked me up and threw me on the bed. Not gently. And it was such a turn-on.

I spread my legs and he hovered over me, his cock nudging my slick pussy lips. His lips were parted, and his fangs descended. I tried not to look away.

But I closed my eyes as he plunged into me.

Such sweet fulfillment. That knobby head pushed its way through, touching every crevice inside me and filling me like no other. He lowered himself until our chests, slick with perspiration, touched.

He moved my arms upward, and I clasped two rungs of my headboard.

The rungs he had bound me to only a day earlier.

I bit my lip to keep from begging him to bind me again. I wanted it yet I didn't. It would happen again, I knew, but not this time.

He pumped and he pumped, and when the tiny tickle began in my clit and grew into contractions in my pussy, I flew.

"Yes, love. Come for me. Come with me."

He pushed into me with one last strong stroke, and I felt each pulse of his penis as he filled me.

Eyes wide open, I looked at his beautiful face, his hair slick around his forehead.

His teeth...

I turned my head, squeezing my eyes shut. "You don't need to tie me down."

"I know, love."

He bit into my neck.

Good pain. Yes, pain could be good. And it morphed into a sweet tugging that swirled through my body and landed between my legs.

My orgasm continued, growing stronger, and I floated beneath him, his body grounding me but taking me away at the same time.

Again, a kaleidoscope of color surrounded us, and the soft jazzy melody played.

Too soon, the tugging stopped, his tongue on my neck.

"No," I said, my eyes still closed. "More. Give me more."

"Open your eyes, Erin."

"No. Please. More. Not done yet."

He gently turned my head to face him. "Obey me. Open your eyes."

Obey me.

Why did I want to obey him so much?

I opened my eyes.

"I can't take any more. I need to work you up to a full feeding. I took a little too much the first time. It won't happen again. Not until you're ready."

"But it feels so...so..." Words escaped me.

"I know, love. Trust me. I know."

His teeth had gone down, but his lips and chin were smeared with my blood. Though I didn't want to find it attractive, I couldn't help myself. It was magnificent. He looked like an animal who had just finished devouring its prey.

Yet I was still here. I hadn't been eaten.

But oh, I had been devoured. In the best way.

He got up and went to the bathroom. I heard the water running in the sink, and when he came back a few minutes later, his face was clean.

He'd done that for me. For my comfort. As much as I appreciated the thought, I wanted to see him covered in my blood.

Yet I didn't want to see him that way just as much.

I was fighting inside myself, my head against my heart, and it was exhausting.

"Dante?"

"Yes, love?"

"I need to sleep. I need to. If I don't, I won't be able to work tonight, and I can't call in sick again. I hate doing that if I'm not actually sick."

"I wish I could help you. I can stay if you'd like. You'll feel protected then."

I bit my lip. "Could you...?" I couldn't believe what I was about to say. "Could you...hypnotize me into sleeping?"

"It's called glamouring, love, and no, I won't."

"But I need to sleep."

"I promised you I would never glamour you, and I won't."

"But if I'm asking—"

He shook his head vehemently. "That doesn't matter. If we're going to have a relationship, if I have any hope of getting you to accept everything about me, I can't use what little power I have over you. I like you to obey me in the bedroom—I almost need it—but that's only in the bedroom. I'm not looking for a subservient partner. I want us to be equals in this relationship. If I glamour you, I destroy that possibility."

I loved him all the more, though part of me was so desperate for slumber that I almost argued the point.

"All right. Then stay. Please. Rub my back. Hold me. Do whatever it takes. I need to sleep."

But then his phone buzzed in his jeans on the floor.

THIRTEEN

DANTE

"Sounds like you got another text," Erin said.

I sighed. Damn! I liked it better when I wasn't at everyone's beck and call. This cell phone bullshit had gone too far.

The text was from River.

Another woman went missing
from University.

I silently thanked the universe that Erin hadn't been at work. I couldn't keep this from her. She'd find out when she went in tonight anyway.

"River says another woman is missing from your hospital."

She sat up in bed.

"Sorry to have to tell you, but you'd find out tonight anyway." A knife of fear jabbed me. "I'm not sure you're safe at work anymore, Erin."

"I'm fine. These are patients, not nurses. And they need me. I have a job to do."

"But if anything happened to you..." I couldn't let myself finish the thought. Couldn't go there.

"Nothing will happen to me. You promised. Remember? Besides, the last woman that disappeared was returned unharmed."

"That doesn't make any of this okay!"

"Of course it doesn't. But I have to work, Dante. It's how I pay my bills. I can't go broke." She paused a moment, massaging her chin. "What was the woman's blood type?"

"I don't know. Why does that matter?"

She shook her head. "Nothing. Just something that's niggling at me."

"What?"

"The first woman who disappeared, Cynthia North, was B positive. And we've had a shortage of B positive at the hospital for a while now. It seems like we're always out. That's why I was at Tulane that morning, to ask for some B pos to be sent over. I'll check her records when I go in tonight. If she's B positive, and the woman who went missing from the free clinic is B positive, then I might look into it more. In fact..." She rubbed her chin some more.

"In fact what?"

"I can't get access to the free clinic's records, but I bet Jay and River can get them. I've been meaning to ask Jay about that, but somehow I always find myself otherwise occupied."

"I can't say I'm sorry if you've been otherwise occupied with me. Do you want me to text River back and ask about the blood type?"

"Yeah. If you don't mind. Though he probably doesn't know yet. I doubt he and Jay are overly concerned about blood types. It's just odd that the first patient had the same blood type that we keep running out of." She sighed. "One of the ER docs commissioned me to do some research on blood types in women with certain characteristics. But she didn't say anything about B positive blood, so it's most likely not related."

"Probably not. Can't the doctors do their own research?"

"Doctors are more overworked than nurses are, believe it or not. Besides, she's paying me fifty bucks an hour, so I jumped at the offer."

"Oh." Research couldn't harm Erin. Could it? "Where will you be doing this research?"

"Here. At home on my computer. She gave me access to all the sites I'll need."

"Okay. Good."

"In fact, I should get on it. She asked me a while ago and I haven't started yet." She yawned. "But not now. Now, I need sleep."

"You do. I'll stay. Do you want to put something on?"

She stretched her arms above her head. "No. I'm comfy in my birthday suit. I'm just going to get under the covers."

She snuggled into bed, and I put on my boxer briefs and got ready to text River back.

Then something occurred to me.

Something disturbing.

Though most vampires didn't feed on humans, I'd learned long ago that a select few could distinguish blood types by their flavors. Vampires actually had the same blood types as humans, though I didn't know what mine was. I'd never been typed, and then I'd been held captive for so long and hadn't given a thought to anything except escaping. I'd call Jack and find out. He'd taken my blood for the labs. It had probably been typed.

Since I had so little experience, I couldn't differentiate

blood types by taste. Erin was the first human blood I'd ever tasted, and I didn't know what type she was.

Except that I *did* know.

A chill swept the back of my neck. I was certain, as if the knowledge had been planted into me telepathically.

She was B positive.

And so was I.

FOURTEEN

Erin

I slept soundly with Dante beside me. He was still beside me when I woke up at nine thirty p.m.

"Did you stay here the whole time?"

"Of course. I'd never leave you alone when you asked me to stay."

I smiled as warmth surrounded me. He was a wonderful man. If only I didn't have to deal with that one little thing...

Not going to think about that now. I had to go to work.

"Did you find out from River about the woman's blood type?"

"I texted him. He didn't know. Wanted to know why I was asking, though. I wasn't sure what to tell him. I just said you were asking and I didn't know why, which I guess is the truth."

"Yeah, pretty much. I'm not sure why. I just have a feeling that it's all connected somehow. Cynthia North's blood type, and the fact that we always seem to be running low on the same type at the hospital."

Dante didn't answer, though one of his eyebrows was raised slightly, making him look pensive. I waited for him to speak, but he didn't.

"I guess I'll get ready for work."

"Are you hungry?" he asked.

"Yeah, actually, though I didn't realize it until now. I'll get something on the way in."

"I can make you something."

"Oh? You can cook?"

"Well...no," he said sheepishly.

"Then don't worry about it. You don't need another mishap with a bread knife." I laughed. I grabbed his arm and looked at it. "All healed up. Wow, you're a fast healer."

"Another thing vampires do very well."

The V word again. I shrugged it off—or tried to—and went into the bathroom to shower.

⚜

When I got to the ER, Lucy was already there. So were Jay and River, who were questioning staff about the newest missing patient.

"Her name is Sybil Downey," Lucy told me. "Young. Only nineteen. I was here when she came in with stomach pains. She was supposed to have an emergency appendectomy but she disappeared before she got to surgery. If it had ruptured, she couldn't possibly have survived."

"I don't know. Cynthia North survived, and she was bleeding to death."

"True. We can always hope."

"Just out of curiosity, was Dr. Bonneville on last night?"

"No. It was Dr. Anderson and all the residents."

Dr. Bonneville hadn't been working the night Cynthia North disappeared.

Probably had nothing to do with anything. I needed to stop worrying about Dr. Bonneville and concentrate on work. Still, something about her bothered me ever since I'd met Mrs. Moore and then hadn't been able to find either Dr. Bonneville or her lookalike anywhere online. But I was being ridiculous. If Dr. Bonneville wasn't on duty, she couldn't have had anything to do with this new disappearance. It was more likely someone who was on duty. I knew all these people, though, including Dr. Bonneville. I couldn't imagine any of them having anything to do with something so heinous.

"Feeling better, I assume?" Lucy asked.

"What? Oh, yeah. I think I must have had food poisoning or something. Whatever it was seems to be out of my system." I logged in to the computer to get a blood type on Sybil Downey.

But wailing sirens stopped me.

"We're on," Lucy said.

Sybil's blood type would have to wait.

A heart attack, a car accident, and a shooting later—no fatalities, thank God—Lucy and I were sharing a cinnamon roll in the break room. Steve came in to join us.

"Update on Sybil Downey," he said. "Her mother said she had her appendix out when she was a little girl. About six or so. We're getting the records."

"That's not a huge deal," Lucy said. "Just a simple misdiagnosis. They would have discovered whatever was causing her distress when they got her open."

"But they never did," I said.

"I know. Weirdest thing. I was on last night. So were you, Luce. How could she have gotten by all of us? The docs, the nurses, the security guards. It doesn't make any sense at all."

"I know," Lucy agreed.

I thought for a moment. "It's almost as if..." I stood.

"It's almost as if...what?" Steve asked.

I ignored him and raced down to the locker room to retrieve my cell phone.

It's almost as if someone erased time.

Those were the words that had been on the tip of my tongue. Even as I thought them, I knew the whole concept was ridiculous. Not only ridiculous, but impossible. Time couldn't be erased.

But memories could be. Drugs, like Rohypnol, could fool with memories.

No, that still didn't make sense. No way could someone have roofied an entire ER night staff for the exact amount of time necessary. No, this had to be something else.

Some kind of...hypnosis.

My skin went cold, a chill sweeping over my neck.

Leave it, Erin. You know Dante didn't have anything to do with this.

No, but he might know who did.

River was on the case. Surely this had occurred to him.

What if it hadn't? Or what if...

Leave it, Erin.

But my curiosity won out. I went back up to the break room with my phone in tow. "Lucy, is River still here?"

"I don't know. He might be. Why don't you text Jay?"

Good idea. Where was my mind? I sent a text and got an immediate reply.

We're getting a bite at a truck stop.

What do you need?

I needed River. I wanted some answers, beginning with why my brother had bite marks on his neck.

Did you see him?

See who?

The vampire.

Dante had told me that vampires didn't glamour unless it was an emergency, but someone had bitten Jay, and the most likely candidate was his vampire partner.

FIFTEEN

DANTE

"Thanks for seeing me on such short notice," I said to Jack Hebert, my vampire physician.

"Not a problem. I prefer night hours. You said over the phone you need to know your blood type. I didn't have you typed when we did your previous work. Any reason why you want to know?"

"Just curious." True enough. What did it matter that Erin and I shared a blood type, and that it was the same blood type of a woman who'd disappeared from a hospital?

And I could be wrong. Hunches weren't always correct.

This seemed like more than a hunch, though. It felt like a fact I'd always known, except I'd only known for an hour or so.

"I can take some more blood right now and do the typing myself in my lab. It only takes about five minutes."

"That would be great. Thanks."

"Make a fist for me."

Jack drew a small vial of blood from my arm. "Sit tight. I'll be back in a few."

I stood and paced around the small examination room. I picked up a magazine, leafed through it, and then put it back down. Paced some more.

Five minutes seemed like five hours.

I closed my eyes just as Jack walked back in, startling me.

"Your blood type is B positive, Dante."

I nodded. Of course. I'd known that. I didn't know how, but I did. A simple fact. But before I could ruminate further—

"There's something curious about that," Jack said.

"What?"

"Blood types are inherited, and vampires are almost always Rh negative. Of course, there have been vampires with Rh positive blood, but that's not the issue here."

"What *is* the issue, Jack?"

"I've been taking care of your family for years, and your father had O negative blood type. Your mother had B negative, and Emilia has B negative. There's no genetic way that I know of for you to have B positive blood, Dante."

I widened my eyes, stunned. "Are you saying I'm not my parents' child?"

He shook his head. "No. You may not know this, but I took care of your mother during her pregnancy with you. I delivered you. You are definitely her child. I witnessed her take you home. We also do extensive genetic testing during vampire pregnancy because of the risks involved. All tests indicated that you were fathered by Julian Gabriel and that Vivienne was your mother." He sighed. "Plus there's the obvious physical evidence. You're a dead ringer for your father, but you have your mother's nose."

"Then how..." I paced around the small room again, rubbing my forehead, thankful that I was who I thought I was but still full of questions.

"We don't have a lot of studies on vampire blood types. Usually we defer to human studies, because our blood mirrors theirs in almost all aspects. But there has to be a reason why most vampires are Rh negative. We do occasionally see an Rh positive vampire, which means one of his parents was Rh positive. The positive Rh factor is a dominant genetic trait, so if one of your parents is positive, you will be positive."

"But neither of my parents were."

"No." He scratched the side of his head. "I've never heard of a spontaneous Rh change, but at this point, I can't rule such a thing out. That could also explain why we do see an Rh positive vampire every now and then. And then there's one other possible explanation, but I can't see how it would apply in your case."

"What's that?"

"Somehow—and I have no idea how or why—someone tampered with your blood."

SIXTEEN

Erin

I knew Dante would be waiting for me when I got off work. The whole twenty-four hour thing and all. I texted him and told him I had a few errands to run before I got home so he wouldn't worry.

Then I headed to the police station. River and Jay would just be getting off their shift, and they'd be clocking out at the station.

I sat in my car and watched as the detectives and officers left the building. I hunched down when I saw Jay. He wasn't who I needed at the moment, and I didn't relish explaining to him what I was doing here.

A few minutes later, River left the building. I opened my car door and walked swiftly toward him.

"Hey," I said.

"Erin. What are you doing here?"

"We need to talk."

"About what? Dante?"

"No. Not about Dante. Dante and I are fine." Sort of. I still wasn't quite okay with everything, but right now I was more concerned about whoever had been biting my brother without his knowledge or consent.

"Good to hear."

"He told me," I said. "About what you and he...are."

"I know. It's probably pretty hard to digest."

"You have no fucking idea. My whole world has been upended."

"No, it hasn't."

"Don't tell me it hasn't. You don't know a thing about me. I know something about you, though. And I need it to stop."

"What are you talking about?"

"We need to talk in private."

"Okay. You want to get something to eat?"

"No. We're going to your place. Not my place, because Dante will be there, waiting for me. Get your car. I'll follow you."

"If it's that important—"

"It is. But we need privacy."

He stared at me hard, as if trying to read my mind. "Fine."

⚜

River's apartment reminded me a lot of Jay's—a typical bachelor pad. Two recliners and a TV in the small living room, and a kitchen littered with pizza boxes and takeout containers.

"You want something to eat?" he asked.

I could hardly eat. In fact, I was feeling pretty sick at the thought of what he'd been doing to my brother.

"No."

"Suit yourself. I'm going to fix some eggs."

"Can it wait? I need to get this off my chest."

He heaved a sigh. "Erin, I'm starving and exhausted. I at least need a glass of blood." He walked toward his refrigerator.

Blood. Of course. The V word. Funny how I could think about vampires but couldn't form the word in my head when thinking about Dante. I wasn't ready to go there yet. Good thing, because right now I was damned angry.

"Why do you need blood? Didn't you get enough from Jay last night?"

He slammed the refrigerator door shut and turned to me, his eyes shining with anger. "What the hell are you talking about?"

"The bite marks on Jay's neck. You've been feeding from him, and it has to stop."

"You've got a lot of nerve, Erin."

"*I* have a lot of nerve? You've been stealing my brother's blood, and—"

"Not that I owe you any explanation, but I have not tasted one drop of Jay's blood. He's my partner, for God's sake."

"So? He's right there beside you all night. And when you get hungry—"

"When I get hungry, I eat. I don't need blood until the morning, when I get home, which is now." He turned back to the refrigerator and took out a white bag. He reached for a glass out of the cupboard and poured blood—God, it was *really* blood—into the glass. He drained it, all the while his back to me. He set the glass down on the kitchen counter and turned back to me. Tiny smears of deep red edged his lips.

He spoke, and his fangs, also tinged with crimson, were apparent. "You're pissing me off. Jay is my partner. We protect each other. I'd never hurt him, and that includes feeding from him. Maybe Dante hasn't clued you in, but we don't feed on humans. We consider it morally wrong."

"That doesn't mean you don't want it."

He advanced toward me, his dark eyes—even darker than Dante's—blazed with anger. "Do you really think I have that little self-control? You know what? Get the hell out of my house, Erin."

My nerves jumped under my skin, but I stood my ground. River wouldn't hurt me, not when he knew what Dante would do to him if he did. "Not until we resolve this."

"You want to know something?" His voice had lowered, and he dropped his head until he was only inches away from my neck. "Your brother smells delicious. So do you. Dante would kick my ass if he heard me say that. But I've stayed away from *you*, haven't I?"

"Y-Yes." Damn the stammer.

"And I've stayed away from *him*." He made a point of showing his fangs as he moved backward, away from me.

Calmness settled over me. I wasn't sure why. Maybe because River was no longer in my face. It was the same calmness I felt when Dante was near. He wasn't here, was he? No, I'd know if he were. Still, I needed answers.

"Then who has been feeding from Jay? Surely you've noticed the marks on his neck."

"It may surprise you to know this, Erin, but I don't look too carefully at Jay's neck. It's part of how I stop thinking about his scent. I don't let myself look at his pulsing veins."

"I—"

"You will never understand the urge for blood that Dante and I have. That all vampires have."

I opened my mouth again, but he held up his hand.

"Let me finish. That's not an insult, it's just a fact. A pure fact. We—"

The door burst open.

Dante.

His dark hair unruly and his eyes feral. He looked crazy and animalistic.

And afraid.

SEVENTEEN

DANTE

Erin. Her delicious scent was thick as it penetrated through the door to River's apartment. The lusty red wine, the truffles, the dark chocolate. And something else. Her adrenaline was spiked. I threw open the door without knocking and stalked inside.

What was she doing here? Why hadn't she gone straight home? Jealousy welled up within me. River was scenting her. I could see it in his face. He was tempted to bite her, tempted to taste her. He was holding back.

But his fangs were out.

That was enough to make my own descend.

"What's she doing here?" I demanded.

"Uh...hello?" Erin said. "I can speak for myself."

"Fine." My rage, though still focused on River, came through with full force. "What the hell are you doing here?"

"Why are you raising your voice? And why are your teeth—" She paused, staring. Then, "I came to talk to River. To find out why the hell he's been biting my brother."

I turned to River, my anger heightening. "*What?*"

"Easy, Dante. She's wrong. I never touched Jay. You know me better than that. And you *know*."

My mind whirled to my sister, and I shrank away from River. I did know. If someone had fed on Jay, it hadn't been River.

"How do you know someone bit Jay?" I asked Erin.

"I saw the bite marks, Dante. I ought to know what they look like by now."

"Bug bites?" I asked.

"Don't treat me like a child. Two puncture wounds about an inch and a quarter apart. Come on."

An inch and a quarter. A smaller jaw.

Emilia. It had to be her, perhaps when he got her pregnant.

I couldn't tell Erin any of this. I didn't want to lie to her, but how could I tell her that her brother was the father of Em's child? Em hadn't even told *him* yet. It wasn't right.

My sister knew better than to bite a human, but during sex, the craving was so strong and intense...and Jay's scent was more than enticing to any vampire. And if Em was fertile, which she obviously had been, the need for blood would have been even greater.

I sighed, my teeth retracting. "River didn't bite Jay, Erin. I promise."

"How can you possibly know?"

"Because he says he didn't, and I trust him."

She turned to River. "You're telling me the truth, aren't you?"

"Yeah. I am."

"I'm sorry. I just thought..."

"Anyone in your shoes would have thought the same thing,

Erin," I said. "Right, Riv?"

"Yeah. Right. I get it. But I didn't do anything to Jay. I swear it. And I hate being accused of something I didn't do."

Erin nodded. "I'm really sorry. I am. But there's still a problem."'

"What's that?" River asked.

"Someone bit Jay," she said, "and I need you to find out who it was."

River and I exchanged a glance. I wasn't about to sell out my sister—not before she had a chance to tell Jay he was going to be a father. But I also had an obligation to Erin. I wanted to be honest with her, and it killed me when I couldn't be.

What was I supposed to do?

"I promise we'll find out what's going on, Erin," River said. "Okay?"

She nodded. "Okay. Again, I'm sorry."

River smiled. Or he tried to, anyway. It was kind of a strange twist of his lips. "You don't have to keep saying that."

"But I am. I thought... It's hard for me. I really don't know what to think half the time. I know so little about...what you are."

"I'll tell you whatever you want to know, love," I said.

She shifted her gaze to me, her eyes fatigued. "I guess I'll go home. Are you coming over? Do you need to...?"

"Only if it's all right with you," I said, knowing full well she needed me to feed as much as I needed to feed. Eventually she'd come to know that as I did.

"Geez, I don't know. Sure. Come on over."

"All right. I need to talk to Riv about a few things first. I'll meet you at your place in an hour."

She nodded and looked to River. "I'm so, so sorry." She left.

"She feels terrible," I said to River. "Don't be too hard on her. She's having a difficult time."

"I get it. I do. But you and I both know who fed on Jay. What are we going to do about this, Dante?"

"Hell if I know."

"I could—"

"No. Just no. You will *not* glamour her."

"I don't want to, but I don't see another way out of it. Not until Emilia tells Jay, if she ever does."

"Bill already glamoured her once, and I'm not sure I'll ever be able to forgive him. Then he glamoured her again and lied about it."

"Bill doesn't lie."

"Then who else could have glamoured Erin?"

He shook his head. "I don't know, cuz. It's just one more mystery to add to the rest of them. I want to help you figure it all out, but I need your cooperation."

I sighed. Last time we'd talked about this, I'd begged him not to go after whomever had taken me. Now, though, I needed to find *her*. I needed answers. "You have it. Because I just found out something really fucked up." I shoved my hand through my hair.

"What's that?"

"Whoever held me for ten years messed with my blood, Riv. I have a blood type that isn't genetically possible for me to have."

EIGHTEEN

Erin

I got home and fixed myself a light breakfast, even though I didn't feel like eating. I believed River. He hadn't fed on Jay. I trusted Dante when he assured me River wouldn't do that. I trusted Dante without question, which was still difficult to wrap my mind around.

River hadn't taken Jay's blood.

Then who had?

And who had taken mine?

I poured myself a glass of wine. Not really my beverage of choice with a raisin bagel, but what the heck? I was just going to bed after Dante and I—

What *did* we do exactly?

We made love, but now that I was allowing him to—

It was still so hard to think about.

I could stop it at any time. Tell him he couldn't take my blood anymore. But without Dante, I'd never find out who was feeding on Jay. And on me.

And without Dante...I'd be incomplete. I'd never again experience such intimacy, and that thought devastated me. I wanted it again. And again. I needed it. After only twice, it had become like a drug to me—a drug that frightened me out of my mind but that I needed more than oxygen.

I took a sip of wine, letting the crisp tannins float over my tongue. I closed my eyes.

Dante. Vampires. What kind of world did I live in?

Did you see him?

See who?

The vampire.

My eyes shot open. Abe Lincoln. He'd said vampires fed on him. He'd know the vampires in the area. He might know the one who'd been feeding on me. I had to find him and talk to him.

But where would I find him?

Homeless people hung out under Claiborne Bridge near University Hospital. That's probably where Abe Lincoln had been found, since he'd been brought to our ER.

I didn't have tonight off, though. I'd have to go today. After Dante and I...

Dante.

He'd promised to take me to the Quarter on my next night off to ferret out whoever was feeding on me. He'd want to go with me today. Or he'd tell me not to go, that he'd take care of it. But how could he take care of it if he didn't have my scent to draw the vampire out?

I was going. I needed to know. I needed to find out who was violating my brother and me.

I jumped at the knock on my door.

Dante, of course.

I opened it, and he grabbed me. "I need you, Erin. Now." He clamped his lips onto mine.

In an instant, my nerves calmed. No longer did I worry about the vampires of Claiborne Bridge or Abe Lincoln or the bite marks on my brother's neck and my thigh.

Only this kiss. This amazing kiss.

Each kiss with Dante was better than the last, more passionate, more urgent.

He was hungry.

Hungry for me. For my blood. I could feel it in his passion, his desperation.

Don't think about that. Think about what comes before. The beautiful lovemaking. The orgasm...

I melted into him, sliding my lips over his, and then kissing his stubbly cheek, his neck, the top of his chest.

"I need you, Erin," he said again. "I need you to take the demons away."

What?

But through my lusty haze, I couldn't ruminate too much about his words. Not when my body was calling out for him. Calling out for what only he could give me.

"Upstairs," he said huskily, and then swooped me into his arms.

In a flash we were in my bedroom undressing each other. Clothes flew about, and my satin underwear ended up torn in two pieces.

He inhaled. "You're already ripe. So wet for me."

"Always." I wrapped my arms around him and tugged him toward the bed.

"I want you on top of me, Erin. I want you to ride me."

Not a problem. I pushed him down on the bed and climbed

on top of him, sinking down on his massive cock.

Foreplay? Who needed it? Not when I was already slick as an aloe vera leaf.

This angle created new friction, and I reveled in it. My nipples hardened, and I grabbed Dante's hands, bringing them to my breasts.

"So beautiful, Erin. You're all rosy. Did you know I can feel your blood flowing beneath your skin? I can feel the pop of your capillaries when you flush all over?"

His words, though strange, ignited something within me. He could sense things I couldn't. He wasn't like me.

He wasn't like me at all.

Yet he *was* like me. Our bodies fit together as if they'd been created to do so, created to perfectly mold to one another.

Dante caressed my breasts and thumbed my hard nipples. I rose and then sank back onto him, elated at how he nudged the tip of my cervix. Then I ground against his pubic bone, letting his coarse black hair tickle my clit.

I closed my eyes. This wouldn't take long. Not with that sweet friction against my clit and his fingers twisting my nipples.

I rode him hard, again, again, again...until—

"Dante! I'm coming!"

The orgasm slammed into me. Quick and urgent, just like this entire lovemaking session had been.

I opened my eyes, and his own were dark with fiery intensity. He parted his lips...and his fangs descended. Literally grew. The irises of his eyes changed too. Only slightly, but I noticed.

An amber rim appeared around the normal coffee color.

Fiery intensity indeed.

How had I never noticed that before?

I was on top of him, perpendicular to him. The two other times he'd been on top of me with access to my neck.

"Let me look at you," he said, his voice a husky rasp. "You're pink all over. Your capillaries have burst. You're still in the last fragments of your orgasm, and I can hear your heartbeat. It's fast, fast and loud, Erin. God, what you do to me. Lean down. Offer yourself to me."

My mouth dropped into an O. He'd said things like this before, that he could feel my blood. Could he hear it too?

"Obey me, Erin. Lean down."

The calmness swept over me, and I did as he bid. I leaned toward him, my nipples brushing against the soft hair on his chest, until my neck was in range of his mouth.

I gasped as he sank his teeth into my flesh.

The pain lasted only a split second, and then, with his cock still inside me, I began my ascent to euphoria.

The colors, the music...could it get any better than this?

It will get better and better, my love. Trust me.

Dante spoke the words directly into my mind. Or so it seemed. I'd probably just imagined them. I couldn't stop to think about it. I wanted to feel, just feel, as I flowed toward the intimate sensations that were similar, that I knew, but that were always a little bit different.

A little bit better.

When the tugging stopped, he swept his tongue over my wounds. Then he thrust his cock so deeply into me, I swore he touched my heart.

"Feel me, Erin. Feel me coming for you."

He hadn't come yet? Or was he coming again? I was still lounging in a cloud of rapture, and I had no desire to leave.

"This is us, my love. This is *us*. Once bonded, never broken."

NINETEEN

DANTE

Once bonded, never broken.

Stay out of my head!

As I came down from the headiness of my feeding and my orgasm, I caressed Erin's shoulders and back.

Three times I had taken her blood. Three times she had allowed me to, even though she hadn't quite come to terms with what I was.

It was the bond that made her feed me. I knew that. For now, it was okay, but I longed for the day when she would look into my eyes and see me for who and what I was.

That day would come.

It had to.

She slid off me, and my cock, now limp, slid out of her channel. She snuggled up against my shoulder, and I wrapped her in my arms.

She lay there in silence for a few moments, her heartbeat still faintly audible, until she opened her eyes and propped her head up in her hand.

"Dante?"

"Yeah?"

"I need you to do something for me."

"Anything, love."

"I need you to help me find Abe Lincoln."

⚜

Most homeless people who hung out under Claiborne Bridge were out begging during the day. At least that was how it had been ten years ago. I didn't see why it might have changed. When I told Erin as much, she insisted we go anyway.

Although I knew who had been feeding on her brother, I *didn't* know who had been feeding on Erin. If this could help me find out, I was all in.

"You realize we won't find any vampires in the middle of the day," I said, as we drove to the bridge.

"I thought vampires didn't burn up in the sun."

"We don't. But we're nocturnal creatures. We prefer night to day, and if vampires are feeding on the homeless, they're doing it at night."

Nocturnal creatures. Erin and her brother were also nocturnal creatures, both working night shifts, due most likely to their vampire blood. Another thing I was keeping from Erin. I couldn't tell her. She had to accept me before she could accept her own vampire heritage.

Another thing I didn't tell Erin was that I'd never allow her to go to the Claiborne Bridge at night. Any human-feeding vampire within a mile radius wouldn't be able to resist her scent. The Quarter was one thing. The bustling nightlife would provide a level of safety. But Claiborne Bridge at night? No way. I'd protect her with my life if I had to, but better safe than sorry. She was not going to the bridge at night. Thank God for her night shift.

We found a place to park the car and then walked under the bridge, cars whizzing by above us. Dome tents were scattered over the cement, and only a few people milled about. As I suspected, most were probably out begging.

An elderly man sat with a mongrel dog near the tent city. We walked toward him.

"Excuse me, sir," Erin said.

"Yeah? You got some change?"

I dug into my pocket and tossed him a few spare coins. "We're looking for someone. Do you know Abe Lincoln?"

"The president? Ain't he dead?"

"Not the president," Erin said. "He's a young man, maybe twenty-five or so, pretty skinny."

"Nah. Don't know no Abe Lincoln."

"Thanks anyway," I said.

"Wait a minute, y'all," he said.

"Yeah?" Erin asked.

"I might know him. If you buy me a bottle."

"Sorry, sir," Erin said. "We'd be happy to buy you a sandwich though."

"Nah. I got a sandwich." He pointed to a dirty paper bag sitting next to him.

We walked over to the next person, a woman with a crimson scarf over her head. She was dark-skinned. Dreadlocks hung below her scarf.

"Ma'am," Erin said, "could we talk to you a minute?"

"Sure. I got nothing better to do."

"Thank you," Erin said. "We're looking for a man who

might hang out around here. He's young, blondish hair, skinny. Goes by the name of Abe Lincoln?"

She laughed, revealing a missing front tooth. "Abe Lincoln? Is that what he calls himself?"

"You know him?"

"You can only be talking about Red Rover." She eyed me. "I can see why *you're* looking for him."

"Why would you say that?" I asked.

"You're a vampire, ain't ya?"

Erin turned to me, her eyes wide.

"I can tell. But don't worry. No one else can. I have the sight."

The sight? That could mean anything, and most likely meant nothing other than she was a loon. "Thanks for your help, ma'am," I said, turning.

"Don't you want to hear about Red Rover?"

"The man we're looking for is called Abe Lincoln," Erin said.

"You described Red Rover perfectly," she said. "I'm Bea, by the way."

"I'll bite," Erin said. "Who is Red Rover?"

"He's a young guy. Skinny. I call him Red Rover because when the vamps come around looking for blood, he goes right on over." She let out a laugh that sounded more like a choking cackle.

"Does he ever go by any other name?" Erin asked.

"Not that I know of. I don't think anyone actually knows his real name. I started calling him Red Rover, and it just stuck. No one else knows what it means though. Except the vamps, of course." She eyed me. "Surely *you* must know him."

"Most of us don't feed on humans, Bea," I said.

"You do. I can see it in your eyes. In fact"—she pointed to Erin—"you feed on *her*."

This was getting more than a little creepy. "What makes you think that?"

"Vamps get a look once they taste human blood. Around the iris of the eyes. It lightens up, like a circle of flame. Shows they've tasted something they can't go without. Addicts get the same look about them."

"Is this making any sense to you?" I asked Erin. She was a nurse. She'd probably seen her share of addicts.

"Not that I've noticed among addicts, but..."

"What?"

"I'll tell you later."

"She sees the mark on you," Bea said. "She's seen it, I tell you."

"All right," Erin said. "Enough. You have no idea what I have or haven't seen. We just want to find Abe Lincoln. Or Red Rover. Whoever he is."

"He has the mark, I tell you. I've been a voodoo high priestess since I came of age. I have the sight."

"So you've told us," Erin said. "If you truly have the sight, tell us where Red Rover is."

"He hangs out on Royal during the day, begging. Sometimes he takes Old John's dog with him, but I see he didn't today." She pointed to the first man we'd spoken to.

"All right," Erin said. "Thank you for your help."

"Ain't you going to give me anything for my help?"

I scoffed. "You're a voodoo priestess. Why don't you just conjure up whatever you need?"

"It don't work that way, Mr. Vampire."

"I'll tell you what," Erin said. "If we find Abe Lincoln on

Royal, we'll come back and reward you."

She hissed at us as we walked away.

"Do you think she's cursing us?" Erin asked quietly.

"There's no such thing as curses," I said.

TWENTY

Erin

Though I felt I'd hidden it well, our encounter with Bea had left me more than a little spooked. I grasped Dante's hand as we walked back to the car.

"Are you sure there's no such thing as curses?" I asked.

"Very sure."

"Forgive my skepticism, but a week ago I would have bet everything I own that there was no such thing as vampires."

"Well, technically, there isn't. Not the way you thought of vampires, anyway. The myths are almost all BS. Our DNA is nearly indistinguishable from humans."

"DNA. This is all so unreal."

Two seconds later, when we got to the car, he pushed me against it.

"Is *this* unreal? You and I? What we've shared?" His dark gaze seared into my own.

"That's not what I mean."

"Then what *do* you mean, Erin? When are you going to

accept all of me?" He nudged into me, his erection apparent. "Just being near you has my cock hard, my teeth ready to descend. We're not animals, Erin. We know how to control our urges, our desires, but when I'm around you—" He shook his head. "*This* is real. I've never known anything more real."

My gaze was glued to his mouth, his full lips, but then inside, those...

I rose onto my tiptoes and kissed him, a current of electricity racing through me. Our tongues tangled, and then—

"Ouch!" I pulled away from him.

His eyes were dark as espresso, but that flaming rim. He said nothing, just burned me with his intense gaze.

I touched my lips. "How do—" God, how to find the words? "What happens with your teeth? Why do they...do that?"

He let out a slow breath. "Give me a minute. You can't just—" He closed his eyes for a few seconds and then opened them. "Teeth are living tissue. They may not feel that way to you, but anyone who has a dead tooth will tell you a living tooth has feeling. Our cuspids are the teeth that make us carnivorous. Humans have them too. Ours just happen to have another use, and they change to fulfill that purpose."

Keep an open mind, Erin. "What does it...feel like?"

"My gums begin to itch, and then they tingle, like tiny pin pricks. Kind of like when your foot falls asleep and then wakes up. Those pin pricks are the oxygenated blood flowing back into the nerves of your foot. The blood flows into my gums and stimulates the nerve in my tooth, and it grows. Once I've fed, the teeth retract."

"But your teeth also come out when..."

"When I'm turned on. Or when I'm angry. Testosterone and adrenaline both stimulate the vampire canine nerve."

Vampire canine nerve? "You make it sound so clinical."

"It *is* clinical. It's a physiological response, just like any other."

Not like any other, actually. I was a nurse. I knew anatomy and physiology as well as most physicians. A thought speared into my head, and I jerked slightly. "I wonder if I've seen vampire patients at the hospital."

"In New Orleans? I'm sure you have. When you lived in Ohio it was probably unlikely. There's no way you would know the difference unless you knew what to look for. We've been living among humans for so long that we've become adept at hiding our miniscule disparities."

"What differences are there? Other than your teeth."

"Our fair and sensitive skin."

"I have that too."

He cleared his throat. "Yes, you do. And our females only menstruate every two to three years."

"Ha! Lucky them. Every human woman in the world would gladly trade places."

"Really? It screws with fertility big time."

Yes, it would. Infertile women who wanted children suffered greatly. I felt pretty stupid for making that comment. "You're right. I'm sorry. It would be almost impossible to get pregnant. You'd have to really watch the timing."

"It's very difficult for vampire women to conceive. That's one of the reasons why there are so few of us left."

"But your sister..."

"Got...lucky, I guess."

Dante's voice sounded funny. I got the feeling he didn't consider his sister lucky at all. I didn't feel comfortable pressing him about it. It was none of my business anyway. Or maybe it was. Maybe Dante and I—

I drew in a breath before the thought could fully form. "Shall we head over to Royal?"

⚜

It was nearing noon, and I should have been sleeping, but my curiosity won out. Dante held my hand as we strolled along Royal Street, looking for Abe Lincoln. We got hungry and stopped for some beignets and coffee at a little shop, and then kept searching. Street musicians were out in abundance, along with beggars and, of course, tourists. We really had to keep our eyes peeled.

Red Rover. What Bea had told us jibed with what Abe had said to me about letting vampires feed on him without hypnotizing him. I hadn't thought to examine Bea's neck for bite marks. If we found Abe, I had every intention of going back and giving Bea some food and money. I made a mental note to check then.

We continued walking, passing the Cornstalk Hotel, where Dante told me his sister worked as a night manager. A few blocks more, past the St. Germain house, where a vampire had reputedly lived. It was a gorgeous red brick residence that was, last I heard, owned by a rich attorney who spent his weekdays in Baton Rouge.

"Dante?"

"Yeah?"

Was Jacques St. Germain really a vampire? The words had formed on my tongue, but I didn't utter them. It was still all too unreal. I wasn't ready to accept that Jacques St. Germain had truly been a vampire. I wasn't ready to let go of my now tenuous hold on reality just yet. It was still too much.

We continued walking, when—

A thin figure emerged from around the corner of the brick building. His head was covered by a tattered orange hoodie, but his build I recognized.

"Abe!" I shouted. "Abe Lincoln!"

He didn't acknowledge me. Maybe I was mistaken.

Then—

"Red Rover!"

TWENTY-ONE

DANTE

The young man stopped and turned toward us.

My nose told me nothing, but my vision told me everything I needed to know. I knew this young man. He was the homeless man whose clothes I had stolen the night of my escape.

He pointed at me. "You!"

Erin's eyes widened. "Abe? You know Dante?"

"He took my clothes. The night... The night I met you, I think. I'm not sure. He hypnotized me."

"Dante? What is he talking about?"

"Let's find a place to sit down where we can talk," I said. "I'll explain everything."

"No," Erin said. "You'll explain *now*."

"We're out in public. I can't. Come on," I said to Red Rover, or whoever he was. "We'll get you a hot meal."

Erin gave me a glare but she went along. We walked a block to Café Amelie and got a table outside, where we would be less likely to be overheard.

I hadn't yet told Erin about my time in captivity. My

memories were so fragmented, and what had been done to me... I wasn't ready yet. I hadn't even told Bill and River most of it. But she deserved the truth. If I expected her to spend her life with me, I owed her that.

But not today. And not in front of Red Rover.

"Listen," I said to him. "You're mistaken about me. But Erin told me that you know a lot of vampires in the city. We're looking for one, and if you can help us, we'll make it worth your while."

"I could swear it's you," he said.

"I said you're mistaken." I didn't trust my ability to glamour, and I certainly didn't want Erin to think I was doing it, but I threw a small wave of energy toward him. Thankfully, it seemed to work.

"Maybe. I know a lot of vamps. Who are you looking for?"

"We don't know, actually," Erin said. "But someone has"—she cleared her throat—"been taking my blood. Without my knowledge or consent. My brother's too. Apparently we smell really good to vampires. And since you seem to know a lot of vampires..."

"It could be—"

A server appeared at our table. "What can I get for you today?"

"Whatever you want, Abe," Erin said.

Red Rover ordered a meal fit for a king, and Erin and I ordered some fruit and water. We'd just had beignets and weren't overly hungry.

When the waitress left, Erin turned back to Abe.

"So anyway, we need your help, Abe. And is that even your real name?"

He nodded. "It is. But no one on the street calls me that."

"No, they call you Red Rover," I said. "We met Bea."

"Yeah. Bea thinks it's funny that I let the vamps feed on me without hypnotizing me. I don't mind. It feels kind of good actually, after the initial bite of course. Then they give me food. It's a win-win situation."

I cleared my throat. "It might interest you to know, Rover, that vampires aren't supposed to feed on humans."

"Why not? You do."

"What?"

"You have the mark. Around your eyes. Bea told me how to recognize it."

"Bea doesn't know what she's talking about," I said.

"Bea knows more than you think."

"She doesn't seem to know how to keep herself off the street," I said.

Erin touched my arm. *Easy, Dante.* I could almost hear her words. She was right. I wouldn't get his cooperation if I slammed the way he lived. He might be a victim of circumstance or shitty luck.

Or he might just be a big loser, but I'd keep that to myself.

"I wish I could help you," he said. "Erin, you were really nice to me at the hospital. But I don't know who else the vampires feed on."

"Do they feed on any of the other people under Claiborne Bridge?" she asked.

"Some. But they hypnotize them, so they wouldn't be able to help you."

Erin tilted her head. "It's called glamouring, Abe. Not hypnosis."

"Is it? They never told me that."

This was no help at all, but I was curious about one thing.

"Abe, or Rover, or whatever your name is, I'm curious. Why do you let them feed on you without glamouring you?"

"I already told Erin why. Because they buy me a meal. They don't have to do anything for the others because they don't even know they've been fed on."

Okay. That made sense on its surface. But I wasn't buying it. "Are these vampires nice people?"

He shrugged. "They're nice to me—" He jerked his head toward the wrought-iron gate. "I have to go."

"Our food hasn't come yet," Erin said.

"Sorry. I have to go. Now." He stood, pulled the hoodie over his head, and walked swiftly out of the courtyard.

"What was that about?" Erin asked.

"I have no idea." But I was just as glad he was gone. Now I had more time to figure out how to tell Erin about my encounter with Red Rover the night of my escape. And I *would* tell her. Eventually. The question was when. She was already having trouble accepting certain things about me.

I gestured to our waitress. "We're going to need to cancel our order. Our...friend had to leave."

"Okay, sir."

I laid out some bills for her trouble. "You want to get out of here?" I said to Erin. "You need to get some sleep."

She nodded.

⚜

I stayed next to Erin until she had fallen asleep, and then I got up and fired up her computer. She had given me the login information, and I wanted to research my Rh factor change. Even as I typed, though, I knew I wouldn't find anything. If

Jack didn't know, I wouldn't find it on the internet.

I could only get information from *her*.

What had *she* done to my blood? I had to find out what was going on with my genetics before Erin and I could even think of having kids.

Wow. That thought had come out of the blue. I'd never given kids a thought before.

I stared at the computer screen until my phone buzzed.

River.

Jay got the blood type of the woman
who disappeared from the free clinic.
B positive.

TWENTY-TWO

Erin

When I woke up to get ready for work, Dante gave me the news about the blood type of the woman from the free clinic. Then I checked my phone. Jay had texted me with the same information, and a little more. Her name was Bella Lundy. I had no way of reaching her, though. Jay and River wouldn't divulge her address. They said they'd been unethical enough getting me her name and blood type.

Just as well. I didn't have time to devote to my amateur sleuthing anyway. I had work tonight, and then tomorrow, on my night off, I had to work on Dr. Bonneville's research—and then I planned to go to Claiborne Bridge to find the vampires. Plus, since we'd found Abe Lincoln, I owed Bea a reward of some kind.

I hadn't told Dante of those plans. He still thought we were going to the Quarter. He'd go with me, of course. I was counting on that. But I knew enough about my enigmatic man to know he'd try to discourage the little trip. On the other hand, he wanted to know who'd been feeding on me as much as I did, so he'd have a big reason to let me go.

I also wanted to run into Abe Lincoln again. Why had he rushed out of Café Amelie, especially after he'd ordered a gigantic meal? It didn't make any sense.

For now, though, I kissed Dante goodbye and drove to work.

An ambulance was pulling up as I parked, and several gurneys carrying what appeared to be car accident victims were being wheeled in.

Nothing like getting right to work.

"Erin!" Dr. Bonneville snapped as I walked in. "Get changed quickly. We need you up here."

Lucy hadn't shown up yet, but several other nurses were running around taking orders. I hurried. Not for Dr. Bonneville, but for the patients who needed me.

I raced back to the ER and went to work on a teenage girl whose care Logan was overseeing.

The girl was unconscious with facial lacerations. I quickly cut off her clothes, only to uncover a huge gash in her chest that had been stitched up. The impact from the automobile accident had caused it to open.

"Doctor! She's had open heart surgery. You need to check this."

"Shit," Logan said. "Get out of my way."

I slinked back. A young kid. She couldn't have been more than sixteen at most, and she'd just had open heart surgery? Crazy.

"Was she the driver?" Logan asked.

"I have no idea," I said. "I just got in."

"Damn. This incision looks almost... I think she's had a

heart transplant. Let's type her right away. She's going to need blood. In the meantime, get some O neg in here stat. I need prednisone too."

I looked around for an orderly. Of course, not one in sight who wasn't busy doing something else. I went to the small fridge and grabbed a bag of O neg.

O neg. What I'd been looking for the night Dante came into my life.

No time to ruminate on that now.

I raced back to the patient, but she was gone. Logan was nowhere in sight. I grabbed Dale, one of the other nurses. "Where's Dr. Crown? And the patient with the heart transplant?"

"I don't know. Sorry, Erin. I have to get back to my case."

Dr. Bonneville walked briskly out of an exam room.

"Doctor, where is Dr. Crown? He and I were working on a case, and he sent me for some O neg"—I held up the bag—"but now he's gone. The patient's gone."

"Erin, I have my own patients to worry about. This accident was brutal. She probably got taken into surgery." She whisked by me.

In the last five minutes? How long had I been gone?

She turned back to me. "Don't just stand there like an idiot, Erin. We've got emergencies here!"

That slapped me out of my stupor. I took the bag of blood back to the refrigerator, and before I had time to think any more about the girl with the heart transplant, one of the residents grabbed me to assist with an older man who had been involved in the same accident.

He didn't make it.

But no break for me. I ran back and forth helping with more

patients for the next two hours. When I finally got a chance to breathe, I remembered the teenage girl. I didn't even know her name, and Logan hadn't resurfaced, which was strange. Even if she'd been taken into surgery, he'd have come back to the ER, where he was assigned. Right?

Lucy walked up to me. "Hey. You okay? You look like you've seen a ghost."

"You know I don't believe in that stuff." *Except vampires are real, apparently.*

"You know what I mean. What's wrong, Erin?"

Where to start? *Oh, my new boyfriend is a vampire and has been drinking my blood. Some other vampire has been feeding on me and my brother, and a patient I was helping seems to have disappeared into thin air. Not to mention I met a homeless voodoo priestess who apparently can tell my boyfriend has been drinking my blood. You know, nothing much.*

"Nothing," I said.

"Wrong. Something's got you agitated. What's going on?"

"Have you seen Logan?"

"Not since I got in. But I've been uber busy with that accident, just like we all have."

"Hey, Luce, what's your blood type?"

"B positive. Why?"

"So is mine. Weird, huh?"

"Erin, about nine percent of the population are B positive. That equals out to roughly six hundred and seventy-five million people worldwide. Not exactly rare."

I quickly filled her in on the fact that two of the disappearing women were B positive, and how we always seemed to be out of B positive here at the hospital.

"I guess we should go in and donate," Lucy said.

"Yeah, we should, but that's not the point I'm trying to make. It's like B positive is all around us."

"Maybe New Orleans just has a higher percentage of B positive people than other places."

I hadn't thought of that. "Maybe. But doesn't it seem strange to you? In fact, what was the name of the woman who disappeared from here the other night? It seems to have escaped me."

"Sybil Downey."

I quickly typed her name into the computer. And ice gripped the back of my neck.

"Check it out." I turned the monitor toward Lucy.

Blood Type: B Positive

"Erin..."

"Come on. This has to all mean something."

"No, it really doesn't. Are you feeling okay, honey? Have you been getting enough sleep?"

"For God's sake, Lucy, I'm not crazy." Or was I? My boyfriend was a vampire—a vampire who had stayed by my side the last two nights to make sure I slept. "And I'm sleeping fine."

"Good. Then stop obsessing over nothing, Erin. You're freaking me out here."

She had no idea how freaked out she was going to be once I told her everything I was currently hiding from her.

But that wouldn't happen today.

The sirens blared, and we headed back out to the ER.

TWENTY-THREE

DANTE

"Riv, come on," I said. "I need this favor."

"This is my night off. I've got stuff to do, and I want to rest. I'm still recovering from a concussion, you know."

"Please." I rolled my eyes. "You didn't want to take any time off for that. They made you, so don't give me that BS. Now you're back on duty, so stop saying you need rest. Come with me to Claiborne Bridge. I need to find the vampire who's been feeding on Erin."

"You were gone for a while, Dante, so there's no way you would know this, but those Claiborne vamps are bad news."

"Red Rover says—"

"Who the hell is Red Rover?"

I quickly explained. "He says they buy him a hot meal after they feed. He told Erin they were nice."

"They might very well be nice to a food source. But they're thugs. They're basically a gang."

"You mean... Well, what exactly do you mean? Specifically?"

"They run drugs and pimp out women. That specific enough for you?"

That was a gang all right. "I didn't know that. But now that I do, I sure as hell need to keep them away from Erin."

"They're dangerous. I can take my piece, but you won't be armed."

"I'll take one of yours."

"Are you kidding? Have you ever even held a gun?"

"Well...no."

"Then it's more of a danger to you if you have it. You're crazy if you want to take on the Claiborne vamps."

"I don't want to take them on. I just want information."

"And what will you do if you find out one of them *has* been feeding on Erin? You'll go mental. And Dante, they'll fucking kill you."

"I'm going, Riv. With or without you."

"Damn you. Give me three minutes."

⚜

River had two pistols on him—one in a shoulder holster and the other hidden under his jeans on his ankle. I had only my fists, my teeth, and my sheer will to annihilate whoever had been violating Erin.

Though logic dictated otherwise, I felt no fear. If I found the vampire who had been feeding on Erin, I'd take him out with my bare hands.

If I didn't find him? Then we had another problem.

It was eerily dark and quiet under the bridge save for the occasional thrum of an automobile overhead. A nearly burned-out streetlight flickered in the distance, the electric static faint in my ears. Crumpled papers drifted by in the light breeze of the night, and a small animal—a rat?—whisked by my feet.

Most of the homeless were probably snug in their tents, and others snoozed curled up with dirty blankets or newspapers up against the poles or in self-made cubbyholes.

Vampires couldn't smell each other, so we had no way of telling whether any were lurking around.

River scanned the area. "I think this is a dead end, Dante. I don't sense any trouble here."

"There's no way to tell," I said.

"Not for you. But I've been a cop for seven years. You learn to feel things in the atmosphere. I'm telling you. Nothing is going on here except homeless people sleeping."

I sighed. Maybe he was right. Still, I wanted to walk the length of the tent city, just in case. "I want to keep exploring."

"Christ. All right."

We walked along in the darkness, until two familiar eyes met mine. I squinted.

"You came back, Mr. Vampire."

Bea, the voodoo priestess.

"You promised to reward me if you found Red Rover."

"I promised nothing. The woman with me"—I couldn't say girlfriend. I didn't want Bea to know how important Erin was to me—"did."

"You found him though."

"How do you know?"

"I told you. I've got the sight."

"Maybe. More likely he came back here and told you he'd talked to us." Still, Erin had promised her a reward. I pulled a few bills out of my wallet and handed them to her. "Thank you for your help. We appreciate it."

River was giving me an imposing stare. "What the hell are you doing, Dante? Put that wallet away now."

"Sorry. But she helped Erin and me earlier. We promised her—"

"Whatever. Be quiet. If someone hears that you're giving away money, you'll have every homeless person in the area awake and holding out his hand."

He most likely had a point. I hastily put the wallet back in my pocket—my front pocket this time.

"Bea," I said, "we're looking for the vampires who hang around here at night. The ones who feed on Red Rover."

"They're around. They stay in the shadows."

"In which shadows?"

"Just the shadows." She tilted her head. "They run drugs for some bigwig."

"Who?" I asked.

"She won't be able to tell you," River said. "We've never been able to ferret out their leader. He's eluded the cops for years."

"I can tell you more than you think I can," Bea said.

"Yeah? What?" River flashed his badge. "Withholding evidence from a police officer is a crime, ma'am."

"What is my information worth to you?"

"Bribing a police officer is also a crime." He put his badge away.

She let out her cackling laugh. "Do you think I care? Cart me off to jail. I'll get three meals a day and a bed."

"You got it," River said. "Stand up. You have the right to remain silent. Anything you say—"

"Riv"—I grabbed his arm—"let's just find out what she knows."

"Are you kidding me?"

"I'd listen to your friend," Bea said. "Unless you want everyone on the force to find out you're a vampire."

"No one would believe you," River said.

She cackled again. "You're probably right."

"Look," I said. "We just want to find these guys. You know I can make it worth your while if you help us."

"They're in the shadows, like I said."

I reached for my wallet.

"You've got to be joking," River said.

"I need to know." I took out a fifty-dollar bill and held it in front of her. "What can you tell me?"

She reached for it, but I whisked it away. "Only if you tell me, and then only if your information leads us somewhere. You know I'm good for it."

"I can't tell you where to find the vamps. They only come out when they need to. But I can tell you something about the person they work for."

"Yeah?" This time River bit. "What do you know about him?"

Bea smiled, her missing tooth a black hole in a sea of yellow that seemed to glow in the darkness. "Only that *he* is a *she*."

TWENTY-FOUR

Erin

Dante was waiting for me when I got home. He looked a little frazzled, his hair in more disarray than usual, and something was off about his mouth. Were his teeth out? I'd find out when he spoke.

I unlocked the door and let him in. "I suppose I should give you a key," I said.

"When you're ready."

Ready. Wow. I so wasn't ready for any of this, but we'd already begun, and I couldn't stop it now. Didn't want to stop it. I sighed. How much longer could I survive this battle inside me?

"Take your clothes off, Erin."

Abrupt. No talk of breakfast. Of my night or his. All right. Two could play this game. "You take yours off too."

He responded with a soft growl. "You forget who's in charge here. I don't obey you. You obey *me*."

His words, though I'd heard them before, unnerved me.

And excited me. I undressed, soon standing before him in my bra and panties.

"The rest," he snarled, "or I will rip them off you with my bare hands."

Shaking, I unsnapped my bra and removed it, letting my breasts fall against my chest.

Dante inhaled and licked his lips. "God. Beautiful. Keep going."

I pushed my cotton panties over my hips and down my thighs until they lay on the floor. I kicked them away.

He closed his eyes and inhaled. "You're ripe. So ripe."

I squeezed my thighs together. My body tingled all over, and my pussy was pulsing. I'd just gotten home, and already I was wet for him.

He inched toward me, and then he buried his nose in my neck, sniffing from my shoulder blade up to my earlobe. "I want to sink my cock inside you, Erin," he whispered. "I need you."

I moaned softly. My juices moistened my inner thighs. I was ready. No foreplay necessary. He still hadn't taken any clothes off.

"Please. Take off your clothes. I want to see you."

He moved backward a few feet, his eyes smoldering. He lifted the T-shirt he wore over his head to display his magnificent chest. His skin was fair, as usual, his nipples a light copper. His abs formed a perfect six pack.

I sank to my knees and unsnapped his jeans. I shoved the denim over his hips. And that perfect cock sprang out to greet me.

I licked the tip, and a shudder raced through his whole body.

He closed his eyes and groaned.

I licked the rest of the salty fluid from the tip until it was coated in the sheen of my saliva. I took him as far as I could and then retreated when the tip nudged the back of my throat. I kissed him, swirling my tongue around the head and then in little figure eights along his shaft until I got to his balls, which were scrunched up against his body. I sprinkled kisses all over them, inhaling his masculine musk. Then I went back to work on his cock.

I plunged my mouth onto it again, this time adding my fist so I could make it all the way to his base. My nipples ached and my pussy vibrated as I blew him. I wanted to give him the blowjob of his life. And I intended to.

He grabbed two handfuls of my hair, and fresh juice gushed from me. But instead of pushing me toward his cock, he pulled my head off of him.

"Upstairs," he growled. Quickly he hoisted up his jeans and then lifted me into his arms and threw me over his shoulder, advancing toward the steps. "Mine," he said under his breath but loud enough that I felt it.

Yours. The words formed in my mind. *Yours forever.*

When we arrived at my bedroom, he laid me—not gently—on the bed and spread my legs.

His eyes widened. Rage poured off of him in waves.

"Wh-What? What is it?"

Dante's eyes were on fire, the "mark" around his irises more apparent than ever. And his teeth...

"The bite marks." His voice was more growling than speaking. "These wounds are new, Erin. Someone has fed on you in the last twelve hours."

EPILOGUE

The Queen

Don't be fooled, Dante.

You have only one blood bond—the one you and I formed together. No human can give you what I gave you.

You are mine.

Once bonded, never broken.

BLOOD BOND SAGA

PART 5

PROLOGUE

Erin

"Take your clothes off, Erin."

Abrupt. No talk of breakfast. Of my night or his. All right. Two could play this game. "You take yours off too."

He responded with a soft growl. "You forget who's in charge here. I don't obey you. You obey *me*."

His words, though I'd heard them before, unnerved me. And excited me. I undressed, soon standing before him in my bra and panties.

"The rest," he snarled, "or I will rip them off you with my bare hands."

Shaking, I unsnapped my bra and removed it, letting my breasts fall against my chest.

Dante inhaled and licked his lips. "God. Beautiful. Keep going."

I pushed my cotton panties over my hips and down my thighs until they lay on the floor. I kicked them away.

He closed his eyes and inhaled. "You're ripe. So ripe."

I squeezed my thighs together. My body tingled all over, and my pussy was pulsing. I'd just gotten home, and already I was wet for him.

He inched toward me, and then he buried his nose in my neck, sniffing from my shoulder blade up to my earlobe. "I want to sink my cock inside you, Erin," he whispered. "I need you."

I moaned softly. My juices moistened my inner thighs. I was ready. No foreplay necessary. He still hadn't taken any clothes off.

"Please. Take off your clothes. I want to see you."

He moved backward a few feet, his eyes smoldering. He lifted the T-shirt he wore over his head to display his magnificent chest. His skin was fair, as usual, his nipples a light copper. His abs formed a perfect six pack.

I sank to my knees and unsnapped his jeans. I shoved the denim over his hips. And that perfect cock sprang out to greet me.

I licked the tip, and a shudder raced through his whole body.

He closed his eyes and groaned.

I licked the rest of the salty fluid from the tip until it was coated in the sheen of my saliva. I took him as far as I could and then retreated when the tip nudged the back of my throat. I kissed him, swirling my tongue around the head and then in little figure eights along his shaft until I got to his balls, which were scrunched up against his body. I sprinkled kisses all over them, inhaling his masculine musk. Then I went back to work on his cock.

I plunged my mouth onto it again, this time adding my fist so I could make it all the way to his base. My nipples ached and my pussy vibrated as I blew him. I wanted to give him the blowjob of his life. And I intended to.

He grabbed two handfuls of my hair, and fresh juice gushed from me. But instead of pushing me toward his cock, he pulled my head off of him.

"Upstairs," he growled. Quickly he hoisted up his jeans and then lifted me into his arms and threw me over his shoulder, advancing toward the steps. "Mine," he said under his breath but loud enough that I felt it.

Yours. The words formed in my mind. *Yours forever.*

When we arrived at my bedroom, he laid me—not gently—on the bed and spread my legs.

His eyes widened. Rage poured off of him in waves.

"Wh-What? What is it?"

Dante's eyes were on fire, the "mark" around his irises more apparent than ever. And his teeth...

"The bite marks." His voice was more growling than speaking. "These wounds are new, Erin. Someone has fed on you in the last twelve hours."

ONE

DANTE

My vision sharpened. I'd felt protective of Erin before, but now that I'd taken her blood, red rage consumed me. In a split second, all of my senses were on alert, and I was ready to spring. My fangs had already descended, but a new sensation took flight within them. My canine nerves pulsed, each throb honing my teeth, until they were longer and more lethal than ever before.

These teeth would kill.

I didn't stop to think about the how or the why of what was happening. One thought only shifted through my mind to the beat of my thundering heart.

Mine.

Then—

Mark her.

Mark what's mine.

With no warning, I lowered my head and sank my teeth into the milky flesh of her thigh.

"Dante!" she cried out, but she didn't try to stop me.

Good thing. I wouldn't have been able to. My mouth, my teeth were without my control now. They took over my mind, intent on plundering what had been stolen. I sucked ferociously, taking what was mine, what had been wrongfully taken from Erin.

My Erin.

Her red nectar flowed over my tongue, infusing me with her strength, her femininity, her courage—everything Erin.

Everything *mine.*

Then it crawled down my throat, feeding me, nourishing me. Calming me. Saving me.

I hadn't climaxed and neither had she, yet still the soft jazz played in the air around us, still waves of pure energy and rapture catapulted through my whole body.

My cock was hard for her, and she was wet for me, and a beautiful climax was in the near future.

But for now, I took. Took from her, and she gave to me willingly. Her body answered my call so sweetly.

Her mind would follow. Soon, I hoped. It had to.

She writhed beneath me, urging me on. What must this feel like to her? To me, it was heaven.

Though my rage hadn't dissipated, I stopped when I needed to. Nothing in the world, not even the blackest anger, could make me harm my love. I licked her wounds and then looked up at her. She'd raised her head off the pillow, and her light-green eyes electrified me.

"Come here," she said. "Come here and kiss me. Please. God, Dante. Please."

I slithered up her body and crushed my mouth to hers. Her sweetness mingled with the blood still on my lips. I took from her in this kiss, took what was mine, gave her what she had begged me for.

Me. All of me.

My teeth were sharp and fully descended, but I didn't hold back as our mouths slid together. My heart was pounding, and so was hers. I could feel as well as hear it thumping to the jazzy beat surrounding us. Her reaction fascinated me, made me ache for her even more. I'd taken blood from her thigh, marked her over the wounds that had been forced on her against her will, and now she wanted more.

Wanted *me.*

My hard cock stiffened further between her legs, sliding over her wetness. I plunged in. Her soft moan reverberated inside my mouth, and her pussy formed around me, a perfect cast for my cock. I continued the feral kiss, holding my cock inside her, relishing the perfect suction, until I could wait no longer. I pulled out and thrust back in with a vengeance.

She wrapped her lithe legs around me, cushioning me in her warmth. I thrust, and I thrust, and she arched into me and cried out. As her slick walls convulsed around me, I pushed inside her once more balls deep and gave her everything.

The soft jazz around us had become faster and louder, in time with my thrusts, and now, with my mouth still clamped to hers, I experienced something new.

I had taken her blood before orgasm, had marked what was mine, covering the wounds made by someone else who had taken her without consent.

An image swirled in my mind, of Erin handing me a newborn son.

Our son.

Downy dark hair and fair skin. He wailed with his first breath, and the nubs of his baby eye teeth protruded through his pink gums.

He was vampire.

TWO

Erin

This orgasm was even more spectacular than the previous ones I'd experienced while Dante took my blood.

When he was feeding from my thigh, the music around us had increased, until it ascended into the familiar colors and shapes I'd seen before.

But this time, we hadn't joined our bodies.

Yet we had. His teeth in my flesh was another kind of joining, a joining I'd come to enjoy despite the reservations I still held on to.

Was this a new kind of lovemaking?

Now that we'd both climaxed, and he lay next to me, his arm strewn across his forehead, these thoughts crossed my mind.

He hadn't asked to bite my thigh. Not verbally. Yet he had somehow. I'd felt it within my soul, and I'd consented. He would've stopped if he'd felt something else from me. I was sure of it.

The tugging on my flesh was familiar, the same as when he fed at my neck, but what made this so intense was that he was covering something else.

The marks from another vampire.

Another vampire who had fed on me within the last twelve hours.

I jerked upward into a sitting position as the thought materialized in my mind.

The only place I'd been in the last twelve hours was the hospital. Also in my car, but mostly at work. Had I stopped? Yes, I stopped this morning to fill my gas tank. I'd forgotten because when I got home, Dante had been waiting for me, and he commanded me to undress. Then...

Then...I hadn't been able to think about anything else once he'd said those words.

"Erin?" Dante rose and sat beside me.

"You said someone fed on me within the last twelve hours."

"Yes." He clenched his hands into fists, his eyes flaming. "And I *will* find out who and put an end to it. Trust me on that."

I did trust him, but we hadn't had any luck questioning Abe Lincoln or the others at Claiborne Bridge. We hadn't gone to the Quarter at night as he'd first suggested.

"Where did you go in the last twelve hours? Retrace your steps."

"I went to work. I was in my car. Then at the hospital. On my way home, I stopped to fill up my tank, but that's it. When I got here, you were waiting for me."

"A vampire could have stopped you during any of that. Or you could have gone somewhere else and been glamoured into not remembering it."

My skin chilled, and I rubbed my arms to ease the

gooseflesh. Nausea welled in my throat, and I swallowed. "I can't stand this. I feel so...so...*used*."

"I know, baby. No vampire should take blood from a human unless he has consented. Outside of an emergency, of course."

"Maybe this was an emergency." But I didn't believe the words even as they tumbled from my mouth.

"We can't rule that out, but I'm not buying it. If it were an emergency, it wouldn't have happened more than once. Your scent is strong, Erin. Strong and delicious and nearly impossible to resist. Someone knows you and has been feeding on you. Not every day, thank goodness, which means it's probably not someone at work."

"Then..." I trembled. I'd been going somewhere, most likely in my car, and I didn't even know it.

Dante stared at me, his fangs lengthening until the points protruded between his lips still smeared with my blood. "Listen to me. I will *not* let anyone harm you. I will find who's been doing this to you and I will put a stop to it. Trust me, Erin. I will do everything to protect you."

"I...know. I think."

The flaming amber ring around his irises seemed to pulse as he spoke in a low rasp. "Never doubt it. You're mine to protect. I've known it instinctively since I first laid eyes on you, first inhaled your scent. I was even willing to stay away to protect you."

I jerked my head. "Stay away? How would that protect me?"

"Erin, I was determined to protect you from *me*."

"I...don't want to be protected from you." The words, though always true, never rang more powerfully or more sincerely than they did at that moment.

He cupped my cheeks, his hands, so often cold, now nearly burning my skin. "I know. That's why I kept coming back. The pull was too great. I couldn't resist it. I tried, but I failed every time."

"I felt it too," I said. "You were pulling me toward you. I kept coming to you. Needed to be with you, even though I didn't understand it."

He wrapped his arms around me, surrounding me in his warmth. His anger and ferocity were dissipating. Because of me. I had that effect on him. I smiled into his chest.

He sighed. "It was almost like a magnetizing force."

I pulled back a little, drowning in his dark eyes. "I've never felt anything like it. I hardly knew you, yet something in you was calling to me. I don't know how else to describe it."

"You described it perfectly. That's how it felt to you, love. But that pull? It was actually *you*. Pulling me to you."

I moved away from him, tensing.

He trailed one finger down my jawline, stopping at the pulsing artery in my neck. "There's a reason for this connection we've formed. At least in theory. It's called a blood bond."

I widened my eyes. "What?"

"I know it's a lot to take. You've had to deal with so much. But I can't keep this information from you. You and I are bonded. By blood."

He was so beautiful. So masculine and majestic. And the love that flowed between us was palpable. Almost visible.

It was real. So real.

And now he was telling me that maybe it...wasn't?

"I don't believe you."

"It's hard for me to believe as well. This hasn't happened

in a long time. I'm talking centuries, maybe millennia."

I shook my head vehemently. "That's not what I mean. Though I don't know what the hell a blood bond is or whether it even exists. I mean that my love for you is... It's not the result of anything paranormal. I love you, Dante. Nothing is *making* me love you. I love you. Period."

"I know. I love you too. But the blood bond was part of the reason for our initial attraction. I was attracted to you anyway. You're gorgeous, Erin. So beautiful."

"So are you."

He smiled. "I'm glad you think so. But remember where I was and what I looked like when you first met me? I looked like a wild man vandalizing your blood bank."

I gasped. Yes. And I'd thought he was looking for food. But no. He'd been looking for... "Blood."

"What?"

"You needed blood that night, didn't you? You didn't want to feed on a human, but you were hungry. And—" Thoughts began to awaken in me—thoughts I'd pushed to the back of my mind because I'd been so focused on Dante and the pull and attraction between us.

"And what?"

"River said you'd been gone a long time. That..." I closed my eyes, trying desperately to remember the conversation. He hadn't really told me anything else. "That you'd been gone. And he sure seemed surprised to see you that first morning."

Dante stayed silent.

"You have to tell me, Dante. The truth. You owe me that much."

He opened his eyes, and the mark Bea had told us about was again clear around his brown irises. "You're right, Erin. I *was* hungry that night. I was desperate. If you only knew how difficult it was not to... Damn."

Not to take your blood.

He didn't finish the sentence, but the words formed in my mind. He didn't have to say them.

"Thank God I'd drunk several bags of blood by the time you found me. If I hadn't, I wouldn't have been able to resist you."

THREE

DANTE

My mind whirled back to that night—the hunger, the desperation. I'd torn open those clear bags and poured the nectar onto my face and down my throat. And then...

Erin.

Her scent, her irresistible scent. That earthy dark chocolate and smoky truffles. The lusty Cabernet. The tin, the copper...

The urge to take her with my teeth had come at me like a raging fire. Somehow I was able to hold back. Even now I wasn't sure how I'd managed. If I'd had a taste of her then, when I was so hungry and desperate, I might have drained her.

Thank God for the bagged blood.

Thank God.

"Why were you so desperate, Dante? River said you had been gone a long time, and he was so surprised to see you. Where *were* you?"

Images hurtled toward me. *Her*. The human goons who smelled like garbage and vomit. Her sharp fangs sinking into me. The knife held over my penis, my foot. Then me sinking my teeth into her flesh. Her blood, thick like tar, acidic as it clawed its way into my body.

All of it.

Humiliation.

And still so much I couldn't remember. Didn't want to remember.

Then Erin. Sweet, beautiful Erin, who'd been tangled within my web through no fault of her own. She hadn't asked for a blood bond, and neither had I.

Yet I felt compelled to be honest with her. So compelled that I wondered if the blood bond required it.

Not yet. I couldn't taint Erin with the horrors of my past. I just couldn't.

"I'll tell you about it," I said. "But not right now."

"Why not? We've shared everything. Everything, Dante."

Sweetness and innocence laced her words. But they reeked of falseness. We *hadn't* shared everything. I'd been deliberately keeping things from her, things I wasn't ready to talk about. Things she wasn't ready to hear. "You deserve to know everything about me. I just can't. Not yet."

"I don't understand. Why did you leave, and why were you gone so long?"

I closed my eyes, trying to tamp down my beating heart.

"Dante?"

I opened my eyes. She was so beautiful, still naked, her green eyes wide and innocent. What I was about to do would shred that innocence a little, and I hated myself for it.

"I didn't leave, Erin. I was taken."

She gulped audibly. "What?"

"I was taken. And I can't talk about it. My memories are a

mess. I'm not sure which ones are real and which ones aren't. I know you deserve the truth, but I'm just not ready yet. Please try to understand."

She left the bed, saying nothing.

She was upset, and I didn't blame her. I'd forced her into my world, and now I was withholding information from her.

I lay back down, closing my eyes and rubbing my temples. I'd just fed from and made love to the woman who was my soul mate and blood mate. I should feel wonderful. Instead, the beginnings of a headache were hammering their way in.

A few moments later, Erin returned. I felt more than heard her approach the bed.

"This is real," she said.

My eyes popped open. "What, baby?"

"You and me. This." She waved her arms in a circle. "What we share together. Our love. It's real."

"Of course it is."

"This conversation started because I was confused. It all seems so real to me, even though I'm having a hard time accepting everything about you. But what underlies everything—the pull, the obsession, the blood bond, as you call it—is *love*. Real love, Dante. Blood bond or not, I love you."

"And you think the blood bond means it isn't real?"

"No. I *do* think it's real, regardless of some outside force dictating to us. You said we had a blood bond, and that was what explained the pull we have toward each other. I didn't like hearing that, because this is real. My feelings for you are not the result of anything other than the fact that I'm completely and hopelessly in love with you."

Warmth filled me. "It *is* real. I never said it wasn't."

"But you said—"

"I said we have a blood bond. That is a physical bond between us, and I honestly can't explain it any more than that because no one really knows much about it. I never said it meant our love wasn't real."

Her cheeks pinked and she bit her bottom lip. "I felt like—"

I stood and pulled her into my arms. "Hey. The blood bond—whatever it might be—doesn't negate the emotion between us, Erin. It only enhances it."

She snuggled her face into my shoulder. "I couldn't bear the thought that you might only want me for my blood."

I pushed her slightly away, gripping her shoulders and staring straight into her green eyes. "Don't ever think that, baby. I want *you*. *All* of you. Your blood is part of you."

She curved one side of her lip in a half smile. "I suppose it is. I just never had a man want it before."

I stiffened. Someone else *did* want her blood. Whether it was a man or a woman, I didn't know. My bet was on a man. I tried to relax my muscles and said nothing.

"I wish I understood it more," she said. "This blood bond thing."

I couldn't help a little scoff. "So do I. Apparently this happened between vampires and humans millennia ago, perhaps before we were even self-aware. If it has happened since, it has been rare and undocumented."

"Then how do you know about it now?"

I sat down on the bed and pulled her down next to me, pushing a few strands of hair out of her eyes. "Bill did some research. He had to dig deep, and he found what might be an explanation for what's happening between us."

"Our love?"

"Our love is real, Erin, but before the love was the pull.

That pull, that need to have and protect, is the result of the blood bond. At least in theory. Like I said, we don't know much about it."

"How did he know to do this research?"

I touched my nose almost absently. "I've lost my sense of smell."

"What?"

"Not completely. I just can't smell the unique scent of other humans."

"Okay..."

"I can still smell food and other things. And I can still smell human hormones like testosterone and estrogen. But what I can't smell is the unique scent of a human, with the exception of you."

She arched her eyebrows. "We each have our own smell." A statement, not a question.

"Yes. Some humans smell really good to us, like you and your brother." The reason was the vampire blood in their line, but I didn't know how to tell her that yet. She was still having a rough time accepting me for what I truly was. "But every human has a unique scent. Natural redheads also smell very good to us. But I can't smell them anymore. I can't smell your brother anymore. I can only smell you."

"Why?"

"The blood bond, as far as I can tell. That's why Bill started the research. I didn't realize it for a while because you had invaded my senses that first night in the blood bank and I literally could think of nothing else. But since I met you, I haven't been able to smell other humans. Like when I found you with that guy." Temper welled within me, and my fangs itched as the pungent aroma of the man's testosterone edged into my memory. He'd been horny and ready to take something that didn't belong to him. Would *never* belong to him.

I willed myself to calm down. A little. Nothing had happened. At least nothing of any consequence. Still didn't make me happy about it. "I couldn't smell him. But I could smell his testosterone. I knew he was turned on. And when I came at him, I could smell his adrenaline, his fear. But I couldn't smell *him*." I sighed. "I know this isn't making any sense to you, because humans don't smell each other."

"So you have the nose of like...a dog."

I chuckled. "Sort of. Probably better than a dog even."

"But you can only smell me now."

"Yeah."

"What does all this mean, Dante?"

"Honestly, Erin, I don't know. It's all theory at this point."

"I don't get it. What's so special about me? Why would you only smell me?"

"What's so special about you? Are you kidding? You're brave and kind and beautiful and smart and protective. And a million other things. You're *you,* Erin. If that's not special, I don't know what is."

And we're dependent on each other now. For our very lives.

I couldn't say that yet. First, she had to consciously accept me for who I was. It wasn't enough that she allowed me to feed, even if she enjoyed it. Or that she was in love with me, and I believed she was.

She had to look at me and see me. Truly see me.

And she hadn't. Not yet.

What a fucking mess.

I raked my fingers through my hair. "I'd answer your questions better if I could, baby. And I promise that one day I'll tell you all about where I was. When I remember everything coherently. And I will. I have to."

"Yes, you have to. Because you have to tell Jay and River everything. They'll find out who did this to you."

"I have. I've been as honest with River as I can be. Trust me. He's been on my ass about it since I got back."

"Of course he has. And now I will be too. And Jay—"

"No, Erin," I said adamantly. "You will tell *no one* about any of this."

FOUR

Erin

Was he kidding? "Dante, I want to help."

"You can help by leaving this to me. To River and me. We know how to deal with it."

A lightning bolt hit me. "Are you saying that whoever took you was—"

"A vampire. Yeah. There's nothing you or Jay can do, because even if you find out who it was, she'll just glamour you—"

I held up my hand. "Wait a minute. This vampire was a *woman*?"

He nodded.

Horrible thoughts formed in my head. "Did she..."

"No. She didn't fuck me or violate me sexually, if that's what you're thinking, though she did other things that I'd rather she hadn't."

A lump formed in my throat. Thank God he hadn't been raped, but what *had* he endured? Shattered images tormented my mind, and though I tried to whisk them away, I couldn't. "Oh my God. I'm so sorry, Dante." Vampire or not, I wanted to mutilate the woman who had hurt the man I loved. No doubt about it. I was irresistible to vampires, huh? Good. I was going back to Claiborne Bridge at night. Not only did I need to find the vampires who were feeding from me and my brother. I had to find the vampire who had hurt Dante. Perhaps my scent would draw them out. Only one problem.

"Is there a way to..." I hedged. "To keep a vampire from glamouring a human?"

He shook his head. "Not that I know of. I wish there were."

"There has to be," I said. "It's such a violation of human dignity."

"It is, which is why most of us won't do it unless it's an emergency. I'm not sure how it evolved, because from everything I know, humans and vampires coexisted peacefully during primitive times."

"Meaning humans let vampires take their blood?"

"That's what we've always been taught. But humans soon outnumbered vampires because human women are much more fertile."

"Right. You told me."

"And then the two species began interbreeding as well. We never knew why. We just accepted it as another reason why vampires began to die out. When they breed, the result is always a human baby—or more correctly, a half-vampire baby that doesn't have any vampire characteristics. No acute senses, no ability to glamour, no physiological need for blood, no vampire canine nerve."

"So if you and I had a baby, it would be essentially human?"

He stared at me for a moment, his eyes unreadable, and then nodded.

A heavy weight I hadn't realized I'd been carrying magically lifted from me. Not that I'd even thought about children with Dante, but we were in love. The logical result was marriage and children. I'd always wanted children. Did he? Was it too soon to think about those things?

This relationship is full of unanswered questions.

"I wish I could tell you everything," Dante said. "But there's a lot I just don't know."

Whoa. Had he read my mind? Though normally such a thought would make me uncomfortable, it was strangely calming—as if we were meant to be so closely bonded that we could know what the other was thinking.

I was probably making things up.

"We don't know much about the blood bond," he continued, "but the theory is that it evolved on the part of humans to draw vampires into breeding with them. Vampires are much like humans, but if the two species ever had to fight for existence, vampires have a few advantages."

"Like your superior senses."

"Yeah. And our ability to glamour. But we're also vulnerable. We rely on blood to survive, and humans have blood. Anyway, the theory—at least what Bill found in his research—is that humans subconsciously created the blood bond to force vampires into interbreeding so that humans could thrive and outnumber vampires. It makes a certain logical sense, because in the wild, species rarely interbreed, even though they can. Lions and tigers, for example, don't interbreed unless they're forced to in captivity."

"So without this blood bond..."

"Without the blood bond, it's possible that humans and vampires never would have interbred, and vampire blood wouldn't have been diluted. We would have always been fewer in number than humans because our women are less fertile. But we wouldn't be as rare as we are today."

"Rare? Are you dying out?"

He frowned. "Sadly, yes."

Two hundred vampires in New Orleans. That's what Abe Lincoln had said. In a city of four hundred thousand.

Sadness tugged at my heart and my gut. How distressing for Dante to be witnessing the extinction of his people. "Why do all babies born in our situation come out human?"

"Human DNA is obviously dominant. We don't really know why."

"Wow." Stupid, but I had no idea what to say. "And you never knew about the blood bond."

"No. Not until Bill researched it. It does explain what has happened between us, though. It also explains how the interbreeding started."

"Why didn't it continue happening, then? The blood bond, I mean."

"Once humans sufficiently outnumbered vampires, maybe it wasn't necessary."

"Why is it happening now?"

"I wish I knew. Remember that music we heard in the bar that night? That Lucy and River and no one else heard?"

"Yeah. I still hear it when we're together."

"It's the blood bond, according to Bill."

I smiled weakly. "I really just wanted it to be from our love being so strong."

He touched my cheek gently. "I will always believe that's part of it, no matter what Bill's research says."

I walked into his arms. "Do you miss being able to smell other people?"

He chuckled into my hair. "Not at all. You're the only person I want to smell for the rest of my life."

Then I jerked backward. "But before... Did all the vampires in a blood bond lose their smell?"

"Yeah. Another thing that led to our demise. Back then, a vampire without the ability to smell a human coming after him was very vulnerable."

"Why would we do that to you?"

"I honestly don't believe it was intentional. Humans as a species were reacting to their survival instinct. Just a part of evolution. Survival of the fittest. They were eliminating a potential threat to their survival. Vampires were, in essence, predators of humans and animals at that time. They took blood for survival. Humans found a way to counteract that. Like I said, this all most likely happened before either humans or vampires were self-aware."

"Doesn't it seem strange that it's happening now? To us?"

He sighed. "Yes. Very strange. But Erin, I'm not sorry it's happening."

Neither am I.

I wanted to say those words. Wanted to with my whole heart and soul.

But they didn't come out.

FIVE

DANTE

Her lack of agreement didn't go unnoticed. I found it odd, especially after how upset she'd been when she thought I was saying our love was the result of some outside force. Still, I held on to her, embracing her warmth, all the while knowing time was what she needed.

Time to accept all of me.

Patience was a virtue. I didn't have a lot of it, but I needed it now. I'd find it, and I'd give her the time she needed. I had no other choice if I wanted this to work. Forcing her into anything was not an option.

In the meantime, she would allow me to feed, and we would make love and take each other to new heights.

Also in the meantime, I would ramp up my work on finding who had been taking her blood.

No one would take what was mine.

Never again.

I pulled away slightly. "You need to sleep now."

"I should. But I'm off tonight, remember? We have a date to go to the Quarter?"

I shook my head. "I've changed my mind about that."

"Why?"

"It's not safe for you."

"How can you say that? You'll be with me."

"I will. And I will die protecting you if I have to. I could fend off three, maybe four strong males. But I don't know what these Claiborne vamps are after."

"They just want blood. That's what Abe Lincoln says."

"Abe Lincoln, or Red Rover, or whoever he is, isn't exactly a reliable source."

River had said the Claiborne vamps were a gang of thugs, and Bea had told us they ran drugs for a female boss. No way was Erin going near any of them.

"Can we go anyway? We'll go to Bourbon Street or Royal, where it's always bustling. I could use a night out, Dante. Even if it's just dinner or something else quiet."

Though it went against my instinct, I couldn't deny her a night out. I kissed her forehead. "All right, baby. You try to get some sleep now, okay?"

⚜

I couldn't leave Erin while she was sleeping, not when we still didn't know who'd been stealing her blood. If only I had the *Vampyre Texts* with me to do some research. Had Bill gotten the translation for me yet? I punched his number into my still-new phone.

"Hi, Dante," he said.

"Hi, Bill. How is that translation on the *Texts* coming?"

"I haven't heard. I'll check into it."

"Good. I need to do some research on this blood bond."

"There's nothing in the *Texts* about a blood bond. I've read the parts I'm having translated."

"Have you? Because you told me the *Texts* were taught through symbolry and example."

"True. All the necessary components are passed down that way."

"Why? Why not just read them?"

"We've always done it this way."

"Then how do you know you get everything accurately? Stories change as they're handed down."

"I don't know, Dante. This is how we've always done it."

"Then I'm ready. Teach me."

"I've been looking into that. I'm not sure I can."

"What?"

"To understand the symbolry, you need a young mind."

"Are you saying I'm too fucking old?"

"I'm only saying that—"

I ended the call. Hanging up was childish, and it would no doubt piss him off, but I was sick to death of his antics. Since I'd returned, he'd been hedging about teaching me what I needed to know. Why? I still wasn't sure, but the grandfather I remembered would never have kept necessary information from me.

I did a quick search to find a linguist who could translate Old French. I was about to send an email when—

What was I thinking? I couldn't give a sacred vampire document to just anyone. I needed a vampire linguist. My only choices were to wait for Bill's linguist to complete the project—and I honestly wasn't sure there even *was* a Bill's linguist—or learn Old French and read them myself. I'd studied French for two years in high school. How difficult could it be?

Again I searched.

Nothing.

Since Old French was no longer spoken, apparently no one was around to teach it. But if I studied Latin along with today's French, maybe I'd get the gist of what I needed and might be able to make sense of the *Texts*. I did some more searches. Apparently the ancestor of Old French was not Latin but something known as Vulgar Latin, a spoken form that evolved during the Roman Empire and differed from the literary Classical Latin that was still taught today.

So much for that idea. However, I did find some tables that showed some of the differences between Old French and modern French.

Since I hadn't yet gotten a job—I really needed to get on that—I had the time to study. I'd begin with French. I quickly found an online course and enrolled, and, keeping a printout of the tables nearby, glided through the first ten lessons. My memory from high school French was better than I'd anticipated.

I fixed myself a small snack in Erin's kitchen and then went back upstairs and lay down next to her.

Now all I had to do was get my hands on Bill's *Vampyre Texts*. Without him knowing.

That would be complicated, but I had no choice.

That's how we've always done it.

Bill's words played over and over in my mind.

Why had it always been done through symbolry and example, and why had no one questioned the approach? If no one had actually read the *Texts*, how did anyone know the material taught was accurate? Why hadn't they been translated long before now? They'd obviously been translated previously.

The *Texts* had been around for millennia, according to what I'd been taught. Old French didn't exist when the *Texts* originated. Who had written them? What was their original importance?

I'd never known Bill to take a dogmatic approach to anything, which is why his stance confounded me.

That's how we've always done it.

In other words, don't question it.

Pure dogma. Bill had changed in ten years. I'd known it since I'd returned. But why?

Were the *Texts* a bible of sorts? Was it a religious document rather than a historical one?

We'd always been told it was history with some philosophy, but why such a sacred approach?

That's how we've always done it.

Not anymore.

I was going to read the *Vampyre Texts* from beginning to end. If there was anything about a blood bond in the pages of that tome, I would find it.

SIX

Erin

"*Bonjour, ma petite.*"

I opened my eyes. Dante lay next to me, propped up on one arm, his other hand stroking my cheek.

"*Tu es belle quand tu dors.*"

French. I recognized the language, but I didn't understand most of it. *Bonjour* meant hello or good day. *Belle* meant beauty or beautiful. Thank you, *Beauty and the Beast.* I'd taken Spanish for a year in high school, and in nursing school, I hadn't been required to take a language.

"French?" I said.

"*Oui.*"

"It's a beautiful language, but I don't speak it. English please." I smiled.

"I said, 'you're beautiful when you sleep.'"

I smiled, my insides melting into a puddle of sop. "That's sweet. Why are you speaking French today?"

"I studied it in high school, and I found an online course. I need to translate some stuff."

"Oh? What?"

"Just some things I found at Bill's. It's in Old French, and I think I can do it if I brush up on my French."

"What kind of things? Documents?"

"Yeah, more or less. I'm trying to find out more about what's happening between us. The blood bond."

"But you said it hadn't happened in a long time."

"Not that has been documented. At least not that I know of. I may be chasing a phantom, but I have to try."

She nodded. "I get it. Will you share with me what you find out?"

"Of course. This affects you as much as it affects me."

I yawned and stretched. "Are we still on for tonight?"

"Yes, love. But we're staying in well-lit areas."

"Fine with me. I just want a nice meal and some time with you." I got out of bed and smiled. "I need a shower. Care to join me?"

His eyes darkened. He didn't need to feed yet. No, this was pure lust in his smoky eyes. He wanted me. On a platter.

I was only too willing to serve myself up.

I walked swiftly to the bathroom and started the shower. We were already naked. When the water was good and steamy, I stepped in, Dante behind me. I turned.

His fangs were out, and my God, he was sex on a stick. I'd never known elongated canine teeth could be so enticing.

"I want you, Erin." His low voice came out with a growl.

I bit my lower lip, the throbbing between my legs already intense. One look from him, one simple touch, and I was jelly.

He turned me around so I was facing the wall, and with no preliminaries, thrust into me from behind, a low moan caressing the back of my neck.

Then chills as he scraped his teeth along the sensitive skin of my shoulder.

Bite me.

The words formed but didn't emerge.

"I don't need blood, baby. I just need you." He plunged into me even harder.

He hadn't read my mind. He knew it instinctively. We were just so in tune with each other that he knew what I was thinking and feeling. Amazing.

He slammed into me again and again, all the while holding one arm around my waist so I wouldn't go crashing against the wall. Always thinking of me, of my safety.

Then my thoughts took a backseat to the incredible orgasm that began to roll through me. The warm water from the showerhead pelted us as I cried out in rapture, in complete euphoria. Colors and vibrations dazzled around me, and he thrust, and he thrust, and he thrust...

And—

"God, Erin! So good. I love you, Erin. I love you so fucking much."

He held himself inside me, and as I continued to fly, each spasm of his cock took me higher and higher into the clouds.

When our respective climaxes subsided in tandem, we stood, joined, letting the shower massage and cleanse us. He lowered his head and kissed my neck. A sweet and tender kiss, his fangs scraping my skin gently. Then he slowly turned me around and clasped me to him, our wet bodies touching everywhere.

"I needed that," he said.

"So did I," I murmured against his shoulder.

"No, I mean I *really* needed that."

I pulled away slightly. "You think I didn't?"

He regarded me, his eyes still smoldering. "I think you haven't quite accepted everything between us yet."

I sighed. I couldn't fault his observation. In the heat of our passion, I accepted him without question. But back on earth?

Not quite.

"I'm trying, Dante."

"I know, love. I'm not rushing you. No pressure." He grabbed my shower pouf from its hook, squeezed some shower gel onto it, and began rubbing it over my shoulders.

I closed my eyes, inhaling the moist steam. He was so patient with me, and I appreciated it so much. I needed his patience.

But I also knew one thing.

His patience wouldn't last forever.

⚜

Dante ordered a bottle of Champagne at dinner.

"Are we celebrating something?" I asked.

"Just us. That's worth a celebration. Don't you think?"

I smiled. "Sure. I suppose."

The server poured two flutes and left the rest of the bottle in an ice bucket.

Dante picked up his glass. "*A nous.*"

There he went with the French again. "To us?"

"Very good. I'll have you speaking French in no time."

I laughed. "I doubt that. Are you French?"

He nodded. "Gabriel is a French name. It's pronounced ga-bree-elle in French. Bill's real name is Guillaume, which is French for William. My grandmother's name was Marcheline, and my mother's name was Vivienne."

SEVEN

DANTE

Saying my mother's name made me pause. I barely remembered her, rarely thought about her. Now, with Em's pregnancy, my mother had been more on my mind.

"Beautiful," Erin said. "What was your father's name?"

"Julian. His name was Julian."

"Is that French?"

"No. Julian is Roman, and his twin brother's name was Braedon, which is Irish. I guess my grandparents got tired of French names."

"So Braedon was River's father, then?"

"Yeah."

"Does he have any brothers or sisters?"

I shook my head. "His mother died after conceiving her second child. From an ectopic pregnancy."

"Oh, no. I'm so sorry."

"It is what it is. Pregnancy is still very difficult for vampire women."

She clasped her hand to her mouth.

"What?"

"I'm sorry. You must be worried about your sister."

Em's pregnancy wasn't something I could discuss with Erin out of respect for my sister's privacy, but I hated keeping it from her, especially because the baby Em carried was Erin's niece or nephew. But it wasn't my news to tell. Emilia had to tell Jay before any of us could say anything.

My neck chilled, and something tugged at me. The urge to tell Erin everything. The truth.

Was it part of the blood bond? I had no idea. But I'd find out as soon as I could, as soon as I could read the *Texts*.

Erin took a sip of her Champagne. "It's delicious. The bubbles tickle my nose."

"You're cute." I smiled.

"So are you. And I mean that in a totally masculine Alpha way."

I let out a laugh. Being with her made me so happy. Almost made me forget how much I'd been through, how much lay ahead of me.

She was still out there. *She* had let me go, but she'd been so obsessed with me and my blood. Surely *she* wouldn't give me up that easily.

You're right. I won't.

Damn it! Not tonight. She would not ruin my night out with the woman of my dreams.

Not the woman of your dreams. The woman of your nightmares.

I stood abruptly.

"Dante?"

"Sorry, love. Just need to use the restroom." I walked swiftly toward the back of the restaurant, only to be guided toward the other side by a busboy.

I raced into the bathroom and grabbed on to a sink, my breath coming in rapid pants. I looked in the mirror. Drips of perspiration slid down my forehead. I grabbed a paper towel from the dispenser and wiped my face. Then I wet it with cold water and slid it over my skin again.

She was in my head. I fought her off most of the time, but she was always there. She had fed from me, forced me to feed from her.

What did that mean? What did it mean for the blood bond with Erin?

What had she done to my blood to change the Rh factor? And what did *that* mean for me? For Erin? For the rest of my family?

No one else was in the bathroom, thankfully, so I looked at my reflection in the mirror and spoke aloud.

"You will not control me."

I already control you.

"You do *not*!" I grasped the edge of the sink once more. The edges of my irises were indeed lighter, and my gums itched as my fangs began to descend.

You are strong, Dante. My blood has made you strong. Her blood is making you even stronger.

Chills erupted through my whole body.

She knew.

She knew about Erin. About the blood bond.

"Get out of my head!" I hurled my fist into the mirror, shattering the glass.

Then I stared at the fragmented image before me. My face, cut into thousands of pieces to render me unrecognizable.

The most apt image of me I'd seen in a while.

I *was* unrecognizable, right down to my blood.

She had changed me.

She'd done more than hold me captive, torture me, and steal my blood.

She'd changed me in a literal way—a way I didn't understand. Didn't want to understand.

And Erin...

I'd dragged Erin into my life. Forced her into this blood bond.

I should have left her alone.

But what if I had? Bill said she would die without giving me blood once the bond had been formed.

Bill...

He had been so strange since I'd returned. Secretive. Unworried.

Blood coagulated on my knuckles, and I wrapped the wet towel I'd used previously around them. Once the bleeding had stopped, I gripped the porcelain edges once more.

Inhale. Exhale. Inhale. Exhale.

"You *will* stay out of my head."

Someone walked in, and I let go of the sink.

"You okay, man?" the guy asked, his gaze edging toward the shattered glass of the mirror.

"Yeah. Fine." What must I look like? "Why?"

"You just look a little rattled."

"I'm good." I walked past him, out the door, and back into the dining room.

Erin sat, studying her menu, her back to me.

Inhale. Exhale. Inhale. Exhale.

Had to appear normal to her. Couldn't let her worry. I'd already forced her into a life she wasn't ready for. I pasted a smile on my face and walked around to sit across from her.

"Hey," she said. "I was starting to get worried. Everything okay?"

"Yeah, fine. Do you see anything you like?" I gestured to her menu.

"I'm thinking redfish tonight. How about you?"

"I haven't looked yet, but I'll be having a steak. Very rare."

"Of course. That's what you ordered—" Her mouth dropped open. "Is that why you like rare beef? Because of the..."

"No, love. There's no blood in meat to nourish us. Most of the blood is drained from the animal before it's butchered. I just like my beef rare. A lot of humans do too."

She reddened. "Drained before it's butchered. Then sold to vampires, right?" She didn't wait for me to respond. "Of course. I knew that. I even like it now. Maybe I'll have a steak with you."

"Have what you want. You don't need to have a steak just to please me."

"I wasn't trying to—" She erupted in giggles. "I guess I was. Isn't that funny? I've never ordered a meal to please anyone but myself before. What was I thinking? I'm having the redfish. And then I want Bananas Foster for dessert."

"Famous in New Orleans," I said. "You shall have it."

"Can you believe I've lived here for three years and I've never tried it?"

"We'll remedy that tonight."

The server came by and took our orders, and I refilled our flutes. I was raising my glass to my lips when—

"Ow!" I swiped the back of my neck.

"What is it?" Erin's eyebrows shot to her forehead.

"Just a chill. I'm fine."

But it hadn't been just a chill. It had been a spear of ice jabbed into my neck.

And I knew, despite my rational mind telling me otherwise.

Erin and I were not alone here.

EIGHT

Erin

"We need to leave."

I widened my eyes. Had I heard him right? "What?"

"I'm not kidding, Erin. We need to leave here. Now."

"But we already ordered."

He threw a few bills on the table. "I know, and I'm sorry. Trust me." He stood.

The server walked toward us. "Sir?"

"I'm sorry. We won't be staying," Dante said. "Please cancel our dinners. The bills on the table should cover the Champagne."

"I can cork it for you, sir—"

"No thank you." He grabbed my hand and pulled me toward the exit.

When we were out on the street, I turned to him. "What was that about?"

"I'm not sure I can explain it. Just a feeling."

"You'd better try to explain it, Dante. We were supposed to have a nice dinner."

"It didn't feel right. Being there."

"It was just a restaurant."

"We'll go to a different one. If you're still hungry."

"Yes, I'm still hungry. Aren't you?"

"Honestly? The sensation kind of zapped my appetite."

"What sensation are you talking about?"

He shook his head. "I never believed much in the paranormal."

"Dante, you are *part* of the paranormal."

He shook his head again, more vehemently this time. "I'm not. Only in myth. Vampires are a mortal species just like any other."

"A mortal species with the ability to glamour their prey."

"Some humans have that ability. Hypnosis is a real thing, Erin. It can be learned. Some humans have psychic abilities too. Is that paranormal?"

My mind was muddled. What was real and what wasn't? I had no idea anymore. "Are you saying you felt a paranormal presence in the restaurant?"

"All I know is that I felt *something.* And it wasn't good, Erin. It felt...dark and ominous. Evil. It felt *evil.*"

Chills scattered over my arms, and I rubbed them. I didn't believe in the paranormal either, but what Dante said freaked me out more than a little. He had run to the bathroom quickly. Had he felt it then?

Before I could ask, he grabbed my arm and pulled me down the street to where a musician was playing guitar and singing folk songs.

"It's better here," he said.

"Meaning?"

"I don't feel the presence anymore. We're safe now."

"You're really scaring me, Dante."

"I know, and I'm sorry. But we had to leave that restaurant. Something wasn't right."

"But everything's fine now, in the middle of the sidewalk?"

"Yeah. I can't explain it. Come on. We can find another restaurant."

"Are you kidding? My appetite just flew the coop. I thought you said yours did as well."

"Yeah, it did. I'm pretty creeped out."

I sighed. "You're not the only one."

He led me to an outdoor café and we grabbed a small table.

"I need to ask you something," I said.

"Go ahead."

"Do ghosts exist?"

He let out a strained laugh. "I never thought so."

"What is that supposed to mean?"

"It means I've always been taught that ghosts don't exist. That the supernatural veil that draws vampires to New Orleans is a result of the voodoo and witchcraft practitioners and the cosmic energy they draw down during their spells. And prayer."

"Prayer?"

"There are a lot of devout Catholics here too, and prayer is just another type of spell casting. It's drawing on the energy of God or the universe or whatever you want to call it."

I wasn't an overly religious person, but this was sounding a little sacrilegious even to me. "Prayer? Really?"

"Prayers are energy, Erin. Every time you commune with a higher power, you're drawing down energy."

"And all this..."

"The prayers, the spells, everything. It all contributes to the supernatural veil around the city. Vampires are drawn to that. A lot of humans are as well."

"But ghosts—"

"Don't exist. At least that's what I was taught. That when you die, you become part of the energy of the universe, and that's what is drawn down here in New Orleans."

"So you cease to exist."

"Yes, as a living creature, but you continue to exist as energy. Energy can't just disappear. It has to go somewhere."

"Then why can't ghosts exist?"

"I don't have a clue. I only know what I was taught. That when a person dies, he no longer exists as a unique individual. He becomes part of the cosmic energy."

"Then what were you feeling at the restaurant?"

"I don't know. And I don't know if ghosts don't exist. Bill, apparently, believes in them."

I dropped the fork I was fidgeting with on the table. "He does?"

"Yeah. He told me so. Big news to me. Apparently a lot of what I was taught as a child is wrong."

"You believe him?"

"I didn't. But I can't deny what I felt at the restaurant. There was a supernatural presence near me, and it was messing with my mind. I felt it. I felt an icicle stabbing my neck, and I had some unwelcome thoughts. We weren't alone there, Erin."

A server approached us, but neither of us were hungry anymore. I ordered a sweet tea, just because we couldn't sit here without ordering something. Dante ordered a black coffee.

When our drinks came, Dante raised his cup to his lips.

His fangs were protruding.

"Are you...okay?" I asked.

He nodded. "They come out when something bothers

me. It's a defense mechanism. Most vampires are better at controlling it than I am."

"Why is that?"

"Because—" He sighed. "I missed a lot. While I was...gone."

"Oh." I wanted to push him on it. Wanted him to tell me everything. I wanted to know everything. Not because I was nosy but because I loved him. But he'd tell me when he could. I was still having trouble dealing with some things myself, and until I could give him all of me, I couldn't expect the same of him.

Even though I wanted it.

We both jerked when some clattering noises drew our attention.

I drew in a breath. "Would you look at that?"

NINE

DANTE

The musician stopped playing his guitar. All eyes focused on a large woman walking toward us, finger cymbals clanging.

"Oh my God."

"It's that woman from under the bridge. Bea," Erin said. "What is she doing over here?"

"I have no idea."

She stopped in front of our table. "I knew I'd find you two here."

"Did you?" I said with skepticism.

"I did. I have the sight."

"So you've told us. What's with the commotion?"

"Bea likes to make an entrance."

"Bea apparently also likes to refer to herself in the third person," Erin said.

I chuckled.

"I need a moment of your time." She sat down at our table without being invited.

"I'm afraid—"

"Fine," I said, interrupting Erin. "What do you want?"

"I came to warn you."

"Of what?"

"I'm not sure."

"That's helpful." Erin rolled her eyes.

"You should take me seriously," Bea said. "'There are more things in heaven and earth, Horatio, than are dreamt of in your philosophy.'"

"Shakespeare," Erin said. "Impressive."

"Don't discount Shakespeare," Bea said. "He was an amazing metaphysician. He knew more than most in his time. As do I."

If she knew so much, why did she live under Claiborne Bridge? Looking at Erin, I could see she was wondering the same thing. I secretly hoped she wouldn't voice her question, though, as I didn't want Bea to get angry and leave. After what I'd experienced in the restaurant, I wanted to hear what this odd woman had to say.

"I'm not discounting Shakespeare," Erin said. "I'm just wondering what you and he could possibly have in common."

"Nothing but an understanding that there is so much more to our world than our brains are capable of processing."

"I'll give you that one," Erin said. "I'm a nurse. I know we only use a tiny percentage of our brains."

"Then you'll understand why I can't tell you exactly what I'm sensing. But I am sensing *something*." She looked directly at me. "There is a dark presence following you."

Erin's lips trembled.

I said nothing.

"You've already sensed it," Bea said.

"I may have."

"I wish I could guide you, but this is something new to me. I've never felt such darkness."

"Is it a single entity?" I asked.

"I'm not sure."

"Do ghosts exist?" Erin demanded.

Bea nodded. "They do."

Erin rubbed at her forehead. "Oh, God."

"What is it?" Bea asked.

"Nothing much. Just the whole constancy of my universe has been bowled over."

"Mine too, believe it or not." Vampires might be new to Erin, but the rest of this stuff was new to both of us. I was now dealing with werecreatures, ghosts, and seers existing. Not to mention some demonic presence that had apparently taken enough of a liking to me to follow me around.

"Not a demon, dearie. A dark presence."

And I was getting damned sick of people reading my mind. "Demons aren't real?"

"They're real, but they have no interest in you. At least not at the moment."

Thank God for small favors.

Erin had gone pale. I placed my hand over hers.

"Just be careful," Bea said. "I don't leave the bridge unless the need is great. I felt I needed to warn you. Heed my warning." She stood and walked away. When she was a few yards beyond us, she began clattering her finger cymbals once more.

"That was freaky," Erin said.

"It was. And I'm not sure it was actually Bea."

"What do you mean?"

"The way she spoke."

Erin nodded. "True. The first time we met her, she said

'ain't,' and her grammar was atrocious. And now she's quoting Shakespeare and telling us to heed her warning?"

"Ain't isn't a huge issue. You're not from the south, but a lot of well-educated people use it. I'm talking more about her general demeanor."

"Good point," Erin said. "She *was* acting differently. But Dante, that *was* Bea. There can't possibly be more than one of them. That would mean my universe is even more fucked up than I think it is."

"You're right. Of course it was. But she was different somehow. And why the finger cymbals? Why announce she was coming like that? You know what I mean?" Truth was, I didn't have a clue what I meant, and trying to convince Erin that some entity had taken over Bea would freak her out even more. "You want to go home?"

"Yeah. I do."

I stood and offered Erin my hand, when icy chills stabbed into my neck once more.

Dante.

A voice spoke in my head.

I stiffened.

I hadn't heard that voice in over ten years.

TEN

Erin

Dante brought me home. He wouldn't need to feed until morning, and I was used to being awake at night, so I decided to work on the research Dr. Bonneville had asked me to do. At fifty bucks an hour, I couldn't refuse.

I fired up my computer, while Dante paced around the townhome.

"Are you going to do that all night?" I asked.

"Sorry," he said. "Just thinking. I need to talk to River."

"Then call him."

"He's on duty. He went back to work after his medical leave."

"Oh. Then call Bill."

He sighed. "Yeah. I should. I should go see him. Will you be okay here?"

"Of course. You can stand outside and listen to me lock my deadbolt. I'm just going to be here on the computer until it's bedtime at eight or nine in the morning."

He kissed me goodbye, and I latched my deadbolt, committing it to memory. I always locked my door. Why I'd gone haywire recently and forgotten, I'd never understand.

After a couple hours of researching and finding nothing except religious stuff explaining the correlation between blood type and hair and eye colors, I gave up. I'd have to tell Dr. Bonneville I couldn't find what she wanted. I took copious notes because I wanted my hundred bucks. According to one site, all B positive people had brown eyes and dark skin. I was so far from that.

I rose and made myself a small snack. We'd skipped dinner, after all, and now I was a bit hungry.

Then I sat back down again and found my fingers typing in *Juan Mendez, Jr*. Jay had gotten back to me with Mrs. Moore's son's phone number, but I'd been so preoccupied with Dante that I hadn't tried to contact him or Mrs. Moore's husband. I still had a strange feeling that Mrs. Moore had known something I needed to know. I'd brushed it off after ruminating on it, but now, with Bea visiting us and telling us something Dante needed to know, I wondered if I should be taking my intuition more seriously.

I did some searching. Juan Mendez, Jr., was a retired attorney who lived in Baton Rouge. I'd have to wait until morning to call him. He wouldn't be up at—I checked the time on my monitor—two a.m. Neither would Mrs. Moore's husband, who was suffering from advanced lung cancer and lived in hospice care.

Nothing more to do until waking hours.

Now I was bored. My fridge was nearly empty. What could it hurt to go to the grocery store? I usually shopped at the twenty-four-hour Walmart nearby on my nights off.

I'd promised Dante I'd lock my door, but I didn't promise I wouldn't go anywhere. I'd gone shopping a hundred times during the night, and never once had I met—

My skin chilled.

What if I'd been glamoured while I was out and about during the night?

No. Dante had said I'd been fed on sometime during my last work shift. Going shopping wouldn't harm me. Besides, I was itching to do something productive. I changed into jeans and a T-shirt and left.

I'd filled my cart with groceries and was headed toward checkout, when I spied a familiar face.

"Hello, Erin," Abe Lincoln said, striding toward me.

"Oh. Hi."

"What are you doing out at night?"

"I work nights, remember? This is my night off."

"Oh."

"What are you doing here?" I wasn't sure what to call him. Last time I'd seen him he hadn't answered to Abe but had come running when I hollered "Red Rover."

"Meeting someone."

"Who?"

He looked over his shoulder and then inched closer to me. "A vampire," he whispered.

I resisted the urge to burst out laughing. "You're meeting a vampire in Walmart?"

"I meet them wherever they tell me to."

I peered behind him, shuddering. "Where is he?"

"He's not here yet. Do you want to meet him?"

Did I? I desperately wanted to find out who was stealing my blood, but Dante had warned that my scent was irresistible to vampires. Any vampire who fed on Abe Lincoln didn't share Dante's scruples about not feeding on humans.

I cleared my throat and decided to change the subject. "Why did you run away the day we bought you lunch?"

"A ghost told me to."

I began to roll my eyes, but stopped abruptly, remembering my conversation with Dante about ghosts earlier.

"What ghost? Was it the same ghost you saw with the vampire the night you came into the ER?"

He shook his head. "No. That was a good ghost."

I chilled again. "There are good and bad ghosts?"

"Of course. Why wouldn't there be? There are good and bad people, aren't there? Everything comes in good and bad."

He had a point. "How did you know the ghost you saw that day was bad?"

"I just knew. I got a weird feeling. So I ran."

"What could a ghost do to you?"

"I don't know. And I wasn't interested in finding out."

This was getting way too freaky. "Look, I need to pay for my groceries. Do you need anything? I'll buy you a sandwich or something. A bottle of water. Whatever you want."

"That's nice of you to offer. But the vampire will buy me a hot meal once we're done."

"Right." I headed toward the checkout line. "It was nice to see you."

"You too. Wait for me after you load up your groceries. I'll take you to meet the vampire."

I opened my mouth to object, but then changed my mind, against my better judgment. My curiosity won out. I began placing my items on the conveyor belt.

"Erin," he said.

I turned back toward him. "All right. I'll wait."

ELEVEN

DANTE

"I didn't appreciate you hanging up on me," Bill said. He sat on the couch in the living room while I paced.

"I apologize." Though I wasn't the least bit sorry.

"You're going to wear down that Persian rug." He eyed my feet.

I plunked down into a recliner. "Sorry."

"What do you need, Dante? It seems you only come to me when you need my help."

I needed his help more than anything, but so far he'd refused to tell me what I needed to know. What was in the *Texts*.

"I was at dinner with Erin," I said, "and I felt a...presence."

"Oh?"

"Something messed with my mind. Took me back to..." It was still so hard to say. "To when I was in captivity. It took me back to *her* while I was in the men's room. Then, when I got back to the table with Erin, I felt an icy stab on the back of my neck. I don't know how else to describe it. I just knew we had to get out of there."

"I see."

Did he really see? I wasn't sure anymore. Though I was hesitant, I went on to explain our subsequent run-in with Bea on Royal Street earlier.

"It was the strangest thing. This homeless woman—she says she's a voodoo high priestess—was quoting Shakespeare."

"Just because someone is homeless doesn't mean she's not educated."

"I know that. But the first time I met this woman, she didn't seem educated."

"Hmm..."

That's not helping. But I didn't say it.

Seconds passed. Then minutes. I was about to say something, when Bill finally spoke.

"I believe the woman. I believe something dark has targeted you."

"How can you believe that?"

"I've learned much in the years you were gone, Dante, a lot of which I didn't want to believe. But I find I have no choice."

"What is it, then? This thing that has supposedly targeted me?"

"I wish I knew."

"Damn!" I brought my fist down on the soft arm of the tan leather recliner.

"Calm down."

"Calm down? Really? You have no idea what I've been through, and now, all I want is peace. A life of peace and love with Erin. Why me?"

"I don't know. But I'm willing to bet it has something to do with your blood."

I hadn't told Bill yet that my blood type had mutated. Or been tampered with.

"And," he continued, "I'd bet it also has something to do with your father and uncle."

"What could it possibly have to do with them?"

"I have reason to believe they were the primary targets when you were taken."

"What?"

"Julian and Braedon are male vampire identical twins. You know how rare that is. Identical vampire twins hadn't been documented since the fourteenth century. And your grandmother lived through their birth. In fact, she had what amounted to an effortless pregnancy for a vampire female. Everything about your father and uncle is extremely rare and worth studying."

"You think they've been..." Nausea crept up my throat as I envisioned my dead father and uncle being autopsied. Cut apart and put under a microscope.

No.

They were alive somewhere. I'd been kept alive. If they were that rare, whoever took them wouldn't kill them. I had to believe that. *Had* to.

"I think you were taken to draw them out, Dante. Whoever took you knew they would go after you."

My mind raced. "Then why keep me? And why take me instead of River? We were both there that night."

"I don't have an answer to either of those questions."

"Then why do you think whoever took me was actually after them?"

"For the reasons I just stated. Their rarity."

"Then they might still be alive. We have to find them."

Bill sighed. "How much are you ready to believe now, Dante?"

"What do you mean?"

"I told you recently that you're safe because a ghost is watching over you."

I jolted. I hadn't believed in ghosts then. But now? I wasn't so sure.

"Is this 'dark thing' that has targeted me a ghost?"

"I don't know yet."

"Bea said it wasn't a demon."

"That's good to know. We need to assume this Bea is telling the truth, at least for now."

"Demons exist, then?"

"I've realized so much in the years you've been gone. Yes, demons exist, unfortunately, but not in the way you might think. When evil embodies a living thing, anyone can gain immortality and become a demon."

I pulled at my hair. This was all too much. Too fucking much.

Dante.

The voice again. The one I'd heard in the restaurant that had sounded familiar.

Very familiar.

"Dante," Bill said, his tone ominous. "Your father is standing behind you."

TWELVE

Erin

After fifteen minutes of waiting in the well-lit parking lot, I rolled my eyes and gave up. Abe Lincoln, as I'd always known, was delusional. Maybe vampires did exist. I pretty much had to accept that. But Abe Lincoln didn't actually know any, no matter what he and Bea said. I was done chasing zebras.

I opened my car door—

I jerked when a clammy hand gripped my other arm. I turned.

Abe Lincoln.

"You nearly scared the piss out of me!" I yanked my arm away.

"Where are you going? I thought you wanted to meet the vampires."

Vampires? As in plural? No thanks. "I changed my mind. I just want to go home."

"But they want to meet you. I told them all about you."

"Not tonight, Abe. Sorry."

He grabbed my arm again. Harder this time. How did a skinny homeless man have such strength?

"They want to meet you. Behind Walmart."

Oh, hell, no. "I'm sorry. I can't. But tell them thanks." I yanked my arm away once more and dived into my car, slamming the door shut and knocking Abe onto his ass on the asphalt. I didn't care. I was so out of there.

I started my engine and peeled out of the parking lot, my heart hammering.

THIRTEEN

DANTE

A chill swept over the back of my neck and I stood and turned.

Nothing.

"You're off your rocker," I said to Bill.

"Believe me. I thought I was too, at first."

"There's no one here," I said.

"You're wrong. He's there. I can see him as plain as day behind the chair. He just appeared."

"Then tell me why I can't."

"Because you don't believe. You need to let go of your skepticism, Dante."

"You taught me long ago that ghosts don't exist, Bill. That the dead join the cosmic energy force and cease to have any uniqueness."

"I did. I taught your father that as well. I was wrong."

"How do you know?"

He laughed. "Because your father is standing right next to you now."

"Can you hear him?"

"Of course. Just as if he were alive."

Dante.

The voice again. It was *his* voice. My father's voice.

But I didn't hear him out loud. Only in my mind.

"That's how it starts," Bill said. "You think your head is playing tricks on you. But it's not. Suspend your beliefs, Dante. Suspend everything you thought was reality. And feel. Have faith."

"How long have you..."

"A day before your return, I began to feel my son's presence. I didn't think anything of it, but the next day, you returned. I knew then that I needed to pay more attention to my feelings and intuition. I opened myself up, and Julian spoke to me. In my mind. A day later, I was able to see and hear him."

"What does he look like?"

"The same as he did when he was alive. You'll be able to see him soon."

"And what does he think about us having a conversation about him as if he's not in the room?" I still wasn't convinced he was actually *in* the room. Before he could answer, I added, "Is this why you've been so...different since I returned?"

"I'm not sure I know what you're asking. I don't think I've been different at all."

Of course not. Now was not the time to get into that anyway. If my father was truly here as a ghost—and I'd heard his voice in my mind three times now—that meant two things. One, ghosts *did* exist. But I could hardly wrap my head around that revelation at the moment. No. The second and more important fact was...my father was dead.

Dead.

He and Uncle Brae weren't alive, as I'd secretly hoped.

And I was responsible.

If I hadn't been taken, my father and uncle wouldn't have gone after me. And if I hadn't disobeyed them and gone to the Quarter on Mardi Gras...

I hadn't mourned my father and uncle. I'd been too wrapped up in what was happening between Erin and me. I hadn't given myself time to grieve, to deal with the feelings that were now plummeting through me like golf-ball-sized hail.

Could I believe? Could I turn my back on everything I'd been taught? Everything I'd always known as truth?

I'd already begun to.

"Dad?" I looked around timidly, feeling like a blind person trying to find the light in the room.

"He says, 'I'm here, son.'"

Not only was I blind, but deaf too.

Or Bill was crazy as a loon.

A chill swept the back of my neck. I swiped at it.

"That's your father, Dante. Ghosts have a cold presence."

The chill. I'd felt it many times since my return—the first when Jay Hamilton had caught me with the homeless man, Abe Lincoln, the night of my escape.

I'd run, and Jay hadn't followed me.

Was that because... "Dad?" I said again. "Were you there with me that night? When I took clothes from a homeless man and a detective found me?"

"He says 'yes,'" Bill said.

"The chill..." I said. "Then...in Erin's apartment. She thought she saw someone."

"He says that was him as well."

"How could Erin have seen...?"

"Once you see a ghost, it's easier to keep seeing him," Bill said.

"That doesn't make any sense. When would Erin have seen him?"

Bill paused a second, appearing to listen. "He says he stopped to help her with her car one day."

"He's been watching over Erin too?"

"Yes."

"Okay. Then...thanks, Dad. I guess."

"He says he'd do anything for both of you."

I let out a huff. "This is getting ridiculous! If he's really here, why can't I see him? Why can't I hear him?"

"Because you don't believe yet. You have to have faith, Dante."

Faith. The second time he'd used that word. How could I have faith after all I'd been through?

Faith was an illusion.

Dante.

His voice again. In my head. What was he trying to say?

I closed my eyes and drew in a breath.

Faith.

What was faith anyway?

We weren't a religious family. Our faith was rooted in our history, in being good, moral people.

Faith was believing without seeing, without having any evidence to substantiate what you accepted as true.

It had been hard to believe a blood bond—something I'd never heard of and that hadn't happened in ages—existed between Erin and me, but at least I had some evidence to substantiate it. The fact that I could no longer smell other humans, the fact that she kept putting herself in danger without knowing it, the music we heard that no one else could. All those things pointed to the blood—

Ice chilled my veins. Panic swelled in me as my heart thundered against my chest like a bass drum.

Erin. She was in danger. Adrenaline surged through me, landing in the nerves in my cuspids. They tingled as they descended.

"Dante?" Bill said.

"Erin," I said, my voice low. "I feel her. Something's not right."

"Are you sure?"

Bill's question lingered in my ears. I'd been wrong before. I'd rushed to the hospital, certain she was in trouble, only to be wrong. Was I wrong now?

I drew in a deep breath and stayed still. I was freaked over my father. That was all.

Calm down. You're imagining things, Dante.

Back to my father. I needed evidence. Tangible evidence that he was here. But what pointed to my father—a ghost—being in this room?

Only Bill telling me so, and I'd stopped putting any faith in what he said weeks ago.

Only that...and the chill on the back of my neck.

I could ask Erin if someone had helped her with her car.

That's what I'd do. I'd call Erin. I reached for my cell phone in my pocket—

She burst through the door without knocking, running from the foyer into the living room. "Dante! I'm sorry to barge in, but I—" She looked over my shoulder. "What are *you* doing here?"

FOURTEEN

Erin

I was still trembling from my run-in with Abe in the parking lot. I hadn't bothered knocking. I charged in and ran through the foyer into the living room.

Behind Dante stood a stranger I recognized. The one who'd helped me with my car. Who'd told me to keep an open mind.

An open mind.

I'd been sure I saw him in the corner of my living room, but I'd been wrong. My imagination had been playing tricks on me.

"Hello, Erin," the stranger said.

He'd had a familiar look about him at the time, but I hadn't placed it. Now, seeing him in the same room with Dante and Bill, it was so apparent.

He was one of them. A Gabriel vampire.

"You're a Gabriel, aren't you?" I said.

"I am."

"Would you stop talking to thin air?" Dante said, standing.

"I'm not. I'm talking to the guy standing be—" I shuddered, as a coolness swept over me. "Wait. What?"

"I'm Julian Gabriel," the man said. "Dante's father. Bill's son."

"Dante can't see him, Erin," Bill said. "He doesn't yet believe."

"Believe what?"

"That I'm real. That I'm here and I'm real."

"That's silly. You're as real as the rest of us." I stepped forward to touch his arm...only to have my hand whoosh downward. I'd definitely felt something, but it was spongy and slick, not at all like a person. I pulled my hand up and stared at it, my heart thundering.

"It's okay, Erin," Bill said. "He's here. But he's a ghost."

Dizziness swept over me, and I gulped. "Uh...what?"

"Erin," Dante said. "I can't see him. Are you sure you see him?"

"Of course I'm sure. But I sure wish I weren't."

My knees wobbled, and Dante steadied me and helped me to a chair. "Apparently my father is here. With us. As a ghost. Which means he's dead."

I felt a little sick. The two half-drunk glasses of blood sitting on the coffee table didn't help my queasiness.

"You can convince him," Julian said. "You can convince my son that I'm real."

"You've got to be kidding me." I sank my head into my hands. Not only vampires, but now ghosts? And demons? According to Bea, anyway.

What new reality was going to foist itself on me next? Werewolves? Zombies? Dancing lobsters?

"You need some water, Erin?" Bill asked.

I shook my head. "I think I need some Valium, to be honest."

"Baby, you really see him? Hear him?"

FIFTEEN

DANTE

She nodded into her hands.

"All right." That was all the evidence I needed. "Dad? Help me. I trust Erin. If she sees you, I believe you're here."

Dante.

"Yes, I hear you speaking into my head. I need to hear you like Erin and Bill hear you."

Dante.

"It might take a little time, son," Bill said.

Erin needs you.

Clear as day. But in my head. It was all I needed though. "Baby, why are you here? You said you weren't going anywhere tonight."

She lifted her head out of her hands. "I nearly forgot. That's why I came here. I went out to get groceries."

"In the middle of the night?"

"Of course in the middle of the night. I work nights and sleep days. My nights off are when I do my shopping. Anyway, I ran into Abe Lincoln." She paused a few seconds. "Yes, he's the one."

"Who are you talking to?"

"Your father, apparently."

"Stay out of this, will you?" I said to thin air. "It's annoying when they can hear you but I can't."

No response. Of course not. I couldn't hear him anyway.

"He says okay," Bill said. "That he understands."

"Great," I said sarcastically. Then I turned back to Erin. "What happened?"

"He said he was meeting a vampire at Walmart."

"At Walmart?"

"Yeah, I thought it was weird too, but that's what he said. Anyway, he asked if I wanted to meet the vampire."

"And you said yes?" Pin pricks covered my skin, and my gums itched.

"Well...yeah. We need to find out who's been—"

"For God's sake, Erin. I've told you how irresistible you smell to vampires. And this is a vampire who has no qualms about feeding on humans if he's the one who's been feeding on Abe."

"I know all that, but I thought—"

"You weren't thinking at all!"

"Dante, would you let me finish? I waited in the parking lot for about fifteen minutes—"

"In a parking lot. In the dark. Waiting for a vampire."

"That's not letting me finish, Dante."

"How do you expect me to just—"

"Let her finish, son."

I looked to Bill...but the words hadn't come from him. "Dad?"

"I'm here."

"I can hear you now. But I can't see you."

"It will come," Bill said. "Now let Erin finish. She's obviously upset."

"I'm sorry. Go ahead, baby."

"So I waited, and then I got sick of waiting, so I went to get in my car, but suddenly Abe Lincoln was there. He told me to come with him, that they wanted to meet me."

"They?"

"Yeah, apparently more than one now. Behind Walmart. No way was I going. He persisted, but I yanked my arm away and got in my car and drove straight over here."

My gut churned. Never again would I ignore my intuition. "Was this recently? Like twenty minutes ago?"

"Yeah. Why?"

"Nothing." Only it wasn't nothing. I'd felt Erin. Felt that she was in danger. Never again would I ignore my instinct. Thank God she'd gotten away. If she hadn't... I couldn't go there. Especially since it would have been my fault. "Please, Erin. Don't ever do anything like this again. Please."

"I won't. Trust me. I learned my lesson. I've never been so scared in my whole life. Except for—" She stopped abruptly, her eyes darkening.

Except for when she learned what I truly was. She didn't have to say the words. I felt them in my soul as if she'd yelled them from the rooftop.

They were a thud to my gut.

She still hadn't accepted all of me.

"She will, son."

My father again. Could he read my mind as well?

"I know what you're thinking. And no, I can't read your mind. At least not in the way you imagine."

Erin let out a huff. "All right. What the heck are you people talking about? I feel like I've walked into crazy town."

"Baby, you and I need to talk in private. Would you excuse us, Bill. And...Dad?" Talking to someone I couldn't see was more than a little disturbing.

"Of course."

I ushered Erin to the bedroom I was using, though I hadn't slept there since I'd started feeding from her. I shut the door.

"I need to move in with you," I said.

She lifted her eyebrows. "What?"

"You heard me. That's the only way I can keep you safe."

"Dante, even if you moved in with me, which you're not going to, you couldn't be with me all the time. I'm a big girl."

"A big girl who got herself into an unsafe situation tonight."

"And who also got herself out of it," she said.

"Yes, you did. But those vamps have smelled you now, and they will hunger for you. They'll go looking for you."

"Well, they won't find me."

"How do you know that?"

"Because you'll be protecting me."

"I can't protect you. Not if you won't let me move in." I gripped her shoulders. "I love you, Erin. I want to protect you. I *need* to protect you. Please. If anything happened to you—"

"Nothing will happen to me. I'm perfectly safe."

"Start having your groceries delivered. Please. Or I'll take you."

She nodded. "All right. I agree. I don't like what happened tonight any more than you do. I was scared out of my mind, Dante."

"You're safe now." I pulled her to me and crushed my mouth onto hers.

She opened, and we kissed with a new fire. A fire that came

from inside me, a desire to protect her always, to keep her in my arms and away from anything that wanted to do her harm.

Vampires. Were they the Claiborne vamps River had mentioned? Thugs, he'd called them. Bea had said they were drug runners for a female boss. She probably wasn't a vampire because females were rare.

I didn't know.

I knew only one thing. Erin had to be protected. And I was the only one who could keep her safe.

SIXTEEN

Erin

Vampires.

Ghosts.

Demons.

My universe had been tilted beyond belief.

But that didn't matter at the moment, because Dante was kissing me. My nipples hardened as he deepened the kiss, devouring my mouth with his. Our lips slid together, and his thigh went between my legs. I ground against it, my hunger deepening, expanding, until I had to have him.

But he broke the kiss, panting. "Not with Bill and... I can't even say it."

I was panting also, and I squeezed my thighs together to ease the throbbing between them. Didn't help.

"Your father," I said.

"My father," he repeated.

"Dante, how did your father...die?"

He sighed. "I don't know. He and my uncle went after me

when I disappeared. They never came back."

Ice sliced into me as my hand flew to my mouth. "I'm so sorry."

"My father is dead because of me." He turned away from me, his shoulders trembling.

I reached forward to touch him, but he inched farther away, as if he could sense me and didn't want to be touched.

"Dante, your father is...*here*." Wow. Totally weird to actually say that. A dead guy was *here*.

Dante turned to face me, his dark eyes sunken. "He's still dead."

Reality was really taking a big hit today. "But he's here. You can make whatever peace you need to make with him."

He shook his head and let out a sarcastic laugh. "Bill said there was a ghost protecting me. I didn't believe him, of course. It was nonsense, and I figured he was losing it. Ghosts don't exist, after all. That's what we've always believed. But I heard my father's voice today. Clear as a bell on Sunday morning. Turns out Bill was right. I just never dreamed the ghost would be my own father."

"Who better than your father to be your protector?" I couldn't believe the words coming out of my mouth.

"In theory, sure. But my father was missing for as long as I was. If he was truly protecting me, then where was he when—"

"When what?"

"I can't go there yet. Not with you."

A spear of fear lanced into me. What had Dante been through? Would he ever tell me? Could he? The thought of him enduring anything unpleasant nauseated me.

"Dante..."

"It's all right, love. I just...can't. Not yet."

"There is something you *can* do, though."

"What's that?"

"You can ask your father. You can find out how he died, why he wasn't protecting you when you needed him to. Maybe he has a good reason."

"I can't. Not when I can't look him in the eye. I need to be able to see him, Erin. Why can everyone see him but me?"

I hesitantly touched his forearm, and he didn't jerk away this time. "I don't know. I wish I did. I think I see him because..."

"Because why?"

"Because I never realized he was a ghost. I didn't know him, so I had no way of knowing he was dead. He helped me with my car one day when it wouldn't start, and then he told me something." The event raced back into my head. "He told me to keep an open mind."

"About what?"

I smiled. "I think he was talking about you. He must have known we were— In fact, I told him I had a date. It was that first night when we went out to dinner. He must have been talking about you. About what...you are." God, I still had a hard time with the V word when it came to him.

Silence from Dante.

"He was trying to help. He must have been. He knew it would be hard for me to accept, and he was asking me to keep an open mind. I had no idea what he was talking about at first, and then..."

"Then what?"

"I was sure I saw him at home that night, remember? But then he disappeared."

Dante slid his index finger over his cheek. "I remember. There was nothing there, but I felt a draft—" He walked swiftly out of the room.

Huh? What could I do but follow. He rushed back into the living room.

"Dad?" Dante said, looking around. "Are you still here?"

"Yes, son."

"You said that coldness on my neck is you."

"It is."

"Earlier tonight, right before we left the restaurant. That spear in my neck. It was more than a chilly draft."

"That was also me, warning you to leave."

"What was there? What was following me? I felt it in the bathroom."

"I don't know, Dante. It's something I've never encountered before."

"Is it a dark presence, like what Bea said?"

"Yes. I believe so."

"Is it a ghost?"

"I don't think so. It's not visible to me."

I took in the conversation, still not able to wrap my mind around all of it. Julian Gabriel stood in my vision, looking as solid as Bill and Dante. Yet Dante still couldn't see him. His gaze flitted around the room, as if he were trying to zoom in on something that was out of his reach.

"I think you need to talk to your father alone, Dante. I should go."

"No," he said. "You're not going out there again without me at your side. It's not safe."

I opened my mouth but closed it before anything came out. I could take care of myself, but I'd had a huge scare, and right now it wasn't worth arguing about. "All right. Then I'll be happy to go back into your bedroom so you can talk to your father and grandfather in private."

This time he opened his mouth. He was going to tell me to stay, but I knew he wasn't ready to talk freely in front of me. I gestured him not to speak.

"Please. Let me do this for you. I understand what you need right now." Without letting him argue, I walked out of the kitchen and back into his bedroom, shutting the door behind me.

SEVENTEEN

DANTE

"She's a special girl, Dante," my father said. "Very understanding."

Hearing a voice out of thin air was really fucking with my head. "She is special, no doubt. I need her. And I really wish I could see who the hell I'm talking to."

"It will come. It took a little while for me too." Bill stood. "Let's move to the kitchen. I need a snack."

I had no appetite at the moment, except for Erin. But I—along with my ghost father, I assumed—followed Bill into the kitchen.

"I was as surprised as the rest of you," my father said after Bill and I had sat down at the kitchen table. "We've never believed in ghosts, despite the alleged hauntings all around New Orleans. I guess we got a little full of ourselves, as a species that no one else believed existed."

"I need to know, Dad. If you're really here to protect me, where were you when..." I couldn't even say the words. The wounds were still so raw and real.

"Dante, when Brae and I went after you, we knew the risk we were taking."

"Bill seems to think you and Uncle Brae were the primary target of whoever took me. But I can tell you—" I drew in a deep breath, gathering my courage. "The person who took me used me, stole my blood." *Let her goons torture me.* But I couldn't say that to the man who'd fathered me. Not yet. It was too humiliating. "If that wasn't her primary purpose, why didn't she let me go?"

"Bill and I have discussed that," he said. "We think she became infatuated with you and decided to keep you."

"But then she let me go. I escaped, but she arranged it. I'm almost sure of it."

"Yes, and we need to figure out why."

I shook my head. "I have questions first. Many, many questions."

"Then ask," Bill said.

"I need to see him!"

"I'm here. I will answer as best I can," my father said. "You'll see me when you're ready to."

"I'm ready now!"

"Dante," Bill said. "I've been telling you since you returned that there are certain things you're not ready to know yet. This should prove that to you. If you were ready to see your father's ghost, your eyes would let you."

I heaved a sigh. No use arguing. Apparently I no longer had control over my vision. Great. I had so many questions for my father, so I'd have to deal with him being invisible for the moment.

"How did you die, Dad? Where is Uncle Brae? What did they do to you? Why didn't you protect me while I was captive?"

"One at a time, son. First, I only died recently, and it was by my own hand."

A slice of rage hit me full force. "You killed yourself? Why would you do that?"

"Dante," Bill said. "Let him explain."

"I don't know where Braedon is. We weren't held together. He is still alive."

"How do you know?"

"For one, I would have seen him by now in the netherworld."

"You can see...others?"

"Only those who have recently crossed over. But recently doesn't have the same meaning to us as it does to you. To us, recent is as long as ten years. So yes, I would have seen Brae by now if he were dead."

As much as I hoped my uncle was still alive, my mind kept going back to what my father had done. "Why? Why would you take your own life?" I shook my head, trying desperately to understand.

"Very simple," he said. "Your mother told me to."

"My mother? She's been gone over twenty years. You just said—"

"She came to me in a dream. All who have crossed over have that ability when the need is dire. Have you ever had a dream, son, where you could swear it had meaning? You could swear in some way it was real?"

I had. About Erin.

About *her*.

I nodded.

"That's how this was. She came to me in a dream. I knew without a doubt that it was Vivienne, and she was still as beautiful as ever."

My mother. I'd been thinking a lot about her since Em's pregnancy. Did my father even know about that?

He continued. "She told me you were still alive, and you needed me. She gave me explicit instructions where to find what I needed. She told me I'd become a ghost and I could watch over you and protect you. She said you had a purpose to fulfill. A nearly divine purpose, and you needed to be protected so you could fulfill your destiny."

I arched my brows nearly off my forehead. "What? I'm just me. I've been through hell. There's no way I have some divine purpose."

"Nearly divine, was how she put it. And no, she didn't elaborate."

"How am I supposed to deal with any of this?"

"You will deal with what you have to deal with," Bill said. "You're a Gabriel vampire, and your strength will see you through. It has already."

"It couldn't help me escape for ten years."

"I'm not talking about your physical strength, Dante."

I hadn't let her break me. That much was true. But at times I'd said what she wanted, did what she wanted, just to avoid the torture. To avoid losing a body part. At times I actually believed what I was saying because I couldn't bear the thought of the pain.

Was that strength?

"It is *all* strength," Bill said.

There he went reading my mind again. I still didn't believe him when he said he couldn't.

"Sometimes we need to do things we don't want to do for the greater good," Bill went on. "You survived, and you survived intact. *That* is strength."

"Your grandfather's right, Dante." My father's voice came out of thin air again. "You were young, but you still faced your fate like a Gabriel. I'm proud of you."

"Then you...know?"

"Only what Bill has told me. The rest can wait. Until you're ready."

It would definitely wait until I could see him.

"Do you know how to find Uncle Brae? We need to tell River."

"I don't. When I passed, I came straight here. It took a little while for my father to see me, just as it's taking you."

"But Uncle Brae..."

"Braedon is alive. I haven't seen him. But more importantly, he's my twin. I would know if he had passed."

"But you're..."

"Dead or alive, I would know. He and I have a connection beyond our bodies, and we *will* find him. But your mother made it very clear that I was to go straight to you, to protect you."

"How can you protect me? You're a ghost."

"I still have the power to glamour humans. As for other vampires, they won't be able to see me. I won't allow it."

"You can control who sees you?"

"I can. It's pretty awesome, actually."

His words made me smile. I could visualize the glint he used to get in his eye when something amused him. Still, I couldn't see him. I sat down at the table with a plunk. This was all too much.

Then Erin's words buzzed in my ears. *Dante, your father is*...here.

He was. Perhaps I couldn't see him, and perhaps he wasn't alive. But he was *here*. I could tell him what he meant to me, how sorry I was that I'd contributed to his terrible fate. How much I wished he'd been there for Emilia the last ten years, and that it was my fault he hadn't been. I could tell him all of this, because he was here. And for that I was thankful.

I raised my head, and—

There stood my father, as plain as day, in front of me. My mouth dropped open.

"So you see me now." His left eye squinted a bit when he smiled, just as I remembered.

"I do." I stood.

"Dante," he said. "I don't know what's going on. Why you, Braedon, and I were taken. But together we will find out. And we'll make sure it never happens again."

EIGHTEEN

Erin

The *Vampyre Texts* tome was large and ornate, leather bound, the printing on thick parchment. I lugged it out of Bill's house and to my car, walking as stealthily as I could. This was why Dante was brushing up on French, to read this book. To try to figure out what was going on between us and why.

I had to help in any way I could, even if it meant stealing—no, borrowing. I had every intention of returning it when we were done.

Still, the idea burned at me. I'd never stolen anything in my life. Back home in Ohio, when I was thirteen, I'd found a fifty-dollar bill on the floor of a small antique shop. I'd turned it in to the clerk. Jay had rolled his eyes when I told him, saying I'd just made the clerk fifty dollars richer.

Stealing definitely wasn't something I took lightly.

I quietly returned to Dante's bedroom. He was still in the kitchen talking to Bill and Julian.

My fingers burned. I hoped I hadn't just made a huge error

in judgment. I'd seen the heavy volume on a shelf in the living room while I was going back to Dante's bedroom. It had invaded my mind, until I made the rash decision to leave his bedroom, grab the book, and haul it out to my car. The others were busy in the kitchen, and I hoped they were involved enough that their acute vampire hearing wouldn't kick in and give me away.

Since no one had come after me and I was now safely back in Dante's room, I was relieved to know it hadn't.

I sat down on his bed, my heart beating rapidly.

I'd just stolen—nope, borrowed—something. Without asking. I'd never done anything like that before. Of course, my entire world had recently been upended. Who knew what I'd do next?

I looked at my watch. Dawn was near, and Dante would need to feed from me soon. Should I go out and remind him? Surely he'd come get me if he needed me.

Plus, I had to get to bed soon. I had work tonight, and the responsibility of telling Dr. Bonneville, if she was in, that I couldn't continue my research work for her because I hadn't found anything. Kissing fifty dollars an hour goodbye wasn't easy, but what could I do?

My groceries were still in my car. Luckily I hadn't bought anything that would spoil. I sat, waiting. Dante would come get me when he was ready.

I didn't have to wait long. He burst into the room.

"I can see him now, baby."

I smiled and launched myself into his arms. "That's great!" Another shift to my reality. I was excited that Dante could see his father...who was a ghost. Life was getting more than complicated.

He gave me a quick kiss on the top of my head. "I know you need to get home. And I need..."

He didn't say the words, but I knew.

"Let's go," I said.

⚜

As soon as we walked through the door, Dante threw my three bags of groceries on the kitchen counter and plastered me against the refrigerator door. "I need you, Erin. Now." His lips came down on mine.

The kiss was devoid of the passion I'd become used to. This was a kiss of pure need.

I responded, letting him take what he desired, what he ached for, as my nipples hardened and pressed into him.

He broke the kiss and rasped, "I can't be gentle right now, baby. I need to get my cock inside you. My teeth inside you." He pushed my pants over my hips.

Already I was throbbing for him, so ready to be penetrated. I hastily stepped out of my jeans and panties while he unbuckled his pants and freed his cock. He trapped me, hoisting me up. A refrigerator magnet gouged into my back, but I didn't care. I existed in this moment to fulfill his need. I had no other reason for being.

And I was okay with that.

He thrust upward into my pussy. I gasped at the intrusion. I was wet for him, no doubt, but the lack of foreplay had me tight as a drum. He speared through my tight tunnel, filling me to the brim with his cock.

Then he opened his mouth with a low growl, his fangs in full descent. "Need you, Erin."

I closed my eyes and turned my head to the side, giving him access to my neck. And when he sank his teeth into my flesh, the stabbing pain morphing to a pleasure so intense, an orgasm hit me out of nowhere.

"Dante!" I cried out, relishing the tugging on my neck, the pulsing in my pussy.

He sucked and he thrust in perfect rhythm, the sound of his mouth on my neck sending me further into ecstasy. And then he plunged upward, taking me so deeply that we were truly one body, joined not only sexually but by blood.

The blood bond.

He withdrew his teeth and licked over my puncture wounds. Then he gently withdrew his cock and set me down until my feet touched the tile floor.

I turned my head and met his gaze, my blood smeared over his lips and chin. Without thinking, I leaned toward him and slid my tongue over his bottom lip, tasting my blood.

It tasted like...blood. I'd tasted my own blood before, when I'd bitten my tongue or had a nosebleed.

"Dante?"

"Hmm?" His eyes were glazed over. He looked...satisfied. Completely physically and emotionally satisfied.

"You said my scent is irresistible. Is my blood, as well?"

"Your blood tastes a thousand times better than your scent smells."

I was oddly flattered. "What does it taste like? To you, I mean. It just tastes like blood to me."

He smiled, his teeth still covered in blood. Oddly, I found him attractive like that.

"Imagine the richest dark chocolate or the most complex Bordeaux. It's hard to describe, because you don't have the need I do. But it's like sinking your teeth into the most succulent piece of rare beef. Or letting the most precious Osetra caviar float over your tongue."

"Oh. Your words. They're so...beautiful."

"My words don't do your flavor justice. You have to also imagine having a base need for blood. Your very life depends on that sustenance. So imagine tasting something so rich and thick and powerful after you've been without food or water for days. That's how you taste to me, Erin. I could take more of your blood right now, and even though I'm full, the effect would be the same as if I'd been starving and finally had found sustenance."

I leaned forward and pressed my lips against his, blood and all. He spoke like a poet when he talked of his need for my blood. I slid my lips across his, tasting my own blood on them. I'd tasted it before when kissing him after he'd fed, but this time I concentrated, trying to taste what he tasted, feel what he felt when he fed.

I closed my eyes, imagining, letting my feelings swirl around us as we kissed.

Though I didn't taste chocolate or wine, I did taste something—something amorphous that I couldn't describe.

It was absolutely delicious.

I deepened the kiss, hungering for more of the elusive flavor. Our tongues twirled together, and my pussy began pulsing again. His cock hardened once more, and I jumped into his arms, our mouths still fused. He carried me up to my bedroom and sat down on the edge of the bed, still holding me on his lap.

We kissed. And we kissed. And we kissed.

The ineffable flavor intensified. I couldn't get enough. Enough of Dante. Enough of my blood on Dante's lips and tongue.

I ground on his lap, against his erection, and then I sank

down on his hardness, still kissing him with everything I had.

I rode him, my nipples poking through my bra and shirt. And still we kissed.

My pussy was so slick as I slid up and down, taking him, releasing him, and then taking him again.

Each time he filled me was a new experience, an emptiness released. Each time. Each fucking time.

Still our mouths didn't separate. I couldn't stop kissing him, couldn't stop longing for that intense flavor I couldn't name.

I moved faster, faster, and then he grabbed my hips and pushed me down on him. Still I kissed him as he contracted inside me. And still I kissed him as I joined him in climax.

Still I kissed him as we came down together.

Finally, when our mouths parted, we each drew in a deep breath of air.

"Damn, Erin," Dante said.

"I know."

"What was that?"

"Amazing, I'd say."

"I mean..."

"Why did I keep kissing you? I love kissing you."

"I know that. I love kissing you too. But I hadn't washed up. And—"

"Didn't matter. I wanted to taste what you taste. What you crave. I wanted to be a part of it."

"And?"

"It wasn't wine or chocolate or caviar. But it was... *something*."

"It's not *exactly* like wine or chocolate or caviar, Erin. It's *you*."

"I know that. I mean, I know that's what you tell me. I just wanted to try to experience what you experience."

"You—"

I touched my fingers to his lips, quieting him. "I know it won't be the same for me. I get that. But what I'm telling you, Dante, is that I tasted something divine. I can't describe it, but it was amazing. Absolutely quenching." I gazed into his dark eyes. "And I want *more* of it."

NINETEEN

DANTE

"I'll give you as much as you want, love."

"I know. I just never dreamed..." She closed her eyes. "I never, in a million years, believed..."

It was no accident that she wasn't finishing these sentences. Was she finishing them in her head? I didn't know, and I wouldn't ask.

Our bond was real, and it was strong.

She'd been descended from a vampire somewhere high in her family tree. Did that help her appreciation for the taste of her blood on my lips? The thought warmed me. Maybe we weren't so different after all.

I loved her, and I knew without a doubt that she loved me.

But until she truly accepted me as vampire, she could never accept anything vampire in herself. And until she truly accepted me as vampire, our relationship wouldn't deepen.

We wouldn't live together. She'd put the kibosh on that anyway. We wouldn't marry, have children—

The image I'd seen before hurled into my mind—of Erin

handing me a vampire child.

Where had that come from? Any child born of a human and vampire was always human. That's what I'd been taught growing up, and Jack had corroborated it. He was a physician—a vampire physician. He would know.

Yet the picture was clear in my mind. A vampire child. My child. Erin's child. Was it a girl or a boy? I didn't know. But I knew beyond a shadow of a doubt that it was vampire.

I shook my mind to clear it. Something was messing with my mind. Maybe the "dark presence" Bea described, which my father had corroborated.

No. This was not a dark image. It was a happy image, an image that filled me with joy.

The darkness had not caused it. I was certain.

I hadn't felt the darkness since the previous evening at the restaurant. Would I feel it again if it was near? I had to believe I would. That I'd be able to escape as I had previously.

"Dante?"

Erin. Her touch on my cheek. The warmth of her palm, the tingle of blood beneath her skin. She brought me back to reality.

"I understand," I said.

"Thank you."

"You don't need to thank me."

"I know this is hard for you, Dante. I know you want me to..."

Accept you. Those were the words she still couldn't say.

"I do. But I also understand, more now than ever."

"What do you mean?"

"You're struggling with the fact that people like me—vampires—exist. I'm struggling too. I was always taught ghosts didn't exist, at least not as unique individuals like they were as mortals. But now, not only do they exist, but my father is one of them."

"He certainly appears to be."

I shook my head. "And he took his own life..."

"He did?" Her mouth dropped into an O.

"Yeah. He was told to in a dream by my mother, apparently. That he needed to become a ghost to protect me."

"I'm so sorry, Dante."

"I can't even begin to deal with what it all means. My father is dead because of me. That's something I have to learn to live with, but I can't right now, because his very existence has me so rattled. It goes against everything..."

She was silent for a moment, and her eyes became glassy with the sheen of unshed tears. She managed to hold them back as she cupped my cheek. "Think of it from his perspective for a moment. He's in the same boat you are. He didn't believe in ghosts either, but your mother came to him in a dream so real he had to believe. He had to do what she asked. He had to protect you. It's what fathers do. He's probably struggling with reality as much as the two of us are."

I truly hadn't thought of it in that way. "You're so smart, Erin. So intuitive. So in tune with others."

"That's part of being a health care provider," she said. "You learn to intuit when patients can't express themselves verbally or otherwise."

"No. It's something unique about you."

She laughed. "I assure you there's nothing unique about me. Any nurse or doctor who cares about what she does develops intuition for others. It's part of who we are."

I smiled. I still wasn't buying it. She was special. Unique.

And I loved her with all my being. "Don't sell yourself short."

"I don't. But it's—"

I placed my fingers over her lips. "I choose to believe you're special, Erin. Because you are. Especially to me."

She wrapped her arms around my neck. "You're special to me too. I *am* trying, Dante. I'll get there. I *want* to get there." She pulled back, her eyes widening. "Oh! I almost forgot. I have something for you."

She jumped off the bed, pulled on a pair of sweats that had been draped across a chair, and ran downstairs.

I zipped up my jeans. All that, and we hadn't even undressed completely. Amazing.

I walked into the bathroom and regarded my reflection in the mirror. My whole face was smeared with dried blood from our make-out session. I couldn't help but smile. She was coming closer to full acceptance. It wouldn't be long now.

At least I hoped it wouldn't be.

I washed my face quickly and returned to the bedroom. About five minutes later, she came back up. "I had to get something out of my car. It's down in the living room."

I arched my brow. "You went outside like that?"

"Yeah. So?"

"Take a look in the mirror."

She went into the bathroom and let out a squeaky scream. Her face was still smeared with dried blood just like mine had been. She turned on the faucet. "Why didn't you tell me?"

"I didn't know you were going to go outside."

"Oh my God."

When she came out a minute later her face had been scrubbed clean. "What if someone had seen me?"

"Did anyone?"

"I don't think so. It's still pretty early. But people could have been in the parking lot going to work." She plunked down on the bed, lay down on her back, and put her arm over her forehead. "Speaking of work, I should get some sleep. I'm back on tonight."

"Do you want some breakfast? I can make something."

"Your famous toast?" she said without moving her arm from her eyes.

"Yeah. That's about it."

She sat up. "I'll make us something. No problem. Come on." She got up and left the room.

I followed.

When I reached the living area, my heart nearly stopped, and I gulped audibly.

On her coffee table lay what looked suspiciously like Bill's leather bound *Vampyre Texts*.

TWENTY

Erin

"What is that, Erin?" Dante asked quietly.

"Oh!" She smiled. "It's for you."

But his brow was furrowed. He didn't look happy about my acquisition.

"Where did you get it?"

"I...borrowed it. This morning. From Bill."

"Does he know you took it?" Dante shook his head. "Of course he doesn't. He doesn't let anyone touch that book. Erin, what were you thinking?"

"I was thinking about *you*. Of all the questions you have. You're learning French so you can read this thing. I wanted to help."

He paced around the living room, raking his fingers through his already disheveled hair. He was upset, angry. And all I could think of was how delicious he looked.

What was wrong with me? How had I made such a stupid mistake?

"I-I'm sorry. I'll take it back."

"No." He turned back to me. "What you did was wrong. You know that as well as I do. But I need this book, Erin."

"That's why I took it. I know you need it. We both need it, to figure out what's going on between us. Taking it wasn't my best moment in life. I'll grant you that. But once I saw it, all I could think about was this thing between us, and how this book might be able to explain it. You know?" Tears welled in my eyes. I'd done something ridiculous that I knew in my heart was wrong. And I'd done it anyway. That wasn't me at all. "I'm so sorry. I really am, Dante."

He came to me swiftly then and took me into his arms. "It's okay, baby. We'll make it all right. And you were right. I do need this book."

"Will Bill understand?"

He didn't respond right away. Just kissed my forehead a few times.

"Dante?"

"I don't know, honestly. I don't really know my grandfather anymore."

"What about your dad?"

"I think he will understand. But it's not his book, Erin. It's Bill's. I have to tell him."

"I know. Tell him I'm sorry, okay?"

He kissed my forehead again. "I will."

"Are you going to return it right away?" I asked.

Again, he took a few moments to respond. "I'm not sure. We both need to get some sleep now. I'll decide tonight."

I nodded against his neck.

⚜

When I got to the ER that night, chaos had broken out. Not only had the missing patient from a few nights ago not been found or returned, Logan was now missing. He hadn't come in two nights in a row, and Dr. Bonneville was livid.

Lucy filled me in once I'd clocked in.

"She's really raging tonight, Erin. Just stay out of her way."

Staying out of her way was easy enough to do on a busy night. All the nurses had to work with all the doctors on a busy night, but so much was going on that no one had a chance to be angry or treat anyone badly.

Unfortunately, tonight was not a busy night.

I'd just finished giving a toddler an asthma treatment when I heard Dr. Bonneville yelling at one of the residents.

"I'll have his medical license," she said. "He'll never practice medicine in this state again. Or anywhere else if I have any say about it. Find him, or I'll have your license too."

"Doctor, we've tried—"

"Try harder! Now I have to get another resident in here to pick up the slack. I'm a doctor, and this hospital thinks I'm an HR person. Somehow I'm responsible because one of the residents is missing. Now get the hell out of my sight."

I walked by the resident, Dr. Nice—yes, that was her name, and it fit her well—trying to make myself invisible.

To no avail.

"Sorry you had to hear that, Erin," Dr. Nice said.

I smiled weakly. "We've all been there."

"I wish I knew why she thinks I have any idea where Logan could be. He and I aren't close at all."

"You're just her target du jour," I said. "She'll be yelling at someone else soon."

"I know. I never seem to get used to it, though."

"You shouldn't have to. But there will be doctors like her everywhere you go."

"I hope I never get like that."

"You won't," I said, chuckling. "Your name won't let you."

She pasted on a nervous smile. "Erin, I don't want to pry, but I know you and Logan dated. Do you have any idea what could have happened to him? It's not like him to leave without calling in."

"First of all, we had one date, and it didn't go well. Second, I honestly have no idea. We're not close at all. I can ask Lucy. She dated him once."

Dr. Nice laughed. "So he's a one-time-only thing?"

I joined her laughter. "Neither Lucy nor I felt a connection, I guess."

"He's cute in a geeky kind of way," Dr. Nice agreed. "But not my type either. I just wish I knew where he was, so I could go yell at him for putting all of us through this."

"I agree, Dr. Nice."

"Erin, please call me Fiona. We've been through this."

We had, but I was more comfortable using doctor in the workplace. "I will, outside of work. If Dr. Bonneville heard me addressing any of you by your first name..."

"I get it." She smiled. "Thanks for the conversation."

I walked away but didn't get far. Dr. Bonneville headed straight toward me, fire in her blue eyes. "Erin, I hear you and Dr. Crown were apparently an item. We need to have a chat."

Great. Not only would I be interrogated on Logan's whereabouts, I'd also get the "don't fraternize with the work colleagues" lecture. Which, unfortunately, I probably deserved.

"My office," she said. "Now."

TWENTY-ONE

DANTE

Once I'd gotten over the fact that Erin had taken the *Vampyre Texts,* I was glad she had. I had every intention of returning them...after I'd had a full look.

The book wasn't as long as it appeared, as the words were printed on thick parchment. It was still long, though—about the size of the *New Testament.*

That was a lot of Old French.

I'd done a little more research on the language, and I'd found that Old French was more of a spoken language. Very little literature written in it still existed.

Whoever translated the *Texts* apparently thought Old French was a good idea. I couldn't say I agreed.

I leafed through the first couple of pages. It might as well have been written in Greek.

Ten online lessons in contemporary French didn't amount to much.

Unless I learned a lot more, I wouldn't be able to read this volume.

After getting over being pissed off about that, I went back to Erin's computer and tried researching again. I was led to the same old thing—paranormal websites claiming to know all about vampires, most of which were filled with one myth after another.

I usually skipped right over these, but today I decided to attack the issue from a different angle. I scrolled through site after site, looking for anything that might ring true.

Nope. Same old thing.

Until—

An obscure site called Nocturnaltruth.com. It was way down on the list. I'd scrolled through at least ten pages of entries before I found it.

Nothing about vampires was mentioned in the blurb on the search engine, but something made me click anyway.

It was only one page with no links.

Do you want the truth?
Email me at lucien.crown@nocturnaltruth.com.

Crown.

The name was familiar somehow. I'd heard it recently. I was sure.

Bill had asked me if I still had an email address. I'd had one in high school, so I logged into it.

Wow. Junk mail galore! I cleared out all the mailboxes and then updated some information. Then I began an email to Lucien Crown:

To whom it may concern:

I want the truth. If you know the truth, you'll know who I am. You'll know why I need the truth.

I struggled with whether to sign my real name and then decided not to. I'd use my father's name. He was dead, so no harm could come to him.

But harm could come to Em. Or me.

"For God's sake," I said aloud.

I deleted the email.

This was most likely a hoax and would lead me down a rabbit hole. That wasn't what I needed. I needed the truth. The real truth.

My phone buzzed. Bill.

Of course. He'd noticed his book was missing.

"Yeah?" I said into the phone.

"Return my book, Dante."

"Is the translation ready for me?"

"No. Not yet."

"Then I'm keeping the book. I need it."

"You won't be able to read it."

"I'll figure it out one way or another."

"You must return it."

"I won't harm it. You'll get it back when I'm done."

"You're not ready for what's in there," he said adamantly.

"I'm nearly thirty years old. I'll decide myself what I'm ready for." I moved the phone from my ear, ready to end the call, when Bill's voice came at me loudly, as if on speaker.

"Dante, *no* one knows what's in the *Texts*. It's too dangerous to know."

I clamped the phone back onto my ear. "Excuse me?"

His sigh whooshed into my ear. "I didn't want to have to tell you this."

"Tell me what? That you don't even know what's in the book? And you expect me to believe that?"

"I don't expect you to believe anything. I expect you to respect me enough to have faith—"

"Respect you? When all you've done is keep me in the dark since I got back? You've been reading my mind, Bill."

"I'm not—"

"Bullshit. I know you have been. It's not only annoying, it's creepy as all hell. I need answers. I need to know why I was taken. Why Erin and I are bonded. Why that bitch who kept me stole my blood. I need to know, Bill. I have the right to know. If the answers are in that damned book—"

"No one knows what's in the book."

"Please don't treat me like a child. That's a lie, and you know it."

"Come over, Dante. Bring the book. We need to talk."

⚜

The book stayed at Erin's. Bill had another copy in his office. If he needed to refer to it, he could use that one.

I wasn't surprised to see my father in Bill's office as well, standing.

"Do you ever sit?" I asked him.

"Ghosts don't really sit," he said. "We're constantly on the move, and we don't really have bodies."

"Fascinating," I said dully, sitting down across from the desk Bill sat behind.

"This will be news to your father as well, Dante," Bill said. "He wasn't old enough when he left—"

"He didn't leave any more than I left. He was taken. He might have gone after me, but it wasn't his idea not to come back."

"Semantics," Bill said. "Can we get past that, please? I'm doing the best I can. I'm about to break old Vampyre law divulging what I'm about to tell the two of you."

I scoffed. "What the hell is old Vampyre law? We follow the laws of the place where we live."

"We do," he agreed, "but when vampires reach a certain age, they learn about old Vampyre law."

"What age is that?"

"Ninety-two."

"So you've known about this for ten years," I said.

He nodded. "Since shortly after the two of you le— were taken." He cleared his throat.

"And who told you?"

"One of the elders. He's gone now. Only two of us on the council know."

"What is there to know?" Then I turned to my father. "You're eerily quiet."

"Only because this doesn't concern me. For all intents and purposes, I don't exist anymore. I'm here only as your protector. I need to know everything you know."

Sounded reasonable enough.

"No one has read the *Texts* in their entirety. Old Vampyre law cautions us against doing so."

"And why is that?"

"Because there are secrets in the *Texts*," Bill said. "Secrets that could ultimately destroy us."

"This is ridiculous," I said.

"I have to agree, Dad," my father said. "None of this makes any sense. You taught me that the *Texts* were historical. What about our history could possibly destroy us?"

"Believe me. It didn't make any sense to me when I found

out either. But it's something we are supposed to accept. On faith."

Faith. That word again. I had to have faith that my father was here, as a ghost, and once I'd accepted that, I'd been able to see him.

But faith was still a foreign concept to me. Religious people had faith, but I wasn't a religious person.

Did I have faith in anything?

Erin. I had faith in my bond with Erin. I accepted it, even though I didn't understand it.

Could I apply my faith to what Bill was about to tell me?

Time would tell.

I'd previously thought Bill was sounding dogmatic. Perhaps I'd been right.

Bill cleared his throat and continued, "Apparently the *Texts* were originally written in ancient hieroglyphs. A vampire scientist named Olivier Le Berre translated them in the early thirteenth century into Old French. It was Le Berre who insisted they never be read by any vampire after him. He devised our current teaching of the necessary elements through symbolry passed to each generation orally, so no one had to actually read the *Texts* in their entirety. What lay between those pages, he said, could be our undoing."

"So you truly don't know what's in the *Texts*," I said, still unbelieving.

"I know some of it. The history. What I taught you," he said to my father. "That is what was taught to me by my father, and what I taught River and Emilia when they came of age.

"And I'm still in the dark," I said.

"There's a reason for that," Bill said. "Hear me out. I was as curious as both of you, and my ego got the best of me. I'm a logical person. What could be in a book that could possibly harm us? I thought I knew more than the elders, so when I was told the truth about the *Texts,* I decided to read them myself."

"You can read Old French?"

He shook his head. "But I can read contemporary French. It was a stretch, but I was able to translate a few sections. Most of what I read I already knew. It was what I'd been taught, and what I taught you, Julian. But I eventually came across a passage so dark that I closed the book and vowed never to open it again."

"What did the passage say, Dad?" my father asked.

Bill closed his eyes. "I can't reveal it to you. It's too dangerous. I'm asking you to believe me. To take it on faith."

I stood. "That's bull."

"Dante, hear him out," my father said.

"I can't repeat it," Bill said. "Not in good conscience."

"Then why are we having this little discussion?" I asked. "You've already refused to teach me what you taught River and Emilia. Are you really having parts of the *Texts* translated for me? Or is that another lie?"

Bill didn't respond.

Yup. A lie.

"It's not what you think," Bill finally said.

"And exactly how is that?" I asked, not nicely.

"Your father is here. He might be dead, but he's here. He will be the one to teach you. I lied about the translation to keep you satisfied until you were able to accept your father as a ghost."

I turned to my father. "Dad?"

He nodded. "I will teach you son. But I can only teach you what I know."

"Then what about Erin and me? What about the blood bond?"

Bill stood behind his desk. When he opened his mouth to speak, his fangs had descended. "Dante, the answers you seek aren't in the *Texts*. The *Texts* will only darken your world. What you seek is light."

"What I seek is understanding of the blood bond between Erin and me. Where else would I find it?"

"I don't know. I was only able to come up with a tiny bit of research, and though it rings true with your situation, we'll never know if it's truly accurate."

"Where did you find your information?" I demanded.

"An obscure site on the web. Nocturnal Truth."

TWENTY-TWO

Erin

I sighed as I sat down beside Lucy at my workstation.

"You okay?" she said. "You look like you've just been through major trauma."

Major trauma? Major trauma was what we saw every night in the ER. Even so, my run-in with Dr. Bonneville had taken it out of me. She'd demanded to know how her research project was going, and when I'd told her I hadn't found anything of substance, she'd gone off the deep end. "You're worthless." Then she'd pulled a hundred-dollar bill out of her pocket and shoved it at me. "I suppose I'd better pay you, or you'll haul me into small claims court and God knows I don't have time for that shit."

At least she hadn't reprimanded me about Logan, which was what I'd been afraid of in the first place. All she asked is whether I knew where he might have gone.

And at least I was a hundred dollars richer.

"I'm fine," I said. "Just another night at the ER with the

hag, as Steve likes to call her."

"She cornered you, huh? She got Dr. Nice earlier."

"I know. I witnessed some of it."

"She hasn't asked me about Logan yet."

"She only asked me if I knew where he went," I said. "Mostly we talked about some research she wanted me to do for her. There's nothing out there to support her hypothesis, and apparently that makes *me* an idiot."

"Maybe it's out there and you just didn't find it."

"Whose side are you on?"

"Calm down. Yours. I'm always on your side, Erin."

I shook my head. "I know. I'm sorry. I just really didn't need this tonight."

"No one ever does." Lucy typed something on her computer. "Seriously, though. What do you think is going on with Logan? He always seemed so dedicated."

"I don't know. Maybe he got called out of town for a family emergency or something."

"But he'd call, wouldn't he?"

"You'd think so."

Lucy turned to me. "Or maybe he's..."

"Dead?" The thought had occurred to me as well. "I don't think so. Someone would have found him. ID'd him."

"Maybe he was abducted by aliens." She smiled.

"Get a grip, Luce." Though if vampires and ghosts were real, why not aliens?

"What other explanation is there? If he's not dead, he would have called in. At least the Logan I know would have."

She was right. The Logan I knew, or thought I knew, was a dedicated physician who took his duty to his patients very seriously. None of this made sense.

"The only thing that might have happened is that whoever took the patient also took Logan, and he's somewhere where he can't make a call or send an email."

That jolted me.

Dante had been taken. Held against his will.

Had the same thing happened to Logan?

No, that was ridiculous.

I turned to my computer and logged in. Not that it was any of my business, but I checked to see if there were any medical records for Dr. Logan Crown.

Bingo! He'd been seen in the ER two years ago for a mild concussion. He was also on a high dose of lithium, a mood stabilizer.

I turned away from the screen. Man. He was probably bipolar. I was really violating his privacy, and I felt like shit for doing it. But I needed to check one more thing. His blood type.

B positive.

I made a mental note and got out of the file.

Lucy was engrossed in her own computer screen, and she'd thought I was nuts when I brought up the rash of B positive blood around the hospital earlier, so I kept it to myself.

Had Logan had any bite marks on his neck? I hadn't been looking at the time. I'd just wanted a quick fuck to get Dante out of my mind.

I had little time to ruminate on it. Sirens shrieked, and Lucy and I ran back out to the ER.

"Pregnant woman, mid-twenties, seven and a half months along. Her water broke. We've got O2 started."

Dr. Bonneville was on it. "Do you have a fetal heartbeat?"

"Yeah, but it's slow."

"The cord is probably compressed. Let's get her in room

four for an ultrasound, stat. This baby is being born tonight. Let the NICU know."

"Please, please," the woman wailed. "Save my baby! Please!"

"We'll do everything we can," I said, trying to soothe the young mother. Whether the baby lived depended on his lung capacity. He was far enough along to survive, but he might have the NICU in his future. "Who's your obstetrician?"

"Dr. Mullaney."

"I'll page the doctor on call at her office."

"No! I want Dr. Mullaney." She gritted her teeth. "And I need to push. Now!"

Her doctor would be Dr. Bonneville, then. There wasn't time for Dr. Mullaney or anyone else to get here. She still had her maternity pants on, but she was most likely crowning.

"It's too soon!" she cried. "Please! Save the baby!"

"We'll do everything we can."

Once in the room, I got her pants and underwear removed and strapped on the fetal monitor. Normally, with bradycardia, I'd use an internal monitor, but that wasn't possible. Just as I'd suspected. "She's crowning, Doctor."

Dr. Bonneville came around swiftly. "No time for that ultrasound. Ma'am, this baby is ready to be born."

"But it's too soon!"

"You're seven and a half months along. Your baby will have a good chance."

"Stop the labor. Please! Give me a shot or something."

"We can't stop the labor now," I said. "Your water has broken and the baby has descended into the birth canal. He's coming."

"She," she said through puffs of breath.

“A baby girl.” I smiled. “How wonderful.”

“Will she be all right?”

“We will do everything we can.”

Dr. Bonneville situated herself between the woman’s legs.

“It hurts!” the patient wailed.

I felt for her, but there was no time for an epidural. This baby was determined to get out.

“I need to call my boyfriend!”

“We’ll take care of notifying everyone,” I said. “Right now, you need to concentrate on bringing your daughter into the world, okay?”

“When you feel the next contraction, I want you to give me a good push,” Dr. Bonneville said. “It should be coming in a few seconds. Here it comes. Now...push!”

The woman screamed as she bore down.

“Good,” Dr. Bonneville said. “Just one more and we’ll get that head out. I don’t like the bradycardia, Erin. Have you called NICU?”

“Yes, Doctor.”

“Okay. One more push, and we should have that head out.”

The woman screamed again, and the little girl’s head broke free. Dr. Bonneville eased the baby’s body out, cut the cord, and handed her off to another nurse. Then she bent back down to deliver the placenta.

The baby’s skin had a gray tinge. That was never good.

“She’s not crying,” the mother wailed. “Why isn’t she crying?”

“They have to suction her mouth out,” I said. “It takes a few seconds.”

“Apgar three,” the nurse handling the child said.

Cry, damn it. Cry!

Then a sound—kind of like an oink. Then another.

"She's breathing," the nurse said.

A couple more oinks...then a louder cry. Thank God!

"I want to see her," the mother said.

"In a minute," I said. "It won't be long."

A NICU nurse arrived to take over. "The on-call pediatrician is on his way," she said to Dr. Bonneville.

"We're going to take her to the Neonatal Intensive Care Unit," I told the woman.

"Neonatal?"

"ICU for newborns. They'll be able to decide whether she needs help getting oxygen.

"But I heard her. I heard her cry. I want to hold her!"

"I understand. But we need to do what's best for her right now. We need to keep her warm and make sure she's healthy enough to keep breathing on her own."

"I'm what's best for her. She's my baby."

"Of course you are." I wiped the sweat off her forehead and forced a smile. "You will see her as soon as you possibly can. Have you named her yet?"

"My boyfriend wants to call her Sally, after his aunt. But I like Isabelle."

"How about Isabelle Sally?" I said.

"That sounds good." She yawned. "Why am I so tired?"

"Because your body just worked harder than it ever has before." I forced a smile. "What's your name?"

"Patty. Patty Doyle."

"Patty, I'm Erin. We'll get everyone notified, all right?"

"May I see the child?" Dr. Bonneville said, putting a fresh pair of rubber gloves on her hands.

"Of course, Doctor." The NICU nurse handed Dr.

Bonneville the bundle. "Her color is quite good. Her lungs must be mature. There's a good chance she won't need incubation."

Dr. Bonneville examined the child, and then she did something odd. She placed one of her gloved fingertips on the child's lips and poked into her mouth.

Very strange.

But the other nurses didn't question her, so I certainly wasn't about to.

"Sucking reflex is excellent," Dr. Bonneville said. "I think she's going to be fine."

I stayed by Patty's side as the orderlies wheeled her to the service elevator to take her to recovery in the maternity ward.

"You were so nice to me," Patty said. "I'd like to name her after you."

"What about Isabelle Sally?"

"It's going to be Isabelle Erin. Who cares what Liam thinks? He won't marry me anyway." She choked out a laugh.

I had no idea what to say to that, so I simply smiled.

Until I was ripped away from her by more blaring sirens. "I'll come visit you when I can," I said as she disappeared behind the elevator door.

TWENTY-THREE

DANTE

"I found that website," I said to Bill. "I almost sent an email, but then I didn't want to risk it. It seemed like it could be a hoax."

"I created a dummy email account to respond," Bill said. "There are a lot of documents on the site, and they're all encrypted. Even if I could read them, it would be like looking for a needle in a haystack."

"How did you find the blood bond stuff then?"

"I couldn't tell you. The documents were all encrypted. I had to put in key words, and then I paid a fee to have the documents with my key words unencrypted. Maybe I should have searched the *Texts* myself, but"—he shuddered—"I couldn't open the book again."

I'd already tried. I'd have to spend a lot more time studying to even attempt to understand it. My grandfather didn't need to know that, though. "Does the site have a translation of the *Vampyre Texts*?" I asked.

"It purports to, but first of all, the fee to unencrypt all the documents is exorbitant. It cost enough as it is to get the stuff about the blood bond."

I had no money. Only what Bill had given me. I truly needed to find a job, but what was I qualified for? I hadn't even finished high school.

"I know what you're thinking," Bill said. "And no, I won't pay for you to access the full documents on the website."

"That's not what I was thinking, and I wouldn't ask you to," I said.

"Do you know who runs the website, Dad?" my father asked.

"He goes by the name of Lucien Crown, but I'm sure that's not his real name."

Crown again. I knew I'd heard that name before. But where?

"Is he a vampire?"

"He calls himself a nocturnal philosopher, whatever that is," Bill said. "I have no idea if he's a vampire."

"Who else would have access to the *Texts*?" I asked.

"I don't know."

"He must be a vampire," I said. "The nocturnal gives it away."

"Maybe that's just what he wants us to think," Bill said.

"But he had the answer to the blood bond."

"He had *an* answer. Whether it's true? Will we ever really know?"

"But everything you said has happened," I said.

"True. That's very true."

"Dad," my father said, "if this book is as dangerous as you say, why didn't you destroy it? You still have two copies in this house."

"One," he said with resignation. "Your son and Erin have the other."

"That makes no difference. Why didn't you destroy them after you found the so-called dark passage?"

"It's not that simple, Julian. The book contains our history. We can't change our history, no matter how dark it is."

"Humankind has a dark history too, Dad."

"I'm not denying that," Bill said. "But the portion of the *Texts* I'm talking about has nothing to do with our history. It has to do with what we're capable of."

I opened my mouth, but my grandfather held up his hand. "Don't. That is all I can say. I've already told you too much."

I wasn't about to fight him. Not right now. "I need to get some sleep," I said. "I'm exhausted."

Bill nodded.

I headed to my bedroom and was about to disrobe to take a shower when my father appeared. I nearly jumped out of my skin. "You might warn me before you do that."

"I'm sorry, Dante. But I need to talk to you. It's important."

"Yeah?"

"You and I need to know what's in the *Texts*. I trust that we can handle any darkness we find. After what we've been through, darkness will not affect us."

Did my father know what I'd been through? Had he been through the same...or worse? A shiver ran through me. Of course he had.

"We can do it ourselves," he continued, "but that would take more time than we have. The alternative is to pay the fee to the website."

"How can we do that? I have no money. I've been living off Bill since I returned, and it's putting a nasty taste in my mouth.

And you're—"

Dead. I couldn't say the word.

"Dante, I have money. Now that I'm dead, you need to file a death certificate and then you and Emilia can collect my property as my heirs."

My eyes popped open. Why hadn't I thought of that? Of course, my father had money. My mother had been rich, and he'd inherited everything when she died. Why hadn't Bill taken care of that when he'd disappeared?

Because he was hoping his sons were alive, of course. He had no proof of death.

"I'm not sure what's going on with my father, Dante," my father said, "but for the first time, I'm not sure I trust him."

"Thank God," I said. "It's not just me. He's seemed off since I got back."

"He's hiding something," my father agreed. "Something that has him scared, and trust me, your grandfather doesn't scare easily. If we're going to figure out what's going on between you and Erin, we need that book. We'll need my money to get the translation from the website. With my death certificate, you can get your hands on it. But there's one thing you'll need to do first."

"What's that?"

"Recover my body."

TWENTY-FOUR

Erin

My shift ended, and after I changed, I decided to head up to maternity to see how Patty was doing. I'd promised her, after all, and I wanted to look in on little Isabelle as well. She'd been over five pounds, so she was probably doing well.

I checked in with the front desk. "Could you tell me which room Patty Doyle is in? She gave birth last night in the ER. I was her nurse, and I want to say hi and see how she's doing."

"Sure. Let me check." She scanned her computer screen. "What was the name again?"

"Doyle. Patty Doyle."

"Hmm. I don't have a Patty Doyle."

"Maybe it's Patricia?"

"Nope. No Doyle, period."

"That's strange. Her baby got transferred to the NICU."

"Let me look there." She typed a few things and regarded her screen again. "No Doyle in the NICU." She tapped again. "Or here in our nursery. Are you sure you have the right last name?"

My heart nearly stopped. “I’m sure. A NICU nurse came to the ER last night for the baby.”

“Her name?”

“I didn’t get her name. But she was there. Ask Dr. Bonneville or the other nurse on duty, Dale. We were both there when she took the baby.”

“I’m sorry. Neither the mother nor the baby are anywhere in this hospital.”

EPILOGUE

THE QUEEN

I'm getting closer to my ultimate goal, Dante. Even without you. I needed to let you go to become what you are destined to be. You are strong, Dante. My blood has made you strong. Her blood is making you even stronger.

But it's not her blood that will ultimately fulfill you.

You will be back.

I already control you.

I always will.

The only blood bond you have is with me.

BLOOD BOND SAGA

PART 6

PROLOGUE

DANTE

I headed to my bedroom and was about to disrobe to take a shower when my father appeared. I nearly jumped out of my skin. "You might warn me before you do that."

"I'm sorry, Dante. But I need to talk to you. It's important."

"Yeah?"

"You and I need to know what's in the *Texts*. I trust that we can handle any darkness we find. After what we've been through, darkness will not affect us."

Did my father know what I'd been through? Had he been through the same...or worse? A shiver ran through me. Of course he had.

"We can do it ourselves," he continued, "but that would take more time than we have. The alternative is to pay the fee to the website."

"How can we do that? I have no money. I've been living off Bill since I returned, and it's putting a nasty taste in my mouth. And you're—"

Dead. I couldn't say the word.

"Dante, I have money. Now that I'm dead, you need to file a death certificate and then you and Emilia can collect my property as my heirs."

My eyes popped open. Why hadn't I thought of that? Of course, my father had money. My mother had been rich, and he'd inherited everything when she died. Why hadn't Bill taken care of that when he'd disappeared?

Because he was hoping his sons were alive, of course. He had no proof of death.

"I'm not sure what's going on with my father, Dante," my father said, "but for the first time, I'm not sure I trust him."

"Thank God," I said. "It's not just me. He's seemed off since I got back."

"He's hiding something," my father agreed. "Something that has him scared, and trust me, your grandfather doesn't scare easily. If we're going to figure out what's going on between you and Erin, we need that book. We'll need my money to get the translation from the website. With my death certificate, you can get your hands on it. But there's one thing you'll need to do first."

"What's that?"

"Recover my body."

ONE

DANTE

You'll need to recover my body.

A brick hit my gut. If I hadn't realized earlier that my father was truly dead, I did now. His body was out there somewhere, probably decomposing by now, and I had to find it.

"Dante?" he said.

"Yeah. I heard you, Dad. It's a lot to process. That's all."

"I know, son."

"I mean, you're here and all. And you look..."

"I look like I did when I died, except my injuries are gone."

A shudder reeled through me. He'd had injuries? Of course he had. He'd been held captive, same as I was. And he'd somehow escaped, only to take his own life. Images of my father's battered and partially decomposed body, vultures circling above it, swirled in my mind.

"This won't be easy for you," he said.

I drew in a breath, trying to compose myself. "Dad, nothing has been easy for me for the past ten years. I can do this."

"You'll need help."

"I have you."

"I'm not exactly corporeal. You'll need someone you trust."

I trusted only three people, excluding my father. Erin, and I couldn't drag her into this. Emilia, and she was in a very fragile state. That left River. He'd be the one.

But Emilia... She had to be told. I opened my mouth, but before I spoke—

"Your cousin is the best choice. But there is the issue of your sister."

I had to trust that my father wasn't reading my mind. Or if he was, that he had no ulterior motive. I had no other choice right now if I wanted to get through what was coming. "Yeah. We need to tell her about you. But she's..."

"I know, Dante. My father told me." He chuckled. "I can't say I'm thrilled, but I also can't say I'm surprised. We all just want her to get through the pregnancy safely."

"She's stronger than any vampire woman I've known," I said. "Not that I've known too many other than Mom and Aunt Simone, and I didn't know either of them for long."

"Your mother and Simone were both incredibly strong women whose devotion to their families was unequaled, but your sister has something they did not. Tenacity. That is what will get her through this."

Tenacious. That was Em all right.

"When should we tell her?"

"*You* will tell her after you and River have recovered my body."

"No, Dad, that's—"

"That's how it will be, Dante. Recover my body first, and she'll know I'm gone. Then it won't be such a shock when I appear to her as a ghost."

"It's going to be a shock anyway," I said.

"It will challenge everything she was brought up to believe, as it did for both of us, but she will accept it as you did. Have faith in that."

I huffed. "Why does everyone keep telling me to have faith? First Bill, and now you."

"Sometimes faith is your only choice. It beats the hell out of having doubts, doesn't it?"

My father always could get a smile out of me. He was charismatic where Bill was stoic. "I suppose you've got me there."

"River is probably just getting off work. You should fill him in on what needs to be done."

"Will he be able to see you?"

"Yes. I don't know how long it will take, but he will eventually."

"What about Bill? The book? Do we tell River everything?"

"We have to, don't you think?"

I nodded. "Yeah. It's just a huge responsibility, upending someone's world. I've already done it to Erin."

"I know. But Erin had a lot more to accept. Right now, all River has to do is accept that I'm dead and agree to help you recover my body. The fact that I'm here as a ghost can wait if it has to."

"Can it? How am I supposed to convince him that I know where your body is? And where is it, anyway?"

"First things first. I know you need to feed, Dante. Go to Erin. Take your sustenance and draw strength from it."

"Wait, you're not going to—"

He laughed. "No, I'm not going with you. And no, those times I was in Erin's apartment, I was not in the bedroom with you. Give me some credit. Not only do I respect your and Erin's privacy, but honestly, a father doesn't want to see that."

Thank God. Not that I thought my dad was some kind of perv, but he *had* been at Erin's. She had seen him when I hadn't.

But that meant—

"Oh my God."

"What is it?" he asked.

"You said you could still glamour people as a ghost. You said..." I shoved my hand through my hair.

"Dante—"

"It was you, wasn't it?" I shook my head, anger boiling beneath my skin. My gums itched as my fangs descended. "All this time I blamed Bill. Thought he was lying to me. You glamoured Erin that first time she saw my teeth. It was you!"

"Son, listen to me."

"You fucking glamoured her!" I grabbed my leather jacket and forced my arms inside. "I'm out of here."

A sharp icicle speared into my neck. I grabbed at it. "Leave me alone!"

"Not until you listen to me."

The freezing jab again. "Damn!" I turned around to face my father's ghost.

"I gave her a nudge, Dante. I asked her to keep an open mind. I did it for you. You *need* her."

"I would have handled her myself. I didn't need you to run interference for me."

"Didn't you? She raced downstairs in a panic because she saw your teeth before she was ready to. I was there to protect you. To protect what had become necessary to you."

"That is not your job," I said through clenched teeth.

"Not my job to protect my son? The hell it's not."

"Protecting me is one thing. Interfering in my personal relationships is another."

"She was panicking. She was ready to walk away from you forever. What was I supposed to do?"

"Maybe let me deal with it myself?"

"How? You'd been gone for ten years, and during those ten years you matured from a postadolescent into a potent vampire male, but without any guidance for controlling your urges. Your immaturity is a danger to yourself and others right now."

I opened my mouth, but he held up his hand to stop me.

"Don't take that as an insult. You can't help what happened to you any more than I can. But you know this about yourself. You can't even control your fangs, Dante."

"I can," I growled. But even as the words emerged. I couldn't will my teeth to retract.

"You see? You get angry, your teeth come out. You get aroused, your teeth come out. You get frightened, your teeth come out."

"They're supposed to do that."

"Yes. Physiologically, that's what happens, but you *can* control it. You just haven't learned how."

"What if I don't *want* to control it?" I said, baring my teeth in a wide grin. Heat flushed through my body, and my pulse seemed to ignite with rapid thrums in my neck.

My father advanced toward me. "Your cuspids are long and sharp, Dante. Even more so than mine, and mine and Braedon's are some of the most formidable Jack Hebert had ever seen. Those are lethal, and you *must* control them."

Another surge of dark anger wrapped around me. "I *can*. I controlled them that first night. I let those animals go, Dad. You were there, weren't you? Don't you remember that?"

"You did, even in the face of desperation. You did well. You have a powerful mind. You used what had been done to you as a reason not to kill a defenseless animal. But you would have fed off the homeless man if the detective hadn't stopped you."

"So what? I wouldn't have killed him."

"Maybe not. But with Erin—"

"What I do with Erin is none of your damned business." I thrust out my chest and held my chin high.

"I never said it was."

"You made it your business when you glamoured her."

"I saved your relationship with her. Not once. Twice."

My ire rose again, this time chafed and sore from his betrayal. "Twice?" I said through clenched teeth.

"Yes. I want total honesty between us. I glamoured her only slightly that day in the kitchen at Bill's. About the dog bite."

In my mind, I flew back to Bill's kitchen that day. Erin had so easily accepted the inane story River fabricated regarding why so much blood was pooled on our kitchen floor. Later that same day, Bill glamoured her into forgetting all about the dog bite anyway.

I opened my mouth to spew more venom at him, but he held up his hand.

I stopped. I wasn't sure why. Maybe just because he was my father and he had that effect on me.

"I'm sorry."

I lifted one eyebrow. My father, at least the father I remembered, had rarely apologized. "Sorry for glamouring her? Or sorry for interfering?"

"Both. But I'd do it again. For you. I'd do anything for you, Dante."

I softened a little—but only a little. "Don't ever glamour her again. Promise me."

He sighed. "If only I could make that promise. But as your father, and as your protector, I will do whatever is necessary to protect both you and Erin. You'll understand one day, when you have children of your own."

Children of my own. Again the image of Erin handing me a vampire child emerged in my mind. Any child we had would be human, so why did I keep seeing it?

I didn't know, but the image calmed me a little more.

"Tell me something," my father continued. "If Erin was in trouble, and the only way you could save her was to glamour her, what would you do?"

I twisted my lips into a semi-smile as I shook my head. "It's a moot question, Dad. I can't glamour Erin."

"You can't?"

"No."

"That means you've tried."

I nodded. "The first time I met her. It didn't work. But I was able to glamour the homeless man that first night." Then something occurred to me. "Or was *that* you?"

"No. That was all you."

"I've never actually mastered glamouring. I can only do it when I'm starving for blood."

"Then you're in luck," he said. "I can teach you. I can now teach you all that I'd planned to teach you before we were both taken."

"Can you still do that? I mean, you're a..."

"Ghost. Yes. I'm dead. But I'm here for as long as you need me to be here. I remember everything from my mortal life, and I am willing to teach you."

A cement block lifted from my shoulders. "Bill has been refusing to teach me. I can't figure out why."

"Bill is not Bill anymore, at least not the Bill we both knew. Something he read in the *Texts* has him spooked. That must be why he's afraid to teach you anything."

"How does he expect me to survive if I don't know how to control my urges?"

"I don't know, son. Together, we'll figure this out. I will teach you what you need to know. It will take time, and unfortunately, we don't have time at the moment. First there's something you need to do."

I cringed. "I know. Recover your body before it decomposes more than it already has."

He smiled. "That can wait. You need to feed."

TWO

Erin

Shivers racked my body. I tried all the calming techniques I knew, but I couldn't stop them.

Patty and her baby. Gone.

Vanished.

Like so many others.

The whole thing was horrifying, but this was the first one that had a profound effect on me personally. I'd helped deliver baby Isabelle. Patty and I had bonded. She was even going to give the baby girl Erin as her middle name.

I drove home on autopilot, and before I knew it, I was pulling into my townhome complex.

Dante was waiting for me outside my front door. Hadn't I given him a key? I couldn't remember. No, I hadn't yet. I threw my own keys in my purse and ambled toward him.

"Erin," he said, his eyes warm. "You're pale as a...ghost. What's wrong?"

How could I begin to describe what was wrong? Since

I'd met Dante, my entire life had been turned upside down. In fact... The first patient had disappeared from our hospital the night he'd appeared.

I gulped, trying to swallow the massive lump in my throat.

No. Dante could *not* have anything to do with the disappearing patients.

Could he?

I closed my eyes and shook my head, trying as hard as I could to clear it of such unwanted thoughts.

"Erin?" he said again.

I pushed him against the closed door. "Don't want to talk." I smashed my lips against his.

He responded to my kiss. He was hungry. He fed in the morning, and I was late getting home because I'd stopped to see Patty.

And had my life upended once again.

He broke the kiss and met my gaze, his eyes dark and hungry. "Inside," he said. "Now."

I fished in my purse for my keys. Apparently I was taking too long, because he grabbed my handbag and drew them out in a flash.

Seconds later, we were inside, and he scooped me into his arms and walked upstairs to my bedroom.

My mind raced, though no thought formed completely. Patty. The baby. Dante. The disappearing women. My ache. My need. My love for him that didn't make sense all the time but that I knew with all my heart and soul was real.

Blood.

He needed my blood. I felt his desire all around me. Could almost see it in a pulsing aura encircling his body.

"Erin," he growled. "Undress."

I hesitated.

And he noticed.

"I said, 'undress.'"

This time I peeled off my T-shirt and bra quickly, letting my breasts fall against my chest. I kicked off my sneakers and then hesitated once more.

I was ready. Wet and ready. No matter where my mind was, my body responded to Dante's voice. Dante's touch. Dante's very being.

He inhaled, closing his eyes. "You're ripe. So ripe, Erin."

I didn't doubt it. My nipples had hardened into tight berries, my areolas wrinkled and taut. I squeezed my thighs together in an effort to suppress my ache.

Didn't work.

So I obeyed him. I slid my sweats and underpants over my hips, down my legs, and then stepped out of them.

"Beautiful," he breathed.

I closed my eyes with a sigh and stroked the swell of my breast. I felt him advance toward me, his feet shuffling on my carpet.

When I opened my eyes, the amber around his dark irises was pulsing, and his teeth had elongated.

The throb between my legs intensified. Yes. He was gorgeous. Beautiful. I loved him like this. Still I fought it, trying to look away, but my head didn't budge. I couldn't take my eyes off him—his dark beauty.

"T-Take off your clothes," I said.

"You seem to forget who gives the orders here." He pinched one of my nipples.

I moaned softly, the jolt plummeting through my body and landing between my legs. The command in his voice got me every time. Still, I resisted.

"You're fighting me," he said, fumbling in his jacket pocket. Seconds later, he held the synthetic rope in his hands. "Do I need to use this?"

Yes.

No.

Yes.

No.

Please. Yes.

"You must accept me, Erin. Accept all of me. Say it. Say you accept me as vampire."

The words formed on my vocal cords but stayed lodged in my throat.

No. Couldn't say it. Not yet.

"Erin."

My body didn't struggle. It wanted him. Was ready to accept all of him. Ditto my heart.

The duel was in my mind. I closed my eyes.

"Open your eyes, Erin."

My body responded. My eyes opened.

"I need you," he said.

I fell onto the bed, reached for the rungs of the headboard, and then nodded toward the rope in his hands. "Take me. Take what you need."

"You want to be tied down, like the first time?"

I nodded. I didn't want to want it, but God, I ached for it with everything I was. The pure strength of the desire surprised even me.

I squeezed my eyes shut again as he bound me to the rungs.

"Easy," he said. "You're so tense. Your blood will flow better if you're relaxed."

And just like that, I relaxed. My eyes stayed closed, but I was no longer clenching them shut. My arms slackened into al dente noodles hanging above my head.

"Easy," he said again. "Spread your legs, love. I need a taste of you."

My femoral artery. He was going to feed there again, covering the marks of whoever had been violating me.

I readied for the sting of his teeth.

Instead, his tongue swiped up along my slit. I inhaled swiftly, the sensation traveling through my whole body when he nipped at my clit. I bit my lower lip, aching to cry out.

"I know it feels good, Erin. Stop resisting me."

Was I still resisting? I'd been expecting his bite, and instead, I was treated to his velvet tongue in my most sensitive place. No reason to resist.

No reason to resist either one, actually. My body wanted both.

"Tell me," he said. "Tell me what you want."

I stayed quiet a few seconds.

"Erin..."

My mouth fell open of its own accord. "I want you to lick me. Suck me. Stick your fingers and your cock inside me. Give it to me, Dante. Give me all of it."

"My pleasure," he growled, and slid his tongue inside my wet channel.

I grasped the rungs of the headboard, pulling, yearning to run my fingers through his dark locks and push his tongue farther inside me. I writhed on the bed, arching my back and bringing my legs upward, baring myself to him as best I could.

"That's it," he said. "Show me what you want, Erin. Show me what's mine. Show me that beautiful pussy."

"Yours," I mumbled on a moan. "All yours."

"That's right," he snarled against my inner thigh. "All mine." He thrust two fingers in me as he sank his teeth into my flesh.

I shattered around him, flying, the climax ripping through me like an electric current. The tugging on my flesh, the pulsing of my pussy, the music floating around us, the colors, the shapes—all of it consumed me.

Take it all. Consume me so that nothing is left. Nothing but the me that is part of you.

A pink cloud surrounded us as we were joined as one, his teeth in my body, a part of me.

Love.

This was love. That real love that I knew we shared.

When my shudders finally started to subside, he licked my thigh, crawled upward, and sank himself deep into me.

And the orgasm began again.

He pumped and pumped, deeper and deeper into the recesses of my soul, until he thrust in hard and groaned, filling me.

"Erin. Love. Baby. God."

Erin. Love. Baby. God.

I felt more than heard his words. They floated around me in a cloudy haze, set to the soft jazz I'd become accustomed to when we were together.

Do you hear it, Dante? The music? Do you see the colors?

Yes, baby. I hear and see all of it. I see you. *It's all you.*

It's all us.

Together we danced, rising above all the turmoil in the world, all the turmoil in my own head, joined in body and blood. In heart. In soul.

Still so much I didn't understand. Couldn't accept.

But none of that mattered on this plane of existence where pleasure was the soup of the day and love was the dessert.

And our bond? That was the main course.

But it couldn't last forever. Our climaxes began to subside, and again, I found myself fighting.

No. Don't want it to end. Let's stay here forever. Just the two of us, joined, where no one can find us. No one can hurt us. No problems that we can't solve. Please.

Still, like all good things, it came to an end, our sweaty bodies clamped together, both of us panting.

Dante rolled over onto his back, dark strands of his hair pasted to his forehead and his cheeks with perspiration. "Damn," he said.

I tugged at my bindings. "Dante."

"Oh, right." He quickly moved to untie the knots in the rope.

I rubbed at my wrists, though they didn't hurt. Then I pushed the moist strands of hair off Dante's forehead after he lay back down.

"That was amazing, Erin," he said. "Every time with you is better than the last. Just imagine how it will be when..."

I heard the words he didn't say.

...when you accept all of me.

THREE

DANTE

As transcendent as our lovemaking had been, Erin had been more resistant than usual this time. I had no idea why. She didn't know about my father having glamoured her, and I had to tell her at some point. I didn't want secrets between us. I truly didn't.

But I also had to protect her.

She lay on her side, her head propped up on her elbow, gazing down at me. Her lips were dark pink and swollen, much like the beautiful lips between her legs. I winced, thinking of the time she'd actually thought I didn't like what I saw down there. How could anyone resist that treasure?

"You're so beautiful," I said. "And I mean so much more than that. I wish there were a word I could use to describe how amazing you are. How much you mean to me. Beautiful doesn't come close. Even love doesn't come close. But I love you, Erin. I love you with all my heart."

She smiled, though she didn't return my sentiment. At least not verbally. Instead, she snuggled into my arms and fell asleep.

An hour later, I got up and called River.

"I'm just getting ready to get some sleep," he said. "I'm on tonight."

"Can it wait? I need to talk to you."

"Talk away."

"No, I need to come over. It's important."

"Yeah, okay. Whatever you need, Dante."

I left Erin a note in case she woke up to find me gone, and then I departed, sliding her key under her door after locking the deadbolt. Hopefully I'd be back before she got up.

I drove to River's in the car I'd been borrowing from Bill. I needed to get a car. I needed to get a job. But if River and I could find my father's body and prove his death, I'd get his money, some of which I could use to get a car. I didn't want to sponge off Bill for much longer, especially since he'd gotten so weird.

"Dad?" I said, as I pulled into River's apartment complex.

No response. Apparently ghosts didn't come when you called. How could I tell River about him, though, without him actually being there?

I had no idea, but I had to try. River wouldn't be able to see him at first anyway.

"Hey." River opened the door before I knocked.

"Good timing."

"Yeah. I thought I heard something out here."

"That was me, shuffling around, wondering how I'm going to tell you what I need to tell you."

"Come on in. Hungry?"

"Just ate."

"Yeah, me too. What's going on?"

Where to start?

River's apartment was sparse. A leather recliner sat in

the corner of his small living area. A large flat-screen TV, a loveseat, and a coffee table completed the room. Would I be living in a place like this if I'd been around the last ten years?

"Are you going to say anything?" River asked.

"Your father's alive, Riv." The words spouted out of me before I could even think about what to say.

His mouth fell open. "What? How do you know?"

"My father told me."

"Uncle Jules is back? That's great!" He pulled me into his living room and shoved me down on the small couch. "Tell me everything."

I drew in a deep breath, trying to find the words, when he continued.

"Funny thing. I had a dream about Uncle Jules last night. He was right beside me, plain as day, and he said he was coming back and had important news for me. And you're saying he's actually here? Crazy."

Crazy, indeed. My father had said my mother had come to him in a dream, and that ghosts had that power when the need was dire. Was it my father? Or was River's dream just a dream? Regardless, he would resist what I was about to say, just as I had at first. I looked around. No sign of my father. *Thanks a lot, Dad.*

I let out the air slowly. "My dad is back, but it's not what you think."

"Shit. Is he okay?"

"Yeah, he's okay. If you consider being dead okay."

River shook his head. "You're losing me, man. What are you trying to say?"

Might as well just spew it out all at once. "You know that ghost story Bill told me? That there was a ghost protecting me?

Turns out it's true, and the ghost is my dad."

River looked at me wide-eyed, his face paler than usual. "You've got to be kidding me. Now he's got *you* believing that garbage?"

"It's not garbage, Riv. I thought so too, at first. But my dad is dead, and he's here. Not here right now." Though I wished he were. I could use a little backup.

"You've seen a ghost." He spoke in a monotone.

"Not at first. It took a while for me to hear him, and then see him."

He looked around, rolling his eyes.

"I just said he's not here right now."

"Right. Are you sure you're getting enough sleep, cuz?"

This time I rolled my eyes, huffing. "Riv, I know it's nuts, okay? I didn't believe it at first either. But once you let go a little bit, you'll be able to see him."

"Not if he's not here, as you say."

"Well, yeah, but—"

"Dante, I'm exhausted, and I'm on duty tonight. If you're only here to tell me phantom tales, then please, see yourself out." He rose and turned toward his bedroom.

I stood as well, grabbing his arm. "It's true, and you'll believe it soon enough. For now, I need your help."

"You're not dragging me back to Claiborne Bridge are you?"

"No. At least, I don't think so. Not right now, anyway."

He sighed. "I'm sorry. You've been through hell, and I haven't always been understanding. You're my cousin and I love you, and I want to help you. What do you need?"

"I need you to help me find my father's body."

Silence, though River cocked his head and lifted a single eyebrow.

"Riv?"

"I can't believe I forgot. You know how after you have a dream you can't remember most of it? I had a déjà vu moment when you said that. Uncle Jules told me the same thing in my dream."

"He told me in real life. Though he's a ghost, so saying 'real life' doesn't make a lot of sense."

"Why isn't he here?" River paced around his living room, darting his gaze to his small kitchen and then to his leather chair in the corner before it landed back on me.

"You believe me, then?"

"No. I mean, yeah. I mean...I don't fucking know."

"Trust me. I know the feeling." I cleared my throat. "When's your next night off? I'm assuming we'll need to do this at night."

"Not until Thursday." His phone buzzed and he grabbed it out of his pocket. "Sorry. I need to take this. It's the body shop."

He walked into the kitchen.

I gazed around the room. Why wasn't my father here? He would have been a big help. River wouldn't be able to see him yet, but he could at least help me with what to say. Though maybe he'd talked to River in the dream and was helping that way. Still, I needed to know how to get in touch with him. Did ghosts carry cell phones?

I laughed out loud at that one.

"What's so funny?" River asked, returning.

"Nothing."

"Good. Because I need a favor. My car's ready to be picked up, and I had to turn in the rental this morning after I got off duty. Jay dropped me off here. Can you give me a lift?"

"Sure."

The drive to the body shop only took about fifteen minutes. River said I could leave, but I went in with him. I still had a lot to talk to him about, and he wasn't getting away that easily.

"You're good to go, Detective Gabriel," the mechanic said over the whir of a heavy-duty oscillating fan. "Looks like insurance covered everything. Here's your itemized receipt. Oh, and here are your personals." He handed River a canvas bag.

"My personals?"

"Just the stuff we found in the car."

"I don't keep anything in my car other than empty pop bottles. You could have thrown those away or recycled them." He opened the bag and pulled out a piece of pink fabric. "I definitely don't wear this color. You must have made a mistake." He handed the bag back.

"No mistake. This stuff was in your car. Thanks for your business, Detective." He ambled away, heading back toward the garage.

River pulled out another piece of the same fabric. "What the hell?"

I grabbed one of the remnants from him and took a look. "It has buttons. It's part of a shirt."

"I don't own a pink shirt. This is way too small for me anyway."

"Let me see." I grabbed the bag from him and pulled out another piece of material that looked like it was part of a denim mini skirt. "I assume this isn't yours either? Unless there's something you want to tell me." I smiled.

"Never seen it before— No, wait. Lucy was wearing pink the night of our date. But she wasn't in the car when I had the accident. I'd already taken her—" He stopped abruptly.

"What?"

"She said I took her home, but I don't recall doing it. Remember in the hospital? They told me I had retrograde amnesia, and that was why I didn't remember taking Lucy home. But I *did* remember the accident, which happened later." He grabbed the bag back from me and pawed through it. He pulled out a pair of silver sandals with ripped straps. Then some lacy tatters.

"Must have been a fun night," I said.

"But we didn't..."

I smiled again. "Retrograde amnesia sucks. You got laid and can't even remember. It must have been something, though, if you ripped her clothes off in the car."

"Why can't I remember this?"

"Amnesia, Riv. They told you at the hospital."

"Did I take her home naked?"

"You probably gave her your coat or something. Don't kick yourself for not remembering. You had a concussion."

"But I—" He shook his head. "This doesn't make any sense."

"Makes perfect sense. I'm just sorry you can't remember such a hot night. That truly does suck."

"It couldn't have happened that way. Nothing about this seems familiar to me."

We walked back out into the parking lot. River kept shaking his head and looking at the bag.

"Okay, let's attack it from a different angle then. What's the last thing you remember the night of the accident?"

"The accident itself."

"Before that."

"A lot of it is fuzzy. We had a great time. We got into the

car. I'm almost sure we decided to go to my place. Why didn't we?"

"You obviously changed your minds, and you took her home. After all, you'd already fucked in the car."

"Yeah, maybe..." He shook his head again. Then, "Uncle Jules!"

I turned, and there stood my father. "You see him?" I asked River.

"Yeah. Oh my God, as plain as day." He walked toward my father, ready for a bear hug, but stumbled instead.

"Sorry, River. I'm here, but I'm not corporeal anymore. At least not corporeal in the sense you understand."

"You can see him?" I said again with incredulity, poking my chin forward.

"Of course! This is great! I mean, I never would have believed it, but here you are!"

"I assume Dante filled you in on what the two of you need to do."

"Yeah, and I'm all in, Uncle Jules. But first you have to tell me. Where's my dad?"

"I'm afraid I don't know yet," he said. "But I do know he's still alive. I promise we'll find him, River."

I promise we'll find him, River.

They were talking like old buddies. I wanted to be happy that River could see my dad. I did.

So why wasn't I?

FOUR

Erin

I woke up in the middle of the day and couldn't get back to sleep.

"Dante?"

Maybe he'd gone downstairs to use my computer as he often did. I wanted a cup of tea anyway.

His note sat on the table in the kitchen.

Baby,

I've gone to see River. I locked the deadbolt with your key and slid it back under the door. Don't worry. I'll be back soon. Call if you need anything.

D

I grabbed my key off the floor near the door. That's what I'd do. I'd go to the hardware store and have some keys made. He really should have his own key.

First, though, I'd have my cup of tea and make a phone call. I'd been waiting for a good time to call Mrs. Moore's son, Juan Mendez, Jr. It was midafternoon. Now was as good a time as any.

I grabbed the number and keyed it into my phone.

A woman's voice answered. "Hello?"

"Hi. May I speak to Mr. Mendez, please?"

"May I ask who's calling?"

"Sure. My name is Erin Hamilton. I'm an emergency room nurse. I knew his mother."

"Okay. Just a minute."

A few seconds later— "Hello. This is Juan Mendez."

"Mr. Mendez, hi. I'm sorry to intrude on your day. I'm Erin Hamilton, one of the nurses who took care of your mother, Irene Moore. I'm so sorry for your loss."

"That's kind of you. But she lived a long and mostly happy life."

"I'm glad to hear that. I was hoping you could answer some questions for me."

"I can try. But I can't imagine what kind of questions you would have."

"Just one, actually. Your mother mentioned a physician who worked with your brother Carlos before his death. A doctor named Zarah, but she couldn't remember her last name."

"You mean Dr. Zarah Le Sang."

"Le Sang, with an S?"

"Yeah. Spelled like 'sang' but it's pronounced like 'song.'"

"She told me it was Le Grand or La Grande."

"Mom's memory was failing a bit."

"Understandable. You're sure it was Zarah Le Sang?"

"I'm sure, though I haven't given her a thought in... Well, since my brother was killed, and that was about forty years ago."

"Thank you. I really only needed her name."

"She's probably retired by now. If she's even alive."

"I don't expect to find her. I'm more interested in any research she might have published on her protocol for your brother and others. Thank you so much."

"No problem."

"Your mother was a lovely woman. I only met her once, but she made quite an impression on me."

"Mom was one of a kind."

"She certainly was. Thank you for your time, Mr. Mendez."

"You're very welcome."

I hastily scribbled down Dr. Zarah Le Sang and left to hit the hardware store and get a key made for Dante.

⚜

Dante had returned and was waiting by the door when I got back with the new keys. I smiled and handed him one. "Now you won't have to wait outside if I'm not home."

"Where have you been?" he asked through gritted teeth. Something was clearly bothering him.

I smiled. "Unclench, Dante. I went out to get the keys. It's broad daylight."

"You should be in bed."

"Yeah, I should, but I couldn't sleep. Since you don't like me going out at night, I figured I might as well run this errand. You're pale. Are you okay?"

"Yeah. I just told River about my dad."

"How did it go?"

"Not great at first, but then, all of a sudden, my dad appeared and River could see him right away."

"That's good. Isn't it?"

"Yeah. Good." He shoved his hands into his pockets.

"You don't sound like you think it's good, Dante."

"No, it is."

"But..."

"He's *my* father." He crossed his arms. "How come it took me so long to see him, yet River sees him as soon as he appears?"

"Maybe he's appeared to River before and River didn't see him. Maybe neither of you did."

"No, this was the first time. He told us. Not only that, he came to River in a dream as well. How come he never did that for me?"

"How do you know he didn't?"

"Because I would have remembered!"

"How do you—"

"I just know. That's all." He followed me into the townhome.

"Do you need anything? A snack. Some..." I twisted my neck toward him.

"No, I'm fine until morning. I don't need a snack. Maybe a bourbon, if you have any."

"I only have wine. We could go out. I can't have a drink, though, because I'm on tonight." Thinking about work hurled Patty and baby Isabelle back into my mind. What had become of them? I looked at my watch. "It's about dinnertime. Normally I'm asleep now, but I could eat."

"A glass of wine is fine," he said.

His teeth were out. Funny. I hadn't noticed until now.

Either they'd just descended, or I was getting used to them. The latter disturbed me more than I anticipated. Definitely less than it had a week ago, though. Perhaps I was making progress. I went to the kitchen and poured a glass of wine for Dante and a glass of water for myself. I set them both on my small table and motioned for him to have a seat.

He took a large gulp. Then another.

"I don't get it," he said. "Riv sees him right off, just like you did."

"I didn't know who I was seeing."

"True. But River did. How was he visible right away to his nephew but not to me, his son?"

"Maybe that has more to do with you than with your father."

"That's what he said. He said I was resisting. That doesn't hold water. River was resisting just as much. You should have seen the look on his face when I told him my dad was a ghost. He thought I'd gone batshit crazy."

I laughed despite myself. When had life become so insane?

"What's so funny?"

"Oh, no. Your situation isn't funny at all. I understand why you're upset. I really do." I patted his muscular forearm. "It's the whole of it. I'm sitting here with my vampire boyfriend talking about how it took him longer than his cousin to see his dead father. My life has gone wonky."

"You said vampire," he said, his eyes darkening. "I mean, you just admitted I'm a vampire."

I had, hadn't I? "Well...you *are*. That certainly doesn't change the fact that my life has gone nuts."

"Yours as well as mine," he said. "Ghosts are real. Demons are real. Werecreatures are apparently real."

"And vampires are—" I widened my eyes. "What?"

"It's all real."

"Werecreatures?"

"Yeah, according to River. Werewolves and werecats. Both exist."

I said nothing. What could I honestly say? My brain was fried.

"Sorry to put more on you."

"What about weresnakes and werebears?"

"Just wolves and cats, as far as I know. But I no longer put any faith in what I know. Or what I think I know."

"Hey"—I caressed his forearm—"we're in this together now."

He regarded me sharply. "Are we, Erin? I mean, are we *really*?"

I knew what he was asking. He wanted me to accept everything that he was. Accept the bond that he was certain bound us.

I stood, grabbing his hands and bringing him with me. "I'm sorry you're struggling about your father, Dante. I truly am. But you see him now. What does it matter that River saw him faster?"

"Because he's *my* father, damn it! All I have left is a ghost. River still has his father. Braedon is alive!"

"He is?"

"Yes, according to my dad."

"That's wonderful!"

"Yeah. It is. I love my uncle. He was like a second dad to me."

"This is good news for both of you. And for your sister. Does she know about your dad?"

"Not yet. Another thing on my to-do list."

"Do you want me to go with you?"

"No, I have to do that on my own, and I'm not sure how to do it, with her pregnancy and all. She's so fragile."

I cupped his cheek, thumbing the stubble rough under my fingers.

"You're the strongest person I know. You'll figure out a way."

He stood, his dark eyes gazing into mine. I traced the contours of his cheeks and jawline, traced his full lips.

He was beautiful.

He was mine.

And he was...*vampire.*

The V word.

Suddenly it was no longer so scary.

"Vampire," I said aloud.

"Yes," he said, stroking my hair. "I'm a vampire. A vampire who loves you."

His words echoed in my mind. He'd said them when he'd first told me what he was.

I cupped his other cheek, pulled him toward me, and pressed a soft kiss to his beautiful lips. "I love you too."

"All of me?" he asked on a whisper.

"All of you." I pulled back, staring into his eyes. "Dante, you are vampire, and I love you."

FIVE

DANTE

I hadn't realized how much her acceptance would lighten my load.

My teeth sharpened, and though I didn't need to feed, I knew now that I no longer had to hide. My teeth knew. My whole body knew.

She'd accepted me.

"You have no idea how much it means to me to hear you say those words." My canines seemed to settle in. They'd retract when they needed to. I inherently knew that. But for now, they were fully descended. I no longer needed to hide from the woman I loved.

"I think I do know," she said. "Blood bond or not, vampire or not, you're the man I'm supposed to be with. I feel it in my innermost soul, in every cell of my body, in the deepest recesses of my heart. I'm yours, Dante, for as long as you want me."

I smiled. "How about forever and a few days after that?"

"Perfect," she said. "You know what? I have plenty of groceries, thanks to my midnight jaunt to Walmart. I want to make dinner for you."

"Erin, you don't have to do that."

"I want to. It's a girlfriend thing. I'm actually not a bad cook, if you like hamburgers and hotdogs and the occasional recipe from the internet."

"I'll love whatever you make. And suddenly, I'm starving."

"Great. How about fried catfish? It's fresh and everything."

"Sounds awesome. Do you need any help?"

"Nope. You're not allowed anywhere near the kitchen. Just relax. I'll take care of everything." She shooed me out of the room.

I took my glass of wine and sat down on her sofa. The *Vampyre Texts* eyed me from the coffee table. I picked up the tome and set it on my lap. I'd gotten in trouble more than once as a kid when I'd touched this sacred book. I'd learned to leave it alone. Now? I had a burning desire to know its secrets.

Screw Bill's wrath.

If the book was truly dangerous and could lead vampires down a dark path, why had he kept it? He'd said it contained our history, and he couldn't bear to part with it. That made a certain amount of sense. Plus, even if he destroyed his own two copies, he couldn't destroy the rest.

I opened the book and leafed through it, recognizing a word here and there. One word, however, stood out as if written in red.

Sang.

Blood. Apparently the word was the same in both old and modern French.

Its appearance wasn't odd at all, given this was the *Vampyre Texts,* and blood was a huge component of who we were. Still, the word flashed at me.

Sang.

Sang.

Sang.

The smell of Cajun spices and the sound of sizzling fish snapped me out of my daydream.

Again, the mention of blood in a book about vampires wasn't unusual at all, so why had I seen it pulsing on the pages in red?

Perhaps Bill was right, and the book would lead to darkness. But who was he to decide that my father and I couldn't know what was inside? True, the person who'd last translated the *Texts* in the fourteenth century had agreed, and so had the elders.

I sighed. I had to know, especially if information about the blood bond lay between these pages. I had a right to know, damn it.

Erin walked over to me and kissed the top of my head. "Dinner's on the table." Then she pointed to the page I had been reading. "*Sang*. What does that mean?"

I cleared my throat. "It means blood. Why do you ask?"

"Blood? Really?"

"Yeah."

"That's just the weirdest thing."

"Why? This is a book about vampires. The word blood is bound to come up."

"No, that's not what's weird. What's odd is that I was just researching a doctor who came up with some sort of protocol for a blood disorder. Her name was Dr. Zarah Le Sang. Isn't that strange? A blood doctor's name is Dr. Blood?"

"That is a little weird," I agreed. "What did you find out about her?"

"Nothing. She doesn't seem to exist online. But a patient

of mine knew her. She apparently saved my patient's son with some kind of miracle for his undiagnosed blood disorder. Unfortunately, he ended up dying young anyway in a car accident."

"Weird that she's nowhere online."

"Yes and no. This was all forty or so years ago. It's possible none of her research got transferred to online resources." She shrugged. "I'd love to know more, and I'm sure the information is in some old dusty medical journal somewhere, but I don't have time for that kind of detective work. Come on. Let's eat."

I followed her to the table and sat down. She'd poured me another glass of wine and a glass of water with lemon for herself. "Still have to work later," she reminded me. "I hope you don't hate broccoli."

"No. I eat pretty much anything," I said. "It smells great."

"Thanks." She took a bite of fish, chewed, and swallowed. "Tell me more about River and your dad. Where were you guys when your dad appeared to him?"

"We were at a body shop picking up River's car."

"Right. The accident." She took a sip of water.

"Poor Riv," I said, chuckling.

"You're laughing?"

"No. Well, yeah. Poor Riv doesn't remember what happened that night. Apparently he and Lucy had quite a night, and he can't recall any part of it."

"What are you talking about?"

"She didn't tell you? Shit. Then I shouldn't say anything. River would never kiss and tell, but I saw the evidence."

"What evidence?"

"I've said too much. I just assumed, since you and she were so close—"

"Damn it, Dante, if you don't spill your guts this minute, I won't give you another drop of my blood!"

She didn't mean it, of course. I really wasn't one to talk about other people's sex lives, but I was in too deep now.

"Lucy's clothes. They were in River's car, and they were ripped to shreds."

"What?"

"I know. Crazy, huh? They had quite a time and poor River doesn't remember a second of it. That retrograde amnesia is something else, isn't it?"

"I don't understand." She held a forkful of broccoli halfway to her mouth.

"Don't say anything to Lucy, please. I just assumed you knew."

"Normally I *would* know. Lucy tells me everything. In vivid detail. But this she didn't tell me. In fact..." The fork still hovered in front of her.

"In fact, what?"

"She told me point blank that she and River did *not* have sex that night."

SIX

Erin

Unbelievable. Not that Lucy had any obligation to tell me her personal business, but she normally did. In living color.

"Now I feel really bad," Dante said. "Can you just forget I told you all of that? I honestly assumed you knew."

"That's a valid assumption usually. Lucy doesn't lie to me. Not about sex, at least. She sleeps with almost every guy she goes out with, and I was pretty shocked to hear she hadn't slept with River. I mean, he's..."

"What?"

"He's hot, okay? He could almost be your twin."

"River's hot?" Dante chuckled.

"Well, yeah. Not as hot as you are, but I wouldn't kick him out of be—" I clamped my hand over my mouth. "Sorry."

His eyes started blazing, the amber around his irises glowing. "No one else will ever be in your bed, Erin. Especially no other vampire. Is that clear?"

"Dante, it was a joke. River is great-looking, but I have no desire for him or anyone else. My point is that Lucy said she didn't sleep with him."

"Then how did her shredded clothes get into River's car?"

"Shredded?"

"Yeah. They were in tatters. Even the leather on her sandals had been torn."

"And that seems normal to you?"

"It didn't seem abnormal. Vampires have very high sex drives, as you probably know by now. I've ripped some of your clothes."

"You've never ripped my shoes, Dante."

"We've never had sex in a car, either. Which maybe we should remedy sometime."

I crossed my legs to ease the tickle between them. Sex in a car with Dante? Sign me up. "Lucy doesn't know River's a vampire. He surely wouldn't tear leather in half in front of her."

"He might as well not have, since he doesn't remember any of it."

I thought back to the night of River's accident, our conversation. Then Lucy had shown up.

River turned to Lucy. "I can't remember taking you home."

"Retrograde amnesia," Lucy said. "It's very common with a concussion, especially if you lose consciousness."

"That's what I told him," I said.

"But it's weird. I don't remember taking you home, but I remember the accident."

I lifted my eyebrows. "Really? That is odd."

"Oh, no, I've heard of that," Lucy said. "Sometimes the amnesia is fragmented. Anyway, the important thing is that you're okay."

I hadn't concerned myself with it at the time, but I'd never heard of *selective* retrograde amnesia. You lost all or nothing. Still, perhaps Lucy had heard of it, and I just didn't know about it. I'd been on duty and had been taking care of several patients besides River, so I hadn't been worried about anything Lucy said.

Until now.

"Where are these ripped clothes of Lucy's now?" I asked Dante.

"Riv still has them. Why?"

"I know vampires are strong, but can you rip leather straps apart?"

"Easily," he said.

"All right," I relented. "Must have been some night. For the life of me, though, I can't figure out why Lucy lied to me."

"I'm sorry I have such a big mouth. I truly thought you knew."

"It was an honest mistake."

"Can you forget I told you? For both of their sakes?"

I nodded. "Consider it forgotten."

Boy, would it be hard *not* to tease Lucy about this.

⚜

First thing I did when I clocked in was check the computer for any information on Patty Doyle and the baby.

Nothing.

Only the intake information when Patty had come to the emergency room. The baby hadn't been transferred to the NICU, and Patty hadn't gone to recovery.

Had they disappeared like the others? If so, why weren't the cops swarming around like they always did? This was too weird. I had a personal stake in this one. I'd bonded with this patient, and I wanted to make sure she was all right.

I picked up the phone to call Jay to find out if anything had been reported, but before I could key in his number, the sirens wailed in the distance.

Time for work.

Three gurneys were wheeled in, one dead on arrival.

I went to work with Dr. Thomas on the second one, a young man whose leg had been crushed under a toppled car.

He didn't make it.

Before I could deal with two deaths, a mother came in with a feverish nine-month-old baby named Bianca. I took the baby's temperature—105.6—and grabbed the nearest resident. If the fever went much higher the child could have a seizure. The resident ordered alternating doses of ibuprofen and acetaminophen, plus a lukewarm bath. I bathed the baby while I tried to calm her mother.

"Babies spike high fevers sometimes. It's usually a virus, but we'll run some tests, okay?"

The mother gulped and nodded.

The child was fussy—feverish children usually were—but I couldn't help but note how beautiful she was, with big brown eyes, long eyelashes, and lovely dark curls. Normally I didn't comment on something so superficial, but the mother was in such distress, I thought it might help.

"She's beautiful. Truly."

The mother sniffled. "She just won a baby beauty contest."

I smiled, even while imagining spoiled children a la *Toddlers and Tiaras* vying for a crown. "I didn't realize there were pageants for babies this young."

"Oh, yes. As young as six months old."

I smiled again.

"I know what you're thinking. A mother shouldn't display her child like that. But she won two thousand dollars for her college fund."

"That's nice." I pulled Bianca out of the water and toweled her off. "You feeling better? You want to see your mama?" I checked her temperature quickly. "Already down two degrees. She's doing great."

"I know why she spikes those high fevers."

"Oh?"

"It's her genetics."

"What do you mean?"

"Her daddy is a werewolf," she whispered.

I cradled Bianca, trying to stay calm. The baby would sense even the slightest tension.

Her daddy is a werewolf.

A flashback jolted into my mind. Of a young homeless man I'd come to know as Abe Lincoln.

Did you see him?

See who?

The vampire.

Abe Lincoln was hardly the first patient who'd come to the ER talking about paranormal creatures. This was New Orleans, after all. I'd heard my share of tall tales, and normally, I'd shrug this off. But a child was involved here. If this mother was delusional, I had to think about the baby. Looked like I'd be calling in the social worker.

But my mind shot again to Abe Lincoln. Yes, he was far from the first patient I'd heard spin a fairy tale.

He *was* the first, however, who'd proven to be truthful.

I nodded to Bianca's mother. "I see."

"Weres, they're always hot, you know? Her daddy's normal body temp is about a hundred. She's not a were, but she spikes those fevers."

High fevers were not uncommon in babies. Bianca's fever was most likely due to a virus, not due to any paranormal heritage.

If weres truly existed—and according to Dante, they did—I'd probably seen one or two in the ER. If a temp read at a hundred, we rarely treated it without other symptoms. Nothing to worry about.

Just like vampires, they could be existing in plain sight.

My world had gone bonkers.

The beautiful baby in my arms had finally stopped fussing. I handed her back to her mother. "Just wait in here. I'll be back to check on you in about fifteen minutes. I'd like to see that fever go down another degree."

"You won't tell anyone, will you? About her daddy? I heard doctors and nurses have to keep their patients' secrets. Confidentiality or something, right?"

"Of course." I smiled, a twinge of guilt niggling at me. I had every intention of bringing in social services. "Please just press that red button if you need me before I come back."

I checked on another patient and then went to the computer station to log in some information.

Lucy sat down next to me. "How's it going?"

"Just another night in the ER. I have a half-werewolf baby in exam room three, apparently."

"Oh?" Lucy laughed. "What next? A mermaid getting a sponge bath? Oops. I have to go." She grabbed her pager.

Funny. I hadn't heard it buzz.

I took care of a little paperwork and then headed back to

exam room three to check Bianca's temperature.

I walked in and had to fight to keep my mouth from dropping open.

Lucy was holding Bianca. "I doubt there's anything to worry about," she said to the baby's mother. "Babies sometimes spike fevers. It's their little bodies' way of burning out viruses."

Nothing at all odd about this scene. Bianca's mother had probably wanted to ask a question, and instead of pushing the button for me, she grabbed the first nurse she saw.

Happened all the time.

So why did this seem so strange?

Selective retrograde amnesia.

Torn clothes.

A big dog at the site of River's accident.

My legs wobbled a bit, and I caught myself.

I had to hold it together.

My best friend was *not* a werewolf, and neither was this child's father.

SEVEN

DANTE

Technically Erin had refused to let me move in with her, but now that I had a key, I stayed at her place while she was at work. I'd need to feed as soon as she got home anyway, and I had nowhere else to go.

I'd spent most of the night on Erin's computer searching fruitlessly for any information on the *Vampyre Texts* or a blood bond.

Nothing.

The only option was to find my father's body, file a death certificate, claim his estate, and use some of the money to get the contents of the *Vampyre Texts* from Nocturnal Truth, the obscure website I'd found.

My father had been absent since the parking lot at the body shop. I'd been jealously imagining that he was with River, but that was ridiculous. River was at work, just like Erin was. It still irked me that River had been able to see my father's ghost right away. What was *wrong* with me?

Her.

My time with *her* had fucked me up.

Once bonded, never broken.

I grabbed fistfuls of my hair. "Get out of my head!"

I'm part of you now, just as you're a part of me. You'll never escape me. Never.

"Get out of my head!" I yelled again.

Never. Never. Never.

I paced around Erin's living room, my hands clasped over my ears.

Still her voice taunted me. I no longer could discern words, just the wicked tone that made me want to throw things.

I picked up the voluminous tome and hurled it across the room. It landed against the wall with a thud and then fell to the ground, open.

I closed my eyes for a minute. This was not my book to destroy or throw around as if it meant nothing.

It belonged to my grandfather.

I drew in several breaths and let them out, willing myself to calm. It didn't help much, but it was enough to get me across the room to the book. I knelt down to pick it up, when four words fell into my view.

Demandez a la royne.

Demandez was the imperative form of the verb "to ask" in modern French. What was it in Old French? I had to assume it was the same. This passage was telling me to ask something. No, to ask some*one*. *La* was the feminine form of the article "the." But *royne*? Obviously an Old French word, and one I didn't recognize.

Do as it tells you.

Get the fuck out of my head, you bitch!

Then I stared at the sentence again. The word for queen in modern French was *reine*.

But the word for king...

During my quick search for Old French words weeks ago, I'd come across *moi*, the word for "me," spelled as *moy*.

The modern French word for king was *roi*. Using the same Old French spelling, perhaps it would be *roy* in Old French. And if *roy* meant king...

Ask the queen.

Bitch was talking to me!

She was no queen of mine.

Wrong. You said so yourself.

I said so because you were torturing me!

Perhaps *royne* meant cunt. That would make more sense, if *she* was guiding me to this sentence in the book.

No. It meant queen. I knew without knowing, as though the information had always been in my head.

She was no queen, and I had nothing to ask her. She didn't have any information I wanted.

Except that she did.

As much as I struggled against it, I needed her knowledge. How else would I find my uncle?

As I readied to send her a thought—could I even do that?—another question formed in its place.

Who has been taking Erin's blood?

Nothing. No words formed in my head.

A chill swept across my neck.

"Dad?"

Not my father. I'd see him if he were here. Besides, it hadn't felt like him. This was something else. Something...sinister.

I'd had the same feeling the first time I'd been in Erin's home. I'd sensed something evil. Something I needed to ferret out and eliminate.

I gulped. Was *she* here?

I shook my head vehemently. Of course not. *She* was a vampire, and we certainly didn't have the power to be invisible. No living entity did.

Or did *she*? I'd told River once that I believed my bindings had been enchanted. Ridiculous, yes, but I should have been able to free myself.

Perhaps *she* had power that the rest of us did not.

No.

She existed only in my head, and perhaps that was just my imagination warped from so many years in captivity serving her my blood.

She wasn't here at all, and the book falling open to that particular sentence was nothing but coincidence.

That made sense. Perfect sense. Logic was always the best choice.

But even I wasn't buying that this time.

Though *she* was the last person in the world I wanted to converse with, I tried again.

Why did you let me go?

It was time.

Time for what?

Time for you to do what you were meant to do. Born to do.

My pulse raced. *What am I meant to do?*

You'll find out...

"For God's sake!" I picked up the book, closed it, and returned it to Erin's coffee table.

Then Erin burst through the door.

EIGHT

Erin

Dante's skin was paler than usual. He was standing next to my coffee table when I entered.

He looked frazzled, about as frazzled as I felt. My reality had taken another hit today.

"Are you okay?" I asked.

"Not even in the slightest," he said, advancing toward me. His eyes were dark with smoking embers, the amber ring around his iris more pronounced than ever.

He was hungry.

He gripped my shoulders and yanked me toward him.

My heart thumped. Pinpricks covered my entire body, surging through me and culminating between my legs. My nipples hardened, pressing against my bra. I closed my eyes, waiting for him to crush our mouths together in the customary kiss.

"Oh!"

Instead his teeth sank into the flesh of my neck.

The sharp pain subsided quickly, replaced by the sucking and tugging sensations I had learned to love. I was happy to please him, happy to give him what he needed and craved—but this was different.

He hadn't warned me, hadn't asked. Not that I would've said no. Still, it was oddly unsettling. Yet completely arousing.

He kept sucking, kept taking my blood, and when it had gone on longer than I was comfortable with, I gripped both sides of his head. "Dante."

He continued sucking.

"Dante," I said again, more urgently this time.

He released me then, licking the puncture wounds before pulling back and meeting my gaze. "Sorry, baby."

"What's bothering you?"

"Nothing."

"Bullshit. You didn't even kiss me."

He pressed his lips, still smeared with my blood, against mine softly. "Sorry," he said again.

"I wasn't asking you to kiss me. But seriously, something's bugging you."

Instead of answering, he bent to his knees, pushed my sweats and underpants over my hips, and inspected my inner thighs. "No new wounds. Good."

Nothing about how turned on I was? Even I could smell it. I knelt down to meet his gaze. "Dante, what's going on?"

"I can't talk about it."

I hastily pulled my pants back up. "Please. If we're going to be togeth—"

"I said I can't talk about it. I'm sorry I wasn't tender with you. It won't happen again." He turned away from me.

"You know I don't care about that. I truly want to help."

He looked around my living room, inhaling. "Do you sense anything here?"

"No. What are you talking about?"

"The first time I came here, I sensed something evil. It seemed to go away, or at least I stopped feeling it, until today."

Goosebumps erupted on my flesh. "You're scaring me."

"I don't mean to. But we need to figure it out. Maybe it's that dark presence that Bea said has targeted me."

"If it was anything like that, why would it have been here the first time you came here?"

"Maybe it followed me." He shook his head. "I don't know. I know I sound crazy."

"Dante, after everything I've seen, you don't sound crazy at all." I walked to the kitchen, poured myself a glass of water, and drank it all down. Dante must have taken a lot of my blood. I was feeling dehydrated and slightly lightheaded. The water helped.

I walked back to him. "Have you talked to River lately?"

"Not since yesterday. Why?"

"Just wondering. A patient and her baby disappeared from our hospital, but no one is doing anything about it. When the other patients disappeared, the police were all over it. With these two, it's like they were never there."

He stared into space.

"Are you listening to me?"

He jerked his attention back to me. "Yeah. Sorry."

"Don't you care that a patient and her baby disappeared?"

"Of course I do. The hospital surely called the police."

"Not that I've seen."

"They were probably investigating during a time you weren't there. They'll get to you. What can either of us do about it, anyway?"

I stared at him, furrowing my brow. "What's wrong with you, Dante?"

"Nothing. Nothing I can talk about at least." He jerked his head to the left, gazing at seemingly nothing.

"Are you feeling the strange presence now?"

He didn't answer.

I tentatively touched his arm. His skin was ice cold, despite the fact that he'd just fed. "You want some breakfast or something?"

"No. I'm good. Sorry, baby, but I need to go. I'll be back as soon as I can."

"Wait. You're not leaving me here with whatever evil presence is lurking, are you?"

He smiled, sort of. "Of course not. I don't feel it now."

"Where are you going?"

"I need to see my cousin." He left without kissing me goodbye.

Strange. I closed the door.

A few seconds later, someone knocked.

I smiled. He hadn't left after all. I opened the door.

Only to see Dr. Zabrina Bonneville. Her long blond hair flowed over her shoulders in sleek tresses. I couldn't help staring a bit. I'd never seen her wear it that way. She wore jeans and a peasant blouse, something else I'd never witnessed.

"Doctor, hi. What are you doing here?"

"I need to talk to you, Erin. May I come in?"

"Uh...sure." I held the door open for her.

"I suppose you're wondering about Patty Doyle and her baby."

Had Dr. Bonneville seen me snooping on the computer? I hadn't actually been snooping. Patty had been my patient too.

"Yes, I was, actually. I wanted to check on her the next morning, but there was no record of her at the hospital. With all the other disappearances, I was wondering why the police weren't around."

Dr. Bonneville scoffed. "They do get in the way, don't they? How are we supposed to run an ER with the cops always snooping around?"

"They're doing their jobs," I said, hoping I didn't sound too condescending. On the other hand, we weren't at work right now.

"I get that, but their jobs interfere with *our* jobs."

"If women would stop disappearing from the hospital, they wouldn't need to be there," I said.

"That's true, and I don't mean to sound callous. Those patients are my responsibility. Their disappearance doesn't make any of us look good." She sighed. "I'm just glad they seem to be reappearing, though the whole thing is a strange mystery."

I could agree, but that was futile. "But Patty and her baby didn't disappear?"

She cleared her throat. "No, they didn't. Patty's parents had them transferred. You might not have realized this, but Patty is only seventeen. She's still under the protection of her parents. They wanted her and the baby transferred to a hospital in Baton Rouge."

"Why? The baby was nearly premature."

"I don't know," she said. "And it's not my job to ask. The baby was fine at the time of transfer. She was breathing on her own and her sucking reflex was good."

"And now?"

"I have no idea. She and Patty are no longer my responsibility."

"No, but they're still—" I stopped abruptly. Dr. Bonneville was right, as heartless as she sounded. We couldn't get attached. It was too emotionally debilitating.

Didn't stop me from getting attached anyway.

"I'll be going," Dr. Bonneville said, turning.

"Doctor?"

"Yes?" She looked over her shoulder.

"Why did you come to my home to tell me this? Why not just tell me at work?"

"I'm taking a few weeks off, Erin. I won't be at work for a while."

"Oh?" I was secretly delighted. "Taking a vacation?"

"Yes. Three weeks in Barbados. The other doctors and the residents will hold down the fort without me."

"You'll be missed," I said, and actually meant it, professionally speaking. She was an amazing physician. "Have a wonderful time."

"My husband and I will." She walked out my door, leaving me with my jaw dropped.

Dr. Bonneville was married?

She didn't wear a ring, but none of us wore any jewelry in the ER. She never talked about her personal life, and I'd just assumed...

But why wouldn't she be married? She was a very intelligent and attractive woman, and maybe she was a different person outside of work.

Either that or she'd married a glutton for punishment.

NINE

DANTE

River had just gotten home after his shift, and was talking to—

"Dad?"

"Hello, son."

"All right, that's it." I was in no mood for small talk. "It takes me forever to see you, but Riv sees you right away. And now I find you here at his place? What about me? I'm your fucking son, damn it!"

"Calm down, Dante," my father said.

"The hell I will. What the fuck is this about?"

"I asked him to come," River said. "This isn't his fault."

"You asked my father to come without me here? What the hell kind of betrayal is this?"

"Dante," River said, "I was trying to be sensitive to your situation. I have questions about my own father, and your dad is...well..."

"*Dead* is the word you're looking for," I said without emotion. "You think I haven't accepted that?"

"You've just been through so—"

"I'm sick to death of rehashing that I've been through so much. Don't you think I want Uncle Brae back as much as you do? If he's where I was, he's probably being tortured or worse. This involves me, River. Don't fucking leave me out of it."

"Dante," my father said, "are you angry about being left out? Or are you angry at this situation?"

I scoffed. "All of the above." I raked my fingers through my hair. "Today I felt something evil in Erin's apartment, and then, when she got home, it was gone just as quickly."

"Are you sure it wasn't your imagination?" River asked. "After all you've—"

"Did I not just say I'm sick to death of that?" I shook my head. "You'll never understand."

"No,. he won't," my father said. "But I do. I understand, Dante. I know what you've been through, because I went through much of the same. And I'd do it all again to protect both of you if I had to."

"Dante, seriously," River said. "I didn't think you'd get mad about me talking to your dad without you. I honestly thought it was the best thing."

I drew in a deep breath and let it out slowly. I was so on edge. "All right. I accept your apology. But please don't leave me out again. We're all in this together. I want Uncle Brae back just as much as the two of you do, okay? No tiptoeing around me. I can take it. I've been to hell and back, and nothing either of you say or do is going to break me. I promise you that. If that bitch didn't break me, nothing will."

"Okay," River said. "In that case, I was just asking Uncle Jules about where my dad might be, what he might be going through. It isn't pretty, Dante, and if you were there going through even half of it, I'm so sorry, man."

"I don't need your pity, Riv. I need your help. We have to find my dad's body. That way we can get the money we need to figure out what's going on. That's the only way we'll be able to find *your* dad."

River nodded. "Uncle Jules told me everything. About Bill and the book. You were right, Dante. Something *is* off about Bill. I don't know why I didn't see it. A good detective should have seen it."

"It was easier for me. I was gone for so long that the differences in Bill stood out to me. You lived them. They wouldn't be as obvious."

"Still..."

"Now is not the time for either of you to put yourselves down," my father said. "I need you both alert and willing to go the distance. Are you all in?"

I looked to my cousin, and we both nodded. "All in," we said together.

"So where do we start?" River asked. "Where can we find your body?"

"Where do you think you'd find a body?" my father said. "In a cemetery, of course."

"How could it be in a cemetery?" I paced across the floor. "All the cemeteries around here are closely guarded. You can only get in during the day as part of a tour."

"I don't know how it got there. Your mother directed me through a tunnel where I came up somewhere behind Bourbon Street. She said I'd find a vial of poison hidden behind a voodoo shop. I did, and I drank it. I died there, behind the shop. A man found me, and rather than call the police, he took my body to the cemetery. I have no idea how he got it there. But it's there.

I saw him take it in."

"Which cemetery?"

"St. Louis One."

"Where?"

My father paused for a few seconds. Then, "I'm not exactly sure. I don't have any attachment to the body anymore. But obviously I'd be buried in one of the grassy areas."

"Wait." River held up his hand. "You don't know where? How are we supposed to find you?"

"I'm sorry I can't give you more accurate information. I'd just died and was getting used to my new ghostly existence. I didn't see everything. But I haven't been dead for very long, and there aren't many grassy areas in that cemetery. You should be able to see where the sod was disturbed."

"How are we supposed to do that? I'm a cop. I arrest people for trespassing in that cemetery. I arrest people for desecrating a person's final resting place."

"Riv—"

"Seriously, Dante, this goes against everything I am."

"I can't do this alone, Riv, and you're the only one I trust."

River sank his head into his hands. "All right. All right. I guess we can glamour the guards into letting us in."

"*You* can glamour them. I'm not all that good at it," I said.

"I can still do it," my father said. "I'll be going with you. I can't help you dig, but I can keep the guards away from you."

"When do we do this?" River asked.

"How about tonight?" I said.

"I told you it would have to wait until my next night off. After that concussion, I can't be taking personal days."

"Right. Okay." My mind raced. "You said your next night off was Thursday. That's a day from now. Let's plan to leave as soon as Erin goes to work at eleven."

"Sounds good," River said, shaking his head. "I can't believe I'm about to vandalize sacred ground."

"It's the only way," my father said. "I'm sorry it's come to this, but we need my death certificate so Dante and Emilia can claim my estate."

"We'll take care of you, Dad." I stood. "You get some sleep, Riv. I'm heading back to Erin's." I turned to my father. "I'd like you to come with me, please. I need your take on whatever presence I'm sensing in her home."

"Of course. I'll see you there." He vanished.

River jerked. "Not sure I'll ever get used to that."

"Me neither. He looks so real."

"I think he is real, cuz. Just a different kind of real. At least he's not in any pain. I can't bear to think—" He shook his head.

"We'll find him," I said to my cousin. "I promise. We'll find your dad."

⚜

Erin had gone to bed by the time I got back to her place. I gave her a chaste kiss on the forehead. She opened one eye and smiled.

"I'm glad you're back."

"If you'd let me move in, I'd always be here."

She chuckled. "You can move in now, Dante. I've made peace with everything. Well, most everything."

"What do you mean by that?"

"Nothing about you. I love who and what you are. You're a vampire, and frankly, I enjoy your feedings. Weird, huh?"

"Not at all. I think it goes without saying that I enjoy them as well."

"Of course *you* do. You're getting nourishment."

"Erin, love, what I get from you goes so far beyond nourishment. You and I both know that. Now what's bothering you? What haven't you made peace with?"

She sat up in bed. "Something weird happened in the ER last night. I had a patient with a sick baby, and the mother told me that the baby's father was a werewolf."

I widened my eyes. "Oh?"

"I know what you're going to say. Believe me, I've heard my share of crazy tales since I moved here. I never believed any of them. Not until Abe Lincoln showed up. And I didn't believe him at first either."

"This might just be another crazy tale," I said. "River says weres are even rarer than vampires."

"Have you ever met one?"

"No. At least not that I know of. I imagine they fly under the radar like we do."

"Still"—she drummed her fingers on her thighs—"that's not the weirdest part about it."

"Oh?"

"Yeah. I told Lucy, and the next thing I know, she's in the exam room holding the baby."

"So? Maybe she was walking by and the mom needed something."

"Yeah. That's what I told myself, anyway. We cover for each other all the time. But then I started thinking."

"About what?"

"About Lucy lying to me about not sleeping with River. About the tattered clothes in River's car. About River not remembering taking Lucy home. About Jay saying someone saw a big dog, like a malamute, at the scene of the accident.

What if River never actually took Lucy home? What if…" She shook her head. "I don't even believe it myself."

"What if your best friend is a werewolf?"

TEN

Erin

I was glad Dante had said the actual words so I didn't have to. I was already certain I'd gone mad.

"Lucy never covers up her sexual exploits," I said. "She tells Steve and me everything. No holds barred. If she had such crazy sex with River that he ripped her clothes into shreds, she would have told me."

Dante caressed my cheek. "Erin, this is highly unlikely."

"Of course it is. It's also highly unlikely that you're a vampire, yet here you are."

"But if River remembers the accident, which he claims he does, then he would certainly remember his date morphing into a wolf, don't you think?"

I laughed into my hands. I truly sounded like a crazy person. "I guess I hadn't thought of that."

He smiled, still skimming my cheek and jawline. "You've had a lot thrust on you recently. Your imagination is bound to go a little nuts."

"You don't think I've lost it?"

"Of course not. You've *found* it. You've found something amazing, and so have I." He brushed his lips against mine. "Now go back to sleep. My dad is here, and I need to talk to him about some stuff. We'll do it downstairs so we don't bother you."

"You'll stay, then?"

"Of course."

"I mean...you'll move in?"

"If you're sure it's what you want. I'm not employed at the moment, though. I'm living off Bill for now, but I can't stomach much more of that. I'm going to find a way to make a living, baby, but until I do, are you sure you want me living here?"

I smiled, shoving his hair back over his forehead and gazing into his dark and intense eyes. "I've never been more sure about anything."

"That makes me very happy. Now go to sleep, and no dreaming about werewolf babies and best friends." He left the bedroom.

I closed my eyes.

A moment passed. Then another.

Relaxation eluded me.

I didn't want to eavesdrop, but I couldn't help myself. I got out of bed and sneaked over to the stairwell, hiding behind a wall.

"You need anything?" Dante's voice.

"No. Ghosts don't need food or blood or anything."

"Yeah. Right. This is still all so surreal."

Silence for a few seconds.

Then, "So do you sense anything here?"

"I've been here many times since I died," he said.

Ick. Had Dante's father been watching us? I couldn't let my thoughts go there.

"I get that. I thought maybe what I was sensing was you, that I was imagining the 'evil' of it, but if you'd been here, I'd have seen you."

"I wasn't here."

"Then what was it?"

"Could it have been your imagination? I know you're spooked by what that voodoo woman told you. She's probably full of shit."

"Yeah, I know. But what if she's not? She was quoting Shakespeare, for God's sake."

"A lot of people can quote Shakespeare," Dante's father said. "He's one of the most quoted people of all time. 'That which we call a rose by any other word would smell as sweet.' I know a fair amount of Shakespeare myself, including Bea's quote. It's a famous one from *Hamlet,* second only to 'To be or not to be, that is the question.'"

"I had no idea you were so well read, Dad."

"I'd have taught you all of that. I'm sorry I couldn't."

"Sometimes I feel so inadequate. I didn't even finish high school! I wanted to be a doctor once. And now..."

Dante hadn't finished high school? What else didn't I know?

"You can still be a doctor, son. You'd be a great one. Jack won't live forever, and we need another good doctor for our kind."

"But I can't. I have to get a GED, and then four years of college, four of med school, four of internship and residency. I'd be an old man by the time I was done. Plus, all that costs a ton of money."

"You'll have the money you need soon."

What? What was Julian talking about? Tension seized my body.

"Still, it's not in the cards for me. That bitch stole ten years of my life. Stole my dream of medical school. I try not to let it get to me, Dad, but I can't help it sometimes."

"I understand."

"Hell, she even stole *you* from me!"

"I'm here, son."

"I know. And I'm happy about that. But you're not *really* here. You won't be able to stay forever. You said yourself that a ghost only has ten years on this plane."

"I can teach you a lot in ten years."

"Even if I did try to become a doctor, you'd be gone before I was done."

"Is that a good reason not to do it?"

"No. I don't know."

Though I couldn't see him, I knew Dante was pacing, shoving his fingers through his hair.

Becoming unhinged.

I'd seen him this way a lot lately.

Something was eating at him. Something he wouldn't tell me.

Yet.

"Everything changed. Riv was supposed to go to business school. What happened to his dream?"

"He actually told me. When you disappeared, and then Braedon and I followed, he decided to become a police officer so he could learn investigative skills and try to find us."

"But he didn't."

"No, but he tried."

"He told you all of this?"

"Yes. We talked a lot."

"Why didn't he tell me any of this stuff?"

"He felt weak. He couldn't save you, me, or his own father. He tried and couldn't find us. He failed. He feels very badly about it."

"He does?"

More silence.

"Dante, your cousin is going through his own kind of hell. It's nothing like what you went through, and he knows that, but it still exists and is very real for him."

Silence once again.

Then, "I had no idea." Dante's voice.

"You've been consumed with your own issues—your abduction and escape, your blood bond with Erin. River understands that."

"I feel like a douche."

"Don't. We've all been through enough. We all need to forgive each other and forgive ourselves. Each one of us was only doing what we thought was right at the time. Always."

"You're talking about Erin, aren't you?"

My ears perked up.

"I wouldn't have glamoured her if it weren't necessary. For both of you."

Say what? I stood and clomped down the stairs. "You *glamoured* me?"

Both Dante's and his father's gazes landed on me.

No words.

"Don't even try to tell me this isn't any of my business," I said. "I want to know who glamoured me and why."

"Tell her, Dad," Dante said. "She deserves the truth."

"It was the first time you saw Dante's teeth. I was here, in your living room, when you ran downstairs in a panic. I glamoured you into getting some wine and going back to him."

I stared at him. I stared at a fucking ghost.

"I'm sorry, Erin. But Dante needed you, and I had to protect my son."

"At my expense!"

"I didn't hurt you. I would never hurt you."

"Then promise you'll never do it again."

"I can't make that promise," the ghost said.

I looked to Dante.

"I tried to get him to promise the same thing. He won't do it. He'll do whatever he has to do to protect both of us. It took me a little time, but I can accept that. I hope you can too."

"That's the only time I was glamoured?"

"Fully. By me," Julian said.

What was that supposed to mean? I lifted one eyebrow and looked to Dante.

"I've never glamoured you. I tried the first time we met, at the blood bank, but it didn't take. I've never tried again, and I won't. I promise."

"Then what did you mean when you said 'by me'?"

I expected Julian to answer, but Dante let out a breath.

"Bill glamoured you the day you came to the house. Remember when I cut myself with the bread knife?"

"Yeah." My heart pounded.

"It wasn't a bread knife. It wasn't a dog bite. I spilled a glass of blood on the floor and I bit myself so I'd have a wound to account for the blood."

"No, it was—" I squeezed my eyes shut and conjured the image in my mind. The pool of blood on the tile floor. Dante's forearm bleeding. The wound.... "A bread knife. I remember so clearly."

But then I flashed to his forearm. Two puncture wounds.

"River told you it was a bite from the neighbor's dog. You went next door to talk to the neighbor, and you learned she didn't have a dog. Bill found out, and he glamoured you. I'm so sorry, Erin. If it makes a difference, I gave him holy living hell for it."

I opened my eyes. Dante's own eyes were sunken and sad. Regretful.

"My father would never do anything to intentionally harm you, Erin," Julian said. "I hope you know that."

"I don't know anything anymore. I only know that I need you to both please leave."

"Erin," Dante said, pleading.

"Please. I can't deal with any of this. I thought I could, but I was wrong."

"I will leave," Julian said. "But let Dante stay. You need each other. He'll protect you."

I tugged at a lock of hair in disarray around my shoulder. Was I overreacting? Maybe. This was nothing compared to someone feeding on me, and we hadn't been able to figure out who'd been doing that yet.

"I need a glass of water." I headed to the kitchen. Instead of water, I poured myself a glass of white wine and took a gulp.

"Baby?" Dante touched my arm.

I flinched, but I didn't back away.

"I know this is a lot to take."

"You have no fucking idea."

"I know you feel like you've taken up residence in crazy town. I get that. But it's not a full moon for another week or so, and—"

"Oh my God." I downed the rest of the wine in one gulp.

"I was just trying to lighten the mood. You know, the

legend that people get crazy during a full moon? Where do you think the word lunatic came from?"

"I know all about the word lunatic coming from the full moon. That's not what I mean."

"What is it then?"

"The last full moon. I remember it. It was so beautiful as I drove into work."

"Yeah?"

"Lucy. Lucy called in sick that night."

ELEVEN

DANTE

I quickly explained to my father what Erin was talking about.

"Weres don't always change on the full moon," he said. "That's a myth. They can control the change. Does she call in sick every time there's a full moon?"

Erin shook her head. "I don't think so. She wouldn't have a job for very long if she called in sick that much. But her nights off aren't always the same as mine. Maybe she takes the full moon off. I'd have to check the calendar at work."

"Okay. You can do that tonight."

Erin tensed her knuckles around her wine goblet. "No. I can't. Absolutely not."

"It might give you some peace of mind," my father said.

"Peace of mind? Are you kidding me?" She poured herself another glass of wine.

"Baby, easy. You're working tonight, remember?"

"I'll sleep six hours before I have to go in. Right now, I need a drink." She took two sips of her wine and then turned to my father. "Tell me all you know about werewolves."

"Yeah, I'd like to know too," I said. "You might as well start teaching me all that stuff I should have learned after I graduated."

"I never knew you didn't finish high school," Erin said. "I didn't realize you were gone that long."

I nodded, hoping she would still accept that I didn't want to talk about my time in captivity yet.

She seemed to.

"Weres are actually more endangered than we are," my father said. "They're surrounded by myth, also. Like us, they are born, not made. A werewolf can bite you and nothing will happen, other than you'll need stitches."

"That's a relief." Erin rolled her eyes. "Not that I think Lucy would bite me."

"I don't see any positive proof that your friend is a werewolf," he said. "With everything new that's been pushed on you lately, though, I understand why you'd be suspicious."

He cleared his throat and went on. "Only two species of shifters remain. Wolves and cats, panthers, to be exact. Also like us, they can mate with humans and give birth to human children. Whatever in their DNA that causes them to shift can only be passed to a baby with two were parents."

"Anything else?" Erin asked. "What about their body temperatures?"

"Ours are a degree or two lower than humans. Weres run a degree or two higher."

"That's it? There are no more differences? What hair color do they have?"

"They can have any hair color, just like we can and you can. Most vampires have dark hair, but so do most humans."

"Lucy has blond hair," Erin said. "What else?"

"That's it. I've never met a were that I know of. They don't go around advertising what they are, just as we don't. We wouldn't be able to exist otherwise."

Erin finished her wine and stared into space.

"You okay, baby?"

She nodded, though the look on her face didn't indicate she was convinced of it. "I'm going to bed. I've had all I can take for now."

"I'll go with you."

She held up her hand to stop me. "No, please. I just need to be alone for a little while. I hope you understand."

I started to say something, but my father shook his head slightly at me.

Maybe he was right.

"Okay, baby. Sleep well. I'll be here."

She nodded and walked up the stairs.

"Give her some space, son," my father said.

"I'm trying. She finally accepted me, and now she has to deal with all of this. I wasn't sure how to tell her she'd been glamoured. At least she knows now, and I don't have to feel horrible about keeping it from her."

"It will all work out," he said. "I'm sure of it. Your mother wouldn't have sent me here for something futile."

I nodded.

"What is it, son?"

"I don't know. Sometimes I feel like I'm on top of all this, that I've got this. And sometimes..." I paced around Erin's living room. "Sometimes I feel completely unhinged."

"You've been through a lot."

"That's got nothing to do with it. Someone has been

feeding on Erin. I have to find out who it is, and I have to stop it. It's making me slowly crazy."

"I understand. First things first. You and River need to recover my body and file a death certificate."

"I've been thinking about that, Dad. How are we supposed to dig up your body and then call the coroner? He'll want to know how and where we found the body, and we'll have to admit to trespassing in the cemetery and everything else."

"Leave the coroner to me, Dante." His tone was firm.

He was going to glamour the coroner.

Well, fine with me. I needed to get my hands on my father's money to do what needed to be done.

"First things first, though," he said. "Tonight, while River and Erin are at work, we go see your sister."

"What about waiting until we recover your body?"

"I thought River would be able to go right away and we'd have my body by now. I can't in good conscience keep my existence from your sister any longer."

I nodded. This was going to be a long night.

TWELVE

Erin

"Did you hear the good news?" Lucy said when I clocked in. "Bitchville is on leave for three weeks."

"I know. She's vacationing with her husband in Barbados."

"She's married?"

"Yeah. I had the same reaction."

"Wait. How did you know? The announcement was just made this morning."

"She came to my house and told me."

"She what?"

"I know. I couldn't believe it myself. But she actually came for another reason—to tell me about the mother and baby that seemingly disappeared."

Lucy dropped her jaw. "Someone else disappeared?"

"No, actually. Turned out the mom was a minor and her parents had her transferred to a facility in Baton Rouge."

"Why would she come to your house for that?"

"I have no idea. Maybe because she found out I had tried

to visit Patty the next morning, and she was gone. I did find it strange that the police weren't around. They were here in droves with the other disappearances."

Lucy harrumphed. "I guess we know why, then. Though I don't know why her parents would transfer her."

"Who knows? But as long as she's okay, I'm good with it." I typed some records into the computer.

When I was done, I turned to look at Lucy, who was going through some lab work that had just come in.

She looked the same as always—blond hair, blue eyes, pretty face with long brown eyelashes and pink cheeks. Her nails were painted light rose, and her green scrubs covered up what I knew was a tight body with curves in all the right places.

Nothing lupine about her in the slightest.

I had truly gone off the deep end.

She was my best friend. She told me everything, all about her sexual exploits.

I'm a horny little bitch.

That epithet I didn't like. Now I examined the double entendre. A bitch didn't have to be a derogatory term for a woman.

It also meant a female dog.

Could it mean a female wolf? I turned back to my computer and searched. Female wolves were usually called she-wolves, but according to some sources were also known as bitches.

I gulped down the lump in my throat and hurriedly logged off and deleted my search. I wasn't supposed to do personal work on these computers anyway, and I rarely did.

Lucy referred to herself as a bitch. So what? A lot of women did. I'd had a roommate during nursing school who considered it a compliment when she was called a bitch. To her, it meant she was a strong woman who wasn't afraid to be assertive. Lucy was certainly that as well.

So far, the evening had been quiet. I sat, almost wishing for sirens, so I could get my mind off all of this.

I got my wish, but not in the form I expected.

Jay and River ambled in.

"Hey, Sis."

"Hey. What are you guys doing here?"

"We're investigating a missing person report."

"Who's missing this time?"

"One of your residents. Logan Crown."

"He's been missing for a while."

"Well, the report was just filed."

"Who filed it?"

"I'm not at liberty to say. They asked that they remain anonymous."

"Okay..."

"When was the last time you saw him?"

"I'd have to check the records, but it was a few nights ago. I was working with him on a case. A teenage female came in. She had a scar that indicated she'd had a heart transplant. I went to get blood for a possible transfusion and when I got back, both she and Logan were gone."

"Right. We got the information on her when it happened."

"But no one filed a report on Logan?"

"Not until now."

"You mean he didn't just take off?" My nerves jumped and my mind raced. "It *was* weird that he just disappeared. Why wouldn't he tell anyone he was leaving? He's always been very professional. I thought maybe he had a family emergency, or maybe..."

"What?"

"Maybe he died, and his body is rotting somewhere. I know it isn't pretty, but he could have had an aortic aneurysm or something alone in his apartment."

"We've already searched his place. He's not there."

River was talking to Lucy, presumably about the same thing. I tried to listen with one ear, but then I ended up not listening to Jay, and he got frustrated.

I concentrated on my brother, until Dr. Nice came and asked me to help her on a case.

"It's a homeless man, Erin. He's been beaten pretty badly. I don't know why, but he's asking for you."

Did you see him?

See who?

The vampire.

Abe Lincoln.

Who else?

I rushed into exam room two, where Abe Lincoln was lying on the table, another nurse tending to two black eyes and some facial lacerations.

"Abe, what happened?" I asked.

"I need to talk to you," he said. "Alone."

I nodded to Dale. "I can take over if you want. I know this patient."

"Sure." She left.

I grabbed some antiseptic towelettes. "This might sting a little. I'm sorry."

He winced when I dabbed a long cut on his cheek.

"What in the world happened, Abe?"

"The vamps. They came after me."

"Why? You always said they were so nice to you."

"They usually are."

I checked his neck. Sure enough, fresh bite wounds.

"You look pale." Paler than usual. Abe Lincoln was never the picture of health after living on the streets.

"They nearly drained me, and then they took turns using my face as a punching bag."

"How many were there?"

"Five. No six. Something like that. My vision is pretty blurry. I lost my glasses a while ago."

"You've told me."

Dr. Nice walked in then. "How's he doing, Erin?"

"He's been beaten pretty badly, and he may have some significant blood loss."

Dr. Nice looked more closely at Abe's face. "These lacerations aren't consistent with significant blood loss. On what do you base that finding?"

Five or six vampire thugs just drank from him.

Nope. Couldn't really say that.

"Just his pallor. I'd like to check his blood counts."

"I see no indication for that," Dr. Nice said.

Of course she didn't. Because there *wasn't* any indication for it, based on his injuries.

"But I always value the opinion of nurses," she continued. "Nurses are the lifeline between physicians and patients. If you feel we should check his counts, I'll order the lab work." She made some notes on the chart. "Go ahead and call a phlebotomist, Erin. Or draw the blood yourself if you have time."

Once Dr. Nice had left, Abe said, "Please don't take more of my blood."

"I won't take much, but I have to. I can't get you a

transfusion without a report from the lab. Hang in there."

"I feel so weak."

"You've lost a lot of blood." I absently touched the healing wounds on my own neck. Was it safe for Dante to be feeding from me every day? I felt fine, and I made sure to drink a lot of fluids during the day.

Dante wouldn't do anything to harm me.

I felt sure of that.

Still...the body replaced blood quickly. White cells and platelets replaced themselves rapidly. Red cells took longer, about four weeks to replace those lost in a pint of blood. Dante obviously wasn't taking that much from me. I'd have to ask him how much he took at each feeding, just to be safe. But so far I had no side effects.

I drew Abe's blood quickly and got it sent off to the lab. "We should have a reading pretty soon," I said. "If it's low enough, you'll get the transfusion you need."

"Thank you."

"What happened, Abe? Why did they do this to you?"

"They asked me for something and I wouldn't give it to them."

"What was that?"

"You."

THIRTEEN

DANTE

"Daddy?" Emilia's mouth dropped open.

"You can see him?" I shook my head, walking toward the front desk at the Cornstalk Hotel.

My sister stood, her eyes round as saucers, and raced toward us. I caught her before she flew through my father and hit the wall.

"Em, are you okay?" I held on to her. "Remember your condition."

She brushed off her linen pants. "I'm fine. But what—"

"This would be easier if you couldn't see him." But she could, just as River could. I resisted the urge to clench my hands into fists.

"What do you mean by that? I don't understand."

"Dad is..." How the hell to say this?

"I'm a ghost, Emilia."

"But, ghosts don't... And that would mean you're..." Tears welled in her eyes.

"Dead. Yes." My father crossed his arms.

"But you're here. You look so real."

"I am real. I'm just not exactly corporeal."

"But you said... Bill said..."

"That ghosts don't exist. I know. Turns out we were all wrong."

"But...are you okay?" She scoffed. "Of course you're not okay. You're dead."

"I'm okay. I'm dead for a reason. I'll explain everything."

I tried to control my envy while he told the story of our mother coming to him in a dream and telling him to take his own life to help protect me.

"So this is all for Dante?"

"I'm here for Dante and you. And for River, at least until his own father can get back to him. Braedon is alive."

"Where is he?" she asked.

"I don't know yet. But I'll find him. Dante and River will help me."

"What about me?"

"You're pregnant, Em," I said. "You need to take care of yourself."

"I'm fine. Jack says I'm progressing as well as any female vampire he's seen. As well as Grandma Marcheline when she was pregnant with twins."

"Jack didn't deliver Braedon and me," my father said. "He was a teenager when we were born."

"He has the records," Em said.

"Don't lie to us, Sis," I said.

She whipped her arms over her chest. "Fine. But I feel fine. I *am* fine. And I'm going with you to do whatever it is you have to do to find Uncle Brae."

"We have something else to do first, Emilia. Dante and

River are going to recover my body so the two of you can collect my estate."

She was silent a moment. Then, "You are absolutely not leaving me out of *that*!"

"Oh, we are," I said. "We have to recover his body from St. Louis Cemetery in the middle of the night."

"I'm just as good with a shovel as you are."

"You'll be working."

"I'll take the night off."

"No, you won't." My father stood rigid, looking more like an angry dad than like a ghost.

He used his "don't fuck with me" tone. I remembered it well from childhood.

"Your brother and cousin have to take care of this. We can't risk you right now in your condition."

Emilia opened her mouth, but my father held up his hand.

She pressed her lips together.

Even as a ghost, my father still commanded an authoritative presence.

"I can't believe any of this." She shook her head.

"I know it's difficult," he said. "It was difficult for me to believe as well. But I trusted your mother when she came to me, and it turned out she was right."

"There's something I still don't understand," I said.

"What's that?" he asked.

"Why the hell Em and River could see you right off. Why not me?"

"Your grandfather didn't see me right away either."

Just what I wanted—to be compared to Bill. Bill, whom I didn't even know anymore.

"This has been hard on him," my father continued. "He'd

already lost his wife and both of his daughters-in-law. Then, within a period of a week, he lost his grandson and both of his sons. Give him a little slack."

I hadn't thought of it that way, and I suddenly felt foolish and self-indulgent. I'd made this whole thing about me, about what I'd been through. About what my father and Brae had been through.

I hadn't given a thought to what Bill had been through.

He wasn't tortured and violated, yet he'd lived through his own hell.

"Bill had River and me," Emilia said.

"Yeah, he did," I agreed. "We had no one while we were imprisoned."

"I'm hardly comparing the severity of the two," he said. "Just remember that you are not the only person who has suffered, Dante, and neither am I. Neither is Bill, for that matter. Emilia lost her brother and her father."

"I'm okay," she said. "River was great. And Bill took care of both of us."

Again, I felt like shit. Par for the course these days. I couldn't seem to find a happy medium between being in love and happy and feeling like my life had been stolen and coming completely unfurled.

Emilia was not one to feel sorry for herself. She never had been. This whole conversation made me feel the size of a rat turd.

I shoved my hair off my forehead, trying to think of something to say that didn't make me sound like a self-indulgent little piss head. Before I could think of anything, however, my sister spoke.

"When do we go to the cemetery?" she asked.

"You're not going, Emilia," my father reiterated.

"The hell I'm not. I'm just as much your child as Dante is."

"Em," I said. "We've been through this."

"If you think I'm not strong enough to do this because I'm a woman—"

"Emilia, you know damn well it has nothing to do with the fact that you're a woman. It has to do with the fact that you're pregnant."

"And only women can get pregnant. I see where you're going with this."

"This discussion is over," my father said.

"I'm not your little girl anymore. I no longer have to obey what you say." She darted her hands to her hips, indignance emanating from her. "Oh, and you're dead."

That got a chuckle out of my father. She still had him wrapped around her little finger, just as she always had.

"You are so much like your mother," he said.

"I never knew her, but I'll take that as a compliment."

"Believe me. It's definitely a compliment. None of that changes the fact, though, that you're not coming with us to exhume my body. It has nothing to do with the fact that you're a woman. If you weren't pregnant, I would have no problem with you accompanying us. But I won't put your life or the life of my grandchild in danger. I love you too much. I don't want you to suffer your mother's fate or your aunt's."

"Jack told me that vampire pregnancies aren't nearly as difficult as they were even twenty years ago. There's no reason why—"

"No." My father's voice was stern.

Emilia closed her mouth.

And that was that. Emilia no longer pressed the issue.

"We will tell you everything when we're done," I said.

"You damned well better."

"We should go now," I said. "We don't want to keep you from your work."

"You're not. It's a quiet night." She turned to our father. "Will you come see me again? Will you be here when the baby is born?"

My father's eyes gave away nothing. "I will be here for as long as I can be."

I wasn't sure what that meant.

I wasn't sure I wanted to know.

FOURTEEN

Erin

An invisible cloak of thin ice wrapped around me.

"They wanted *me*?"

He nodded. "Ever since the other night, when I failed to bring you to them, they've been badgering me. Tonight they got tired of waiting. But I won't sell you out, Erin. You've been kind to me."

"Why do they want me?" I asked, my lips trembling.

"I don't know. But they're determined to taste you."

Although I was still shuddering, my mind whirled. They wanted to taste me. Meaning they probably *hadn't* tasted me yet, which meant these were not the vampires who had been feeding on my thigh.

The thought should've offered me comfort. Or at least a tiny bit of solace in my mind.

It did not. Not only was there a gang of vampires craving my blood, there was also another vampire who had been feeding on me. One I didn't know about.

One who could be in this hospital at this very moment.

"I won't tell them where you are, Erin. But they want you. They will find you eventually. They will follow your scent."

"Why are you telling me this?"

"Because I want you to be careful. They mean business. I never knew them to be violent before—at least not toward me—but something has brought it out in them. They're no longer satisfied with my blood and the blood of the others under the bridge. They smelled you, and now they want you."

I cleared my throat. "Let me go check on your lab results. Blood counts don't take very long."

My invisible icy cloak squeezed around me as I walked to the lab. I wished with all my heart that Dante was here to comfort me. But I was on duty. I could not fall apart. My patients, including Abe Lincoln, needed me.

"Do you have those blood results that were just sent up?" I asked the technician on duty.

"Just finishing them up. Let's see... looks like his hemoglobin is... Wow. 6.9. That's low."

No surprise to me. "He's lost a lot of blood. Looks like he's in for a transfusion. What's his type?"

The tech glanced down. "B positive."

My stomach dropped.

B positive.

Same as mine. Same as Lucy's. Same as all the women who had disappeared from our hospital.

Why was I not surprised?

I forced my legs to move as I mumbled a quick "thank you" to the technician. Abe Lincoln needed me. More than me, he needed a transfusion before he went into hypovolemic shock. I found Dr. Nice in an exam room with a mother and a feverish child. Once I got the necessary order to administer a transfusion to Abe, I went to the small unit in the ER to get a bag of B positive.

As usual, there wasn't any. Once again, I'd have to make a trip to the blood bank in the main hospital.

With each step, I remembered the fateful night I'd met Dante. The night he vandalized our blood bank because he was starving.

Starving...

For blood.

Had he just been released from wherever he'd been held captive?

Was that why he'd been so manic, so obsessed?

So much I still didn't know. So much he wasn't ready to tell me. To tell anyone.

I had to help him.

I opened the door to the blood bank and eyed the shelves. O neg and O pos. Always a ton of those types. We had everything, including AB neg and pos, the rarest of all.

But no B positive.

I didn't have time to dawdle. I grabbed a bag of B negative and hurried back to the ER. Once the transfusion was underway, I left Abe to assist on some other minor cases. I checked back on him as often as I could during the next hour. He was resting comfortably, and his pallor was improving.

Then Lucy grabbed me.

"Erin, I need you."

"What for?"

"There's a problem with the baby from last night."

"Bianca?" The half-werewolf baby.

"Yeah. She and her mom are back. She's spiked another

fever, and we can't get it down."

"Why are you telling me this? Grab a doctor. I can't do anything for her."

"I need you to listen to me. Dr. Nice ordered the same thing as last night. Meds plus the tepid bath. It's not working."

"Then tell Dr. Nice. She'll probably order some blood panels to screen for infection. Start some antibiotics."

"We're working on that. But it won't help. Bianca needs a special kind of treatment."

"What are you talking about? You know the standard protocol as well as I do."

"She needs an herbal infusion. It's common in... God. Erin, I need you to really hear me, okay?"

The wail of a siren interrupted us, and gurneys began appearing.

That was the end of a conversation I didn't want to have.

I wanted to live in blissful ignorance for a little bit longer.

Bianca would get the treatment she needed. She was a strong and healthy baby. Dr. Nice knew what to do.

Lucy and I both assisted with a heart attack victim. He didn't make it.

Before I could deal with that loss, five victims of an automobile accident arrived. Two were dead on arrival, and three were transferred to ICU.

Exhaustion weighed on my shoulders. I sighed. Dawn was breaking, and it was almost time to clock out.

Abe. Bianca.

What had happened to them? The ER staff had been inundated.

I did some quick research. Bianca had been transferred to the pediatric unit. Good. She'd get the care she needed there.

But Abe?

Abe was nowhere to be found. He'd checked himself out after his transfusion.

"How could you let this happen?" I said to the receptionist on duty.

"He's a grown man, Erin. We can't keep him here against his will. He got up and left."

"Why wasn't I notified?"

"You were needed in the ER. All the staff was. You really wanted me to take you off of a life or death case for a homeless man who just wanted to leave?"

"He just had a transfusion. He needed to be monitored."

"We explained all that to him. He was determined to leave anyway."

I sighed and muttered a quick apology. I shouldn't have gone off on her. It had been an exhausting night, and I needed to get out of here.

Apparently I had a gang of vampires stalking me.

But there was one vampire who needed me, who would be waiting for me at home.

I needed to get to him.

Not just for him, but for me.

FIFTEEN

DANTE

I was hungrier for Erin than I'd been in a while. The last time I'd fed, I hadn't made love to her. She hadn't seemed to mind, and now, as I waited, I wondered why.

She'd accepted me as a vampire, accepted my need for her blood. She'd even seemed to accept her own need to feed me.

Still, something was missing.

And I wasn't sure what that something was.

Plus, I had a lot to tell her, most important of which was that tonight, River and I would be trespassing in a cemetery to exhume my father's body.

I wasn't looking forward to her reaction to that piece of news.

My gaze landed on the *Vampyre Texts* still sitting on her coffee table.

This enigmatic book, which I'd learned at a young age was to be respected and never touched, had quickly become the bane of my existence. The vintage brown leather was distressed with age, its scent a combination of old-style tanning and nostalgic must. As a child, I'd found its fragrance—indeed, just its existence as a fixture in Bill's house—soothing, comforting.

Now?

The aroma held only questions. Hundreds of unanswered questions that I couldn't even begin to put into words.

"What secrets do you hold?" I asked aloud. "What has Bill so scared?"

All will soon be revealed.

Her.

Her voice in my head again.

And though everything within me screamed to blot it out, ignore it, hurl it from my mind, this time, I acted differently.

I listened.

I listened to *her.*

What do you have to teach me? What have I missed?

All will soon be revealed.

No, damn it. I need answers!

You will have answers. But first you must learn to ask the questions.

You told me to ask. You showed me the passage. It said, "ask the queen." I am asking.

Ask. But ask with specificity. There are questions you do not know exist.

Then tell me. Tell me what I need to know. Tell me without my asking.

Are you ready?

Was I? Ready for what? I'd been hearing from Bill since I returned that he could not teach me because I wasn't ready. I'd considered it bullshit from the beginning, but now, I knew that he knew something. Something big. Something with potential for destruction.

Something that perhaps *she* knew as well.

A gladiator duel erupted within my mind.

Evict her. Cast her out. She *is evil. You know this. You know what she did to you. Whatever you need, you do not need it from her.*

Then—

But Bill won't tell you. Perhaps she *will.*

I paced around Erin's living room, my gaze continuing to be magnetically pulled back to the *Texts*.

The giant tome that seemed to be pulsing with its own heartbeat.

The book was alive somehow, with information that had been left dormant far too long. The contents seemed almost under pressure. They were pushing to get out, to be known...

Seriously?

I was unhinged.

How could I even be thinking of letting *her* into my head even more than she already was?

Because I know, Dante. I know the secrets you're yearning for. Just ask. Ask me.

Demandez a la royne.

No!

She was no queen.

But you said it.

My queen.

My queen.

My queen.

"Because you were torturing me! You let those assholes clamp me, cut me, electrocute me! You threatened to mutilate my body! Anyone would have caved! Anyone would have said, 'yes, my queen!'"

Not anyone.

"I kept my strength! I stopped shouting out during the torture. I held it in! I was strong. I *am* strong!"

You submitted to me. You opened your flesh for me. You fed me your blood.

"To avoid death!"

You called me your queen.

I tugged at my hair again, pacing, my heart pounding. "Anyone would have!" I yelled again. "Anyone!"

Not anyone.

I squeezed my eyes shut, pushing her out of my head.

Not your father.

I stiffened, my taut muscles the only thing keeping me from crumpling to the ground.

Not your father.

I hadn't talked to my father about what I'd been through. About what he'd been through. It was enough that we each knew what the other must have suffered. How could we discuss it? How could he, my father, admit any weakness to me, his son? And how could I admit to my father how I'd let myself be humiliated and tortured, unable to escape?

I broke you, Dante.

"No. I didn't scream. I didn't. I didn't break."

My queen, you said.

My queen.

My queen.

My queen.

"No! No! No!"

Just ask. I have the answers you seek, Dante. I broke you once. Submit to me now, and I will show you all you want to know.

No. I could not align myself with *her*.

You will find the answers no other way. Accept your weakness. I am your queen. You said so yourself. You submitted to save yourself. You are mine.

"No," I whispered on a sob. "No."

Just ask, Dante, and all will be revealed.

"No. No. No."

Yes. Yes. Yes.

This time I fell to the ground and curled into a fetal position. "No. No. No." My voice barely audible.

My queen.

My queen.

My queen.

Just ask.

So close to answers. So close...

Darkness descended around me, enshrouding me in a black cloak. I was weak. Weak and useless. I'd been a target, and she'd taken me. I'd allowed it.

Weakness. Vulnerability. Dante. The words were all synonymous.

And now I could have the answers I sought.

Show me. Show me what I seek.

My queen.

SIXTEEN

Erin

An invisible burden strained my shoulders as I unlocked the door to my townhome. Dante would need to feed at some point this morning, but not before I had a long, relaxing bath—

"Dante!"

He was curled on the floor of my living room, his eyes squeezed shut, whispering words I couldn't make out.

I ran to him and knelt down, gripping his shoulders and shaking him. "Dante, baby. What is it? What's wrong?"

"Show me," he whispered, urgency lacing his quiet voice. "Show me what I seek. My qu—"

"No!" I pushed him as hard as I could, rolling him onto his back. "Stop it, Dante. Stop it right now!"

His eyes shot open, and his lips trembled. "Show me..."

"No!" I had no idea what he was talking about or to whom, but inside me I knew I had to stop him. It was a life or death thing at this point, and it was drumming in my head like a Native American chant.

Stop him. Stop him. Stop him.

I pushed him again. "No! Stop it, Dante. Stop it!"

His eyes were glassy as he gazed at me. His pupils were dilated. He still wasn't focusing.

Stop him. Stop him. Stop him.

"Dante, stop it. Wake up. I love you, Dante. It's Erin. I love you."

His gaze was still thick, as though he were looking through fog.

One more push. "Dante! I love you! You are vampire, and I love you!"

His pupils responded, and his gaze softened. I heaved a sigh of relief. My heart was stampeding against my chest. I hadn't realized how worked up I was until I was able to release the tension binding me.

"Erin. My love," he whispered.

"I'm here, baby. I'm here. Are you all right?"

He closed his eyes, inhaled, and then opened them. "I am now."

"That was scary. You kept saying, 'show me.' What were you talking about, Dante?"

He attempted to sit up, and I steadied him until we were both upright.

"I let the book take me to a bad place."

"The book? You mean the *Vampyre Texts*?" I pointed at the coffee table.

"Yeah. I let my curiosity... God, Erin, I came so close to succumbing to *her*." He cupped my cheek, caressing it with his thumb. "Her. The woman who took me. Kept me away from my family all that time. She gets in my head sometimes. I try to stop it. Usually I can, but today..." He shivered.

"It's okay." I massaged his forearm. "I'm here."

"You saved me. Thank you."

"I was so scared. But somehow I knew I had to stop whatever was going on with you. Your eyes were dilated, Dante. You were having a physiological response to something. I think you need..." I breathed in, unsure of how to continue. "Maybe get some help. I know some good therapists at the hospital."

That got a chuckle out of him. "I've considered it. I have. But how could I be honest? Any therapist worth his degree would have me locked up after hearing my story."

I couldn't fault his observation. But I could help. If he would let me. "Talk to *me*, Dante. Tell me what happened."

"I...can't. It's too humiliating."

"Baby, do you really think anything you tell me could make me stop loving you? I know you. I know how strong you are. How determined. If you were held against your will..."

It sank in as if lightning had struck my brain.

Still so much I didn't know about this vampire I was in love with.

Still so much...

None of that mattered right now, because a wave of need swept over me.

My blood boiled in my veins, warming and reddening my skin, and a desire so profound swept through me that it almost seemed as if it had a divine purpose.

I needed to feed Dante.

I needed to feed the man I loved.

I moved toward him, embracing him, leaning to the side and offering my neck. "Take from me, Dante. Take what you need. Please."

He pierced my flesh.

Emotion instantly overpowered me.

I'd fed him before, but this time the feeling was so raw, so powerful, that my eyes closed and I fell limp into his arms.

True submission to the man I adored. The man who needed me as no other ever had or would.

As my blood flowed into him, the purpose of my existence came to me so swiftly that I knew it had always been lying within me. To nourish Dante Gabriel, and as I did so, he nourished me as well.

He completed me.

Quenched my thirst and sated my hunger.

The sweet tugging of his lips and teeth on my flesh sent pinpricks of delight swirling through me. The more of my blood that flowed between his lips, the more of him I felt flowing within me.

His strength. His passion. Even his uncertainties, and I welcomed them as my own.

His curiosity. His torment.

Oh, such torment!

Questions. He was so full of questions, and so hungry for answers that he had almost succumbed to the devil herself.

Along with my blood, I let my strength flow into him. Although I was exhausted from my shift, as I gave him my strength, his flowed back into me, rejuvenating me.

Awakening me.

Arousing me.

My pulse quickened, and honeyed warmth surged through me. *I'm yours,* I said to him with each drop of my blood he ingested. *I'm yours and you're mine. You'll protect me and I'll protect you. We will protect each other from whatever threatens either or both of us. We exist together now. As one.*

A low growl emerged against my tender flesh.

Dante released me, licking the two puncture wounds.

"I love you, Erin."

"I love you, Dante."

He swept me into his arms and headed up the stairs, stopping at my bedroom door.

"I need you," he said, his voice a husky rasp.

"I need you too."

He pushed through the door, depositing me on the bed. "Undress," he growled.

I'd just come from work, so I wore only sweats and a T-shirt with sneakers. The shoes I kicked off without untying them, toeing off my socks as well.

"You're going too slow," he snarled. He yanked my sweat pants and underwear over my hips.

His touch ignited me. He unbuttoned his jeans, pushing them over his hips in a flash.

Then he was inside me, thrusting, thrusting, thrusting. His grunts fueled my desire. We were fornicating like a couple of animals in the wild, and I couldn't have loved it more.

This coupling was the very essence of what we were, what we had become to each other.

We were animals. Animals fated to be together. Though our love existed on a higher plane, right now, we were giving in to our most basic desires.

He had taken my blood, had let me nourish him, and in so doing he had nourished me. Now we fucked. A celebratory fuck to commemorate our bond.

Dante called it a blood bond, and for the first time I understood exactly what that meant.

All of the questions he had, all of the research he was doing to figure out this crazy thing between us—and now I knew what it was. I felt it in my very soul.

The blood bond.

Once bonded, never broken.

SEVENTEEN

DANTE

She had saved me, this amazing woman. And now, as I did nothing more than fuck her, I knew she would always save me. When I needed her, Erin would be there, as she had been today when I had nearly succumbed to *her*. She accepted me, not only with her words but with her actions—with everything that was Erin.

That last bit that had been missing was now in place. We had come full circle.

I was fucking her with primal ferocity, but I needed her to feel what I was feeling.

"I do," she said on a whisper.

"Touch yourself, Erin. Touch yourself, and come for me."

She slid her hand down her still clothed torso and found her clit, so perfectly swollen and pink. Her first two fingers slid over her hard nub. I inhaled, her fragrance thick with pheromones and lust. Such a sweet perfume, made—no *created*—solely for me.

She arched her back as I continued to plummet into her.

I plunged again and again into her sweet suction. She gloved me, and the sensation was so perfect that heaven itself couldn't have felt any better. And when she cried out in climax, I buried myself in her exquisiteness, letting go.

Letting all of it go...

Mine. Mine. Mine.

"Erin," I growled, my eyes closed, as I emptied myself into her. "You. Are. Mine."

I fell down upon the bed, next to her, trembling and sweating, my jeans and boxer briefs around my knees. I breathed in. Breathed out. Breathed in again.

"Dante..." she whispered, half moaning.

"Mine. Erin. Mine."

Nothing mattered. Nothing but Erin and me and the blood bond between us.

⚜

I awoke a while later, my jeans still scrunched around my knees. Erin slept soundly next to me, still wearing her T-shirt and bra. I stroked her soft hair falling out of her ponytail. A magnitude of emotion bubbled up inside me as I gazed at her, her cheeks pink, her lips still soft and not swollen.

I hadn't even kissed her. I'd only taken what I needed, and with such sweetness and giving, she had allowed me to.

This woman was my life. *Once bonded, never broken.*

For a dark second, *she* burst into my mind, reminding me of where I first heard those words.

I stared at my Erin, my only love, and banished *her* from my mind.

She had lied to me, told me I was weak and vulnerable. *She* might not be gone forever, but for now, as I looked at my sweet love, I had the strength to exile her.

Erin rustled softly and then opened her eyes. She met my gaze and smiled, warming my heart.

"Hey," she said.

"I didn't mean to wake you. I know you worked all night and must be tired."

As if on cue, her lips split into a yawn, making us both laugh a little.

"It was a pretty rough night actually, but none of that matters now. You're here. I'm here. That's all I need."

"You saved me today."

"I just brought you here. Back where you belong. Next to me."

"I don't know how I can repay you," I said. "For everything."

She smiled, that sweet smile I'd come to need as much as air. "Love isn't something you repay, Dante. It isn't something you earn. It's something another person gives to you freely. I give you my love because I want to. I give you my blood because I want to. I will give you whatever you ask of me. What makes you happy makes me happy."

She was so special, this woman. "I want to tell you everything."

She stroked my cheek, the soft pads of her fingers warm with her blood flowing beneath them. "When you're ready. I can wait."

I leaned down and pressed my lips to hers in a soft kiss. "Thank you. Thank you for everything. Mostly, thank you for loving me."

"Love isn't something you have to thank me for either."

"Then how can I let you know how much your love means to me?"

"I already know that, my love. Just like you know how much your love means to me."

Warmth flowed into me, almost as if balmy chocolate syrup had been drizzled over me. I felt perfectly safe wrapped in a cocoon of love where nothing could hurt either of us.

I wished we could stay here forever.

But we couldn't. I had an obligation to my father. I had to recover his body, and tonight was the night. I had to tell Erin. I couldn't, in good conscience, keep something of this magnitude from her.

But for now, we could lie together. I eased her T-shirt over her head and then removed her bra. Her beautiful breasts fell, her nipples already tight and hard. I took one between my lips and sucked gently.

"Dante..." she sighed. "I love you so."

I let her nipple go with a soft pop and quickly removed my clothes. I settled in next to her, kissing her lips, her cheeks, the sweet flesh of her neck. I trailed my lips over her shoulders and chest, the round swell of her breasts, until I again found her lovely hard nipple. I sucked gently again, relishing the soft sighs from her throat. The texture of her skin was like silk on my tongue, and her fragrance wrapped itself around me in an almost visible shield.

Slowly, her hand traveled over her breast and she began playing with the other nipple. My dick hardened again.

"Yeah, baby. Touch yourself. It's so hot. You make me want you so much."

Her hips began undulating slowly, almost undetectable, but I could sense it.

I let her nipple drop from my mouth again, and I trailed my tongue over her soft flat abdomen. I spread her legs until her beautiful pussy was fanned out before me like a smorgasbord for all of my senses. My eyes took in its glistening pinkness, the sweet swells of her labia, the hard little nub of her clit. With my fingers, I touched the slickness of her folds. The moist softness of her inner thighs. And I inhaled. That sweet musky fragrance that was part arousal and part simply Erin. Apples. Chocolate. Musky truffles and Cabernet. With my ears, I heard the breathy sighs that morphed into lower tones when I swept my fingers over her clit.

And my sense of taste... I inhaled once more, gleaning everything I could from my other senses before I dived in to that sweet pie.

"Please," she breathed, still playing with her nipples. "Please, Dante. Lick me. Suck my pussy."

I could hold out no longer. I pushed her thighs forward and swiped my tongue from her cute little asshole all the way up to her clit.

My cock hardened into granite.

"Please. Your fingers, Dante. I need them inside me."

"In good time, love." I sucked on her labia, tugged on them, swirled my tongue back to her clit and sucked some more.

Her silky texture, her sweet female scent, her arousing pinkness—it all combined to offer an explosion on my senses.

I shoved my tongue into her heat, letting it dance inside her as I savored every nuance of her flavor. She wriggled beneath me, first arching her back and then taking handfuls of my hair and pushing me farther into her depths. She lifted her hips and ground against me, wetting my cheeks with juices.

"Feels so good. I'm going to come, Dante. Oh my God!"

She exploded around my face, fresh honey gushing over my lips and tongue.

I opened my mouth wide and took as much of her as I could. Still her climax continued, and only when the contractions started to slow did I thrust two fingers into her heat.

She ascended again into orgasm.

My aching cock needed her now. I quickly replaced my fingers with my hard dick, slamming into her. She was still working her nipples, her whole body flushed with burst capillaries thrumming in my ears.

My fangs had long since descended, and her breasts were red and swollen. I leaned down and punctured the soft flesh above her areola.

Though she was flushed, the blood didn't flow as quickly in this spot. This wasn't about feeding. No, this was about lovemaking. This was about my needs merged with hers. This was about her being mine. I sucked gently, taking very little of her red nectar, and she flew into another orgasm.

I thrust once more into her until I emptied myself again.

We stayed together then, joined. My cock inside her, my teeth inside her.

And we fell asleep together.

EIGHTEEN

Erin

Despite the exhausting previous night, I slept better than I had in weeks. When I woke snuggled next to Dante, inhaling his salty masculine aroma, I felt at peace. More at peace than I had since we'd met.

But when he awoke and looked at me with a frighteningly serious gaze, I knew my feeling of Nirvana would be short-lived.

I couldn't say I was surprised. Life would never be completely normal with Dante, and until we figured out who'd been feeding on me and my brother, not to mention whatever else was plaguing Dante that he couldn't tell me about, life wouldn't even be close to routine.

"What is it?" I asked, stroking his hair.

"River and I have to do something tonight."

"Whatever it is, I'm pretty sure I'm not going to like it, am I?"

"I can't see how you could."

I listened, forcing myself not to tune out, as he told me his plans.

"I suppose you've considered the fact that you could be arrested for trespassing and all that other stuff. River must know this, being a cop and all."

"He does. And he resisted at first. But I need help. My father doesn't have a body anymore, so he can't realistically help me. My sister is pregnant, and I certainly can't drag you into this. River is the only option, and you know that as well as I do. So does he."

"Does your grandfather know about any of this?"

Dante shook his head. "And we'd like to keep it that way, not that I think you'll go running to him."

"I'm sure you have your reasons," I said with resignation.

"I do."

"And your father?"

"He'll be with us, making sure anyone who comes near us is glamoured so we can do what we need to do."

"I see." Julian had glamoured me, something I still wasn't comfortable with despite his good intentions. "When do you leave?"

"Tonight. After you go to work."

"What if I decide to take the night off and go with you?"

"You can't, Erin. Not this time, not when I can't guarantee you'll be safe."

"I'm not sure I could be any safer, Dante. You, your cousin, and your father will be there. Who better than the three of you to protect me?"

"This is the cemetery. Supernatural forces are thick there, and River and I will be busy."

"So you'll have better things to do than look after me. Is that what you're saying?"

"The most important thing in my life is looking after you, Erin. You know that. I shouldn't have to keep saying it. But you have your shift at night. They need you there."

"What if *you* need me? Something is gnawing at you, Dante. Anyone can see it, and I can see it more clearly because we're so close, so bonded. What if you need me tonight and I'm not there?"

"I promise, baby, that we will take good care of ourselves. My father won't let anything happen to River or to me."

I let out a slow sigh. "I can't talk you out of this, can I?"

"I have to do it. I have good reasons for doing it, and I will tell you eventually. I promise."

I nodded slightly.

He placed his finger under my chin and tilted my face upward. His eyes were dark and beautiful, and love shone within them.

"Trust me?" he said.

I nodded again, a little more firmly this time.

"I'll stay with you until you leave for work if you'd like."

"No, that's okay. I'm sure you have a lot to do. I just need to shower and get dressed. I love you."

He pressed his lips to mine in a sweet kiss. "I love you too."

⚜

Lucy was already in the locker room when I arrived at work. We hadn't continued our conversation about baby Bianca last night because of the influx of emergencies. I didn't particularly want to talk to my best friend right now, but being her intuitive self, she picked up on my vibe.

"Hey, what's wrong?"

Normally I would spill my guts to Lucy, but lately I didn't feel like I knew her anymore. Plus, was it even my place to tell her what Dante was doing? What River was doing? That Julian Gabriel was a ghost?

"I'm okay, Luce."

"Erin, you're not okay. Spill it."

Though I tried to hold it back, a tear rolled out of my eye.

She wiped it away. "Now I know something's wrong."

"I'm just worried about Dante. That's all."

"Why? Is he okay?"

Before I could stop myself, I spilled the whole story about Dante and River breaking into the graveyard tonight. I conveniently left out the part about Julian being a ghost and glamouring anyone who crossed their paths. Oh, and I also left out the part that all three of them were vampires.

"Oh my God," Lucy said.

"I know. But what can I do? I can't call the cops. I don't want to get them in trouble. And River *is* a cop."

"We could call Jay," Lucy suggested. "Maybe he can talk them out of it."

"That wouldn't do any good."

"Why not?"

Because they would glamour him. I couldn't say that to Lucy. She would think I was more of a nutcase than the nutcase I was currently channeling.

Lucy picked up her cell phone from the bottom of her locker. "Oh!"

"What is it?"

She bit her lip. "Family issue," she said after glancing at her phone. "It's a good thing I have a few personal days available. I'm going to need to take some time off."

"Is everything okay?" I wanted to sound more concerned. I wanted to *be* more concerned. I just couldn't get my mind off Dante and River desecrating a cemetery.

"Yes, everything's fine. Don't worry."

She fumbled in her locker and pulled out an envelope, handing it to me. "This is for you."

"What is it?"

"It's personal. Please, just trust me. If baby Bianca comes back into the emergency room, open it. Do what it says."

"Luce..."

"Don't open it unless she comes back."

"But—"

"Trust me. Everything is okay. Trust me." Her tone was almost hypnotic.

The white envelope burned like a heated coal against my palm. I opened my mouth to speak, but Lucy raced out, disappearing in a flash. My fingers itched to rip the paper. But I'd made a promise to Lucy, and no matter where my mind had gone during the last couple of days, she was still my best friend and had been there for me when I needed her.

I snatched my purse out of my locker and buried the envelope in the bottom of it, determined to forget it.

I was on duty, and now, with Lucy gone at the last minute, we would be shorthanded.

I changed into my scrubs and hurried out of the locker room. I still had a few minutes before I needed to clock in, so I decided to visit the blood bank to make sure the B positive had been restocked. As I walked down the corridor, a strange sound resonated off to my right. A supply closet, and the door was cracked.

Another sound, like a squeak.

"Hey, anybody in there?"

I pushed the door slightly. Another squeak.

My skin chilled as I opened the door farther.

Then—

"Oh my God! Logan? Is that you?"

NINETEEN

DANTE

Shovels, check.

Gloves, check.

Garbage bags, check.

River donned a black leather duster and handed another to me. "This is my old one," he said. "Should fit you fine. It's supposed to get cool tonight."

"Vampires wearing dusters. So cliché."

"They're warm. And they're black. They'll help us stay invisible in the dark." I didn't own a pair of black jeans, so I was wearing dark blue denim. River's jeans were black.

He handed me a black ski mask. "We'll need these too."

My father stood quietly in the corner as we prepared for the evening's event. How did he feel about all this? About seeing his body? I had to mentally prepare myself as well. He hadn't been gone very long, so flesh wouldn't be falling off his bones yet. Still, it would show signs of decomposition.

Humans often defecated upon death. Did vampires? We'd find out. Whether my father had or not, there would still be an unbearable stench. The body would have started to digest the intestines upon death, eating outward, helping the decomposition process.

Rigor mortis would have ended by now. Since he was underground, his body might have been spared the infestation of larvae. But probably not. I'd read that maggots could digest sixty percent of a body within a week. My father had been dead for several.

His skin, what was left of it, would be turning purple, and his body would be cold.

Yes, I'd had to mentally prepare myself.

But had my father?

Didn't matter. It was time.

I looked to River.

"Let's roll," he said.

EPILOGUE

THE QUEEN

I'm part of you now, just as you're a part of me. You'll never escape me. Never.

You're getting closer to the truth, Dante. Ever closer.

All will soon be revealed.

You simply must ask the right questions.

***This story continues in* Undaunted**
Blood Bond Saga: Volume Three!

ALSO AVAILABLE FROM

HELEN HARDT

Keep reading for an excerpt!

EXCERPT FROM
MISADVENTURES WITH A ROCK STAR

HEATHER

Several hours earlier...

"I know you love this band," Susie said. "Come on. Please?"

Susie was my roommate and a good friend, but she was a notorious rock and roll groupie. The woman had a pube collection, for God's sake. She'd sworn me to secrecy on that one. She hadn't needed to bother. Who the heck would I tell? Pubic hair didn't regularly come up in conversation. Also, keeping locks of rock stars' gorilla salad in zippered bags made me kind of sick. I'd turned her down when she offered to show it to me.

"Sorry, Suze. Just not up for it tonight."

"I'm so sorry Rod Hanson turned down your rewrite. But sitting around wallowing in self-pity on a Friday night won't make it any better."

"And going to a concert will?"

"A concert *and* an after-party. And watching Jett Draconis and Zane Michaels on stage is an experience every woman should have at least once."

I did love Emerald Phoenix's music, and yes, Jett Draconis and Zane Michaels were as gorgeous as Greek gods. But...

"Not tonight."

She pulled me off the couch. "Not taking no for an answer. You're going."

♦♦♦♦

Why was I here again?

I stifled a yawn. Watching a couple of women do each other while others undressed, clamoring for a minute of the band's attention, wasn't my idea of a good time. The two women were gorgeous, of course, with tight bodies and big boobs. The contrasts in their skin and hair color made their show even more exotic. They were interesting to watch, but they didn't do much for me sexually. Maybe if I weren't so exhausted. I'd pulled the morning and noon shifts, and my legs were aching.

Even so, I was glad Susie had dragged me to the concert, if only to see and hear Jett Draconis live. His deep bass-baritone was rich enough to fill an opera house but had just enough of a rasp to make him the ultimate rock vocalist. And when he slid into falsetto and then back down to bass notes? Panty-melting. No other words could describe the effect. Watching him had mesmerized me. He lived his music as he sang and played, not as if it were coming from his mouth but emanating from his entire body and soul. The man had been born to perform.

A true artist.

Which only made me feel like more of a loser.

Jett Draconis was my age, had hit the LA scene around the same time I had, and he'd made it big in no time. Me? I was still a struggling screenwriter working a dead-end job waiting tables at a local diner where B-list actors and directors hung out. Not only was I not an A-lister, I wasn't even serving them. When I couldn't sell a movie to second-rate producer Rod

Hanson? I hadn't yet said the words out loud, but the time had come to give up.

"What are you doing hanging out here all by yourself?"

Susie's words knocked me out of my barrage of self-pity. For a minute anyway.

"Just bored. Can we leave soon?"

"Are you kidding me? The party's just getting started." She pointed to the two women on the floor. "That's Janet and Lindy. Works every time. They always go home with someone in the band."

"Only proves that men are pigs."

Susie didn't appear to be listening. Her gaze was glued on Zane, the keyboardist, whose gaze was in turn glued on the two women cavorting in the middle of the floor. She turned to me. "Let's make out."

I squinted at her, as if that might help my ears struggling in the loud din. I couldn't possibly have heard her correctly. "What?"

"You and me. Kiss me." She planted a peck right on my mouth.

I stepped away from her. "Are you kidding me?"

"It works. Look around. All the girls do it."

"I'm not a girl. I'm a thirty-year-old woman."

"Don't you think I'm hot?" she asked.

"Seriously? Of course you are." Indeed, Susie looked great with her dark hair flowing down to her ass and her form-fitting leopard-print tank and leggings. "So is Angelina Jolie, but I sure as heck don't want to make out with her. I don't swing that way." Well, for Angelina Jolie I might. Or Lupita Nyong'o. But that was it.

"Neither do I—at least not long-term. But it'll get us closer to the band."

"Is this what you do at all the after-parties you go to?"

She giggled. "Sometimes. But only if there's someone as hot as you to make out with. I have my standards."

Maybe I should have been flattered. But no way was I swapping spit with my friend to get some guy's attention. They were still just men, after all. Even the gorgeous and velvet-voiced Jett Draconis, who seemed to be watching the floor show.

Susie inched toward me again. I turned my head just in time so her lips and tongue swept across my cheek.

"Sorry, girl. If you want to make out, I'm sure there's someone here who will take you up on your offer. Not me, though. It would be too...weird."

She nodded. "Yeah, it would be a little odd. I mean, we live together and all. But I hate that you're just standing here against the wall not having any fun. And I'm not ready to go home yet."

I sighed. This was Susie's scene, and she enjoyed it. She had come to LA for the rockers and was happy to work as a receptionist at a talent agency as long as she made enough money to keep her wardrobe in shape and made enough contacts to get into all the after-parties she wanted. That was the extent of her aspirations. She was living her dream, and she'd no doubt continue to live it until her looks gave out... which wouldn't happen for a while with all the Botox and plastic surgery available in LA. She was a good soul, but right now her ambition was lacking.

"Tell you what," I said. "Have fun. Do your thing. I'll catch an Uber home."

She frowned. "I wanted to show you a good time. I'm sorry I suggested making out. I get a little crazy at these things."

I chuckled. "It's okay. Don't worry about it."

"Please stay. I'll introduce you to some people."

"Any producers or directors here?" I asked.

"I don't know. Mostly the band and their agents, and of course the sound and tech guys who like to try to get it on with the groupies. I doubt any film people are here."

"Then there isn't anyone I need to meet, but thanks for offering." I pulled my phone out of my clutch to check the time. It was nearing midnight, and this party was only getting started.

"Sure I can't convince you to stay?" Susie asked.

"Afraid not." I pulled up the Uber app and ordered a ride. "But have a great time, okay? And stay safe, please."

"I always do." She gave me a quick hug and then lunged toward a group of girls, most of them still dressed, thank God.

I scanned the large room. Susie and her new gaggle of friends were laughing and drinking cocktails. A couple girls were slobbering over the drummer's dick. The two beautiful women putting on the sex show had abandoned the floor, and the one with dark skin was draped between the legs of Zane Michaels, who was, believe it or not, even prettier than she was. The other sat on Jett Draconis's lap.

Zane Michaels was gorgeous, but Jett Draconis? He made his keyboardist look average in comparison. I couldn't help staring. His hair was the color of strong coffee, and he wore it long, the walnut waves hitting below his shoulders. His eyes shone a soft hazel green. His face boasted high cheekbones and a perfectly formed nose, and those lips... The most amazing lips I'd ever seen on a man—full and flawless. I'd gawked at photos of him in magazines, not believing it was possible for a man to be quite so perfect-looking—beautiful and rugged handsome at the same time.

Not that I could see any of this at the moment, with the blonde on top of him blocking most of my view.

I looked down at my phone once more. My driver was still fifteen minutes away. Crap.

Then I looked up.

Straight into the piercing eyes of Jett Draconis.

This story continues in
Misadventures with a Rock Star!

MESSAGE FROM HELEN HARDT

Dear Reader,

Thank you for reading *Unhinged.* If you want to find out about my current backlist and future releases, please like my Facebook page and join my mailing list. I often do giveaways. If you're a fan and would like to join my street team to help spread the word about my books. I regularly do awesome giveaways for my street team members.

If you enjoyed the story, please take the time to leave a review on a site like Amazon or Goodreads. I welcome all feedback.

I wish you all the best!
Helen

Facebook
Facebook.com/HelenHardt

Newsletter
HelenHardt.com/Sign-Up

Street Team
Facebook.com/Groups/HardtAndSoul/

ALSO BY HELEN HARDT

Blood Bond Saga:
Unchained: Volume One

Unhinged: Volume Two

Undaunted: Volume Three

Unmasked: Volume Four
(Coming Soon)

Undefeated: Volume Five
(Coming Soon)

The Steel Brothers Saga:
Craving
Obsession
Possession
Melt
Burn
Surrender
Shattered
Twisted
Unraveled

Misadventures Series:
Misadventures of a Good Wife
Misadventures with a Rock Star

The Temptation Saga:

Tempting Dusty
Teasing Annie
Taking Catie
Taming Angelina
Treasuring Amber
Trusting Sydney
Tantalizing Maria

The Sex and the Season Series:

Lily and the Duke
Rose in Bloom
Lady Alexandra's Lover
Sophie's Voice
The Perils of Patricia
(Coming Soon)

Daughters of the Prairie:

The Outlaw's Angel
Lessons of the Heart
Song of the Raven

ACKNOWLEDGMENTS

This portion of the Blood Bond Saga was particularly fun with the addition of a ghost. I've enjoyed creating my own version of the vampire and ghost worlds, and I hope you love them as much as I do. Dante is struggling with a lot, as this installment makes clear. His bond with Erin is keeping him sane...for now.

As usual, no book is the work solely of the author. Thank you to my editor, Celina Summers, my line editor, Scott Saunders, and my proofreaders, Amy Grishman, Chrissie Saunders, and Michele Lehmann. You each added your own special touch to this story, and I'm forever grateful.

Thanks as always to the team at Waterhouse Press—Meredith, Jon, David, Dave, Robyn, Haley, Jennifer, Jeanne, Kurt, Amber, Yvonne, and Jesse.

To the ladies of my street team, Hardt and Soul—you rock! The love and support you give me lifts me to new heights. Thank you for spreading the word about the Blood Bond Saga and for your wonderful reviews and general good vibes.

Thank you to my family and friends and to my two local RWA chapters, Colorado Romance Writers and Heart of Denver Romance Writers.

Most of all, thank you to all my readers. I'm so glad to know you love Dante and Erin as much as I do!

ABOUT THE AUTHOR

#1 *New York Times*, #1 *USA Today*, and #1 *Wall Street Journal* bestselling author Helen Hardt's passion for the written word began with the books her mother read to her at bedtime. She wrote her first story at age six and hasn't stopped since. In addition to being an award-winning author of contemporary and historical romance and erotica, she's a mother, an attorney, a black belt in Taekwondo, a grammar geek, an appreciator of fine red wine, and a lover of Ben and Jerry's ice cream. She writes from her home in Colorado, where she lives with her family. Helen loves to hear from readers.

Visit her at HelenHardt.com